Bello:
hidden talent rediscovered

Bello is a digital-only imprint of Pan Macmillan,
established to breathe new life into previously published,
classic books.

At Bello we believe in the timeless power of the imagination,
of a good story, narrative and entertainment, and we want to
use digital technology to ensure that many more readers
can enjoy these books into the future.

We publish in ebook and print-on-demand formats
to bring these wonderful books to new audiences.

www.panmacmillan.co.uk/bello

Richmal Crompton

Richmal Crompton (1890–1969) is best known for her thirty-eight books featuring William Brown, which were published between 1922 and 1970. Born in Lancashire, Crompton won a scholarship to Royal Holloway in London, where she trained as a schoolteacher, graduating in 1914, before turning to writing full-time. Alongside the *William* novels, Crompton wrote forty-one novels for adults, as well as nine collections of short stories.

Richmal Crompton

MERLIN BAY

First published 1939 by Macmillan

This edition published 2015 by Bello
an imprint of Pan Macmillan
20 New Wharf Road, London N1 9RR
Basingstoke and Oxford
Associated companies throughout the world

www.panmacmillan.co.uk/bello

ISBN 978-1-5098-1021-5 EPUB
ISBN 978-1-5098-1019-2 HB
ISBN 978-1-5098-1020-8 PB

A CIP catalogue record for this book is available from the British Library.

Typeset by Ellipsis Digital Limited, Glasgow

Visit www.panmacmillan.com to read more about all our books
and to buy them. You will also find features, author interviews and
news of any author events, and you can sign up for e-newsletters
so that you're always first to hear about our new releases.

Chapter One

THE Cornish Riviera Express hurtled noisily through the slumbering peace of the mid-summer afternoon. Newbury, Salisbury, Taunton, Exeter . . .

Fertile valleys, bare sweeps of upland, woods that nestled at the foot of friendly little hills or adventurously scaled the summit, cattle browsing in the meadows, rivers sleeping between banks of willows, villages with straggling sun-baked farms and church spires that floated dreamily on a sea of swaying tree-tops . . . and above all a sky of cloudless blue.

Old Mrs. Paget, sitting upright in a corner of a first-class carriage, watched the swiftly changing scene with childlike interest. The grander effects were wasted on her. It was the small, the inconsiderable—above all, the human—that caught and held her attention. The fleeting glimpse of a woman throwing corn to some hens at a farm-house door, children playing see-saw on a plank set across a log of wood, a boy holding up a stick for an excited ungainly puppy, an old man sunning himself in a cottage garden gay with sweet-williams and snapdragons. . . . The pictures vanished almost as soon as they appeared, but Mrs. Paget's bright blue eyes had missed no detail of them. They were safely stored up in her mind. Probably she wouldn't be able to sleep to-night (one didn't in a strange bed), and it would help pass the time to go over it all again, the woman feeding the hens, the children playing see-saw, the boy holding up the stick. . . . It was strange to think that just for those few seconds her life had, to ever such a slight degree, impinged upon theirs, that one small moment of their existence had detached itself, as it were, from the whole to live in hers. The boy would grow up and marry perhaps, have children, be happy or unhappy, and she would never see him again, but she would always remember him standing there holding the stick and laughing down at the puppy. It was the trivial sort of thing she *did* remember, she thought ruefully. Really important things, such as dates and politics and who had married whom and the ramifications of the royal family, she invariably forgot. She would never be able to tell anyone who had been Home Secretary this year, but she would always see the woman throwing corn to the hens, and the old man sitting, silent, motionless, worshipping the sun. . . . She thought: My mind's like one of these scrap-books we used to make when we were children. Ridiculous little pictures, cut out of magazines and advertisements and stuck in anyhow with no sort of connection or meaning. . . .

A group of children sitting on a gate waved as the train went past, and Mrs. Paget leant forward to wave her handkerchief in reply. She kept her handkerchief on her knee for the purpose. She had already waved to five or six groups of children since the journey began. Every time she did it, Florence, her daughter, who was sitting opposite, looked up from her knitting in disapproval. Florence thought it undignified to wave to strangers, even if they were only children. Mrs. Paget was fond of children and always felt vaguely sorry that they had to grow up. Her own three—Florence, Martin, Pen—had been delightful as babies, but she had to admit that they meant very little to her now. It isn't that I'm not fond of them, she assured herself hastily. I'd do anything in the world for them (at least I think I would), but I don't really *love* them. They've grown up so dull. . . .

Florence had been dull even as a child, but her dullness had been quaint and attractive in those days. Pen needn't have been dull. A clever, high-spirited girl before marriage, she had made herself dull by deliberately limiting her interests to those of household and family. She lived entirely for her children and did it with an air of conscious virtue that exasperated Mrs. Paget, seeming to think, moreover, that the mere fact of having had six children gave her a moral superiority over everyone else. Mrs. Paget sometimes felt a little sorry for Charles, Pen's husband, but his business kept him away from home a good deal, and, in any case, he didn't seem to mind.

Martin was self-contained rather than dull. And, of course, they'd seen so little of him since he left school and went out to Malaya. It had been a friend of Michael's who got him the job, and Martin had been wild with excitement at the prospect. Rubber planting sounded romantic and adventurous and out of the ordinary. His enthusiasm had, naturally perhaps, waned with the years, and on his last leave he had seemed to avoid talking about his work. He had come home again on leave last month, staying with Mrs. Paget for a week before setting off on a round of visits, after which he was to join her at Merlin Bay. Mrs. Paget had looked forward to his home-coming, but time had inevitably raised a barrier between them, and she found it oddly disturbing to be united by a bond of intimate relationship to a stranger. She supposed, however, that it happened to most parents. Or was she peculiarly inadequate? Certainly one couldn't imagine its happening to Pen. "I understand all my children perfectly," Pen would say proudly, and so far Mrs. Paget had resisted the temptation to reply, "Then you've no business to." No one, of course, should understand anyone else. It was the element of surprise and uncertainty in a relationship that kept it alive.

She glanced speculatively at Florence. Perhaps even Florence wasn't really dull. Perhaps she had lovely exciting thoughts that she never told to anyone. Perhaps it was because she lived in a secret world of her own that she seemed so uninteresting on the surface. She was at present engaged in knitting a dish-cloth for Mrs. Pettigrew's stall at the Parish Sale of Work. She always knitted three dozen of them and they always sold, as Mrs. Pettigrew said, "like hot cakes, my dear, if you'll excuse the expression." At other times of the year she knitted bed-socks for the local hospital—long, shapeless, bag-like affairs that did not appear to have any particular end or beginning. Mrs. Paget did not mind the bed-socks so much (they were like large, clumsy, tame animals and she felt almost an affection for them), but the dish-cloths were apt to get on her nerves. There was something so stupid and spiritless about a dish-cloth.

She looked at Florence's thin face bent over her work and wondered with sudden interest what she was thinking about. Florence had been quite pretty as a girl, in the fluffy fly-away style that ages quickly. Her soft brown hair was now almost grey, her fair smooth skin wrinkled, and her slenderness had settled down into a spinsterish angularity. Her manner was still the manner of her girlhood—fluttering, nervous, shy—but, whereas it had been rather charming in those days, it was almost ridiculous now. She was touchy and easily offended, so that she did not make many new friends and was apt to quarrel with her old ones.

Her greatest friend was Violet Coniston, who was coming to join them for the month at Merlin Bay. Violet was a schoolmistress—good-looking, successful, popular, not at all like Florence. The friendship dated from school days and had from the first been characterised by slavish devotion on Florence's side and good-natured, slightly contemptuous tolerance on Violet's.

Violet would, of course, make a determined effort to catch Martin these holidays. She was forty-six and he would be her last chance. She was the sort of woman about whom people said "It's strange she hasn't married," and yet weren't really surprised. Mrs. Paget knew that she had been paving the way ever since Martin's last leave by writing to him. He'll be a fool if he lets himself get caught by her, she thought, but she had long ago given up trying to stop people being fools.

Suddenly Florence looked up and met her eye.

"I was wondering whether to hem a few dusters as well as making the dish-cloths," she said. "I should think they'd sell quite well, wouldn't you?"

"Yes," said Mrs. Paget, faintly disappointed. (So Florence's thoughts weren't wonderful and exciting, after all. . . .)

Florence glanced at her watch, then put her knitting into its cylindrical imitation leather bag, lifted a suitcase from the rack, opened it, and took out a small air-cushion.

"I think it's time you had a little nap, dear," she said to Mrs. Paget.

Mrs. Paget sighed. She hated the air-cushion and she didn't want a little nap, but to have said so would have hurt Florence's feelings, so she allowed her to arrange the air-cushion behind her back, and dutifully closed her eyes. Satisfied, Florence returned to her dish-cloth. The air-cushion was uncomfortable, but Mrs. Paget knew that Florence was watching her with faint suspicion and waited till her thoughts should be wholly absorbed by her dish-cloths and her plans for the Household Stall again before she made the furtive little movement that allowed it to slip down to the seat beside her. She was over seventy, and Florence liked her to be frail and helpless. Her frailness and helplessness justified Florence's existence.

"I've given up my whole life to Mother," she would say. "She needs me so much now that I've really no time for anything else."

Conscientiously Mrs. Paget tried to need Florence. From childhood, painfully timid and nervous, Florence had refused every opportunity, shirked every responsibility that life had offered her. Even when she had been attracted to men they had only to show themselves attracted in return for her to retreat in panic behind her defences of icy reserve. As a girl she had tried to evade all the social contacts that most girls crave for, refusing invitations, shrinking from fresh acquaintances. Her attitude was generally approved ("She's such a home bird, is Florence"), except, secretly, by Mrs. Paget. She had made a supreme effort to combat it on one occasion when Florence was twenty and wished to refuse an invitation to go to Egypt with some friends. ("Oh, I *couldn't*, Mother," she had wailed. "I shouldn't know what to *do*. I shouldn't know what to *say*, I'd be *miserable*.") Mrs. Paget had tried to insist on her going, but the only result bad been an attack of hysterics that had prostrated Florence for several days. After that, Mrs. Paget had resigned herself to the inevitable. Florence was like that. It was no use trying to make her different. Psychologists, she believed, called it by some special name, something about a longing to return to the warmth and darkness of the womb. The mothers of other daughters didn't call it that. They held her up as a shining example to their own daughters. "Look at Florence Paget," they would say. "*She* isn't always wanting to gad about here, there, and everywhere. She's content with her own home, as you ought to be."

When they congratulated Mrs. Paget on the possession of such a paragon, Mrs. Paget smiled and said nothing.

And here Florence was, at the age of forty-nine, still the exemplary "home bird" of her youth, as innocent and inexperienced and intolerant as a girl, with no more knowledge of life than is implied in household routine and a social round of village tea-parties. Mrs. Paget suspected that she occasionally caught a terrifying glimpse of the emptiness and frustration of her existence, and then she would become frenziedly active in house and garden in order to shut it out.

She reminded Mrs. Paget of Mrs. Hague in *England Reclaimed*, who had

> ... wisely broken up her life
> With fences of her own construction.
> Monday was Washing Day,
> Tuesday was Baking Day ...

Monday, Florence got the laundry ready; Tuesday, she did her district; Wednesday, she cleaned the church brasses; Thursday was the housemaid's afternoon out, and the week-end was very busy, with the laundry to be checked, the tradesmen's books to be gone through, and Violet to be written to. And every day, of course, there was the dog to be taken out and things to be done in the garden. And Mother to be looked after. . . .

"Really," Florence would say at such times, with an odd look of terror in her pale goat-like eyes, "I'm so busy I hardly know which way to turn."

And Mrs. Paget would be sorry for her and become old and helpless and very dependent on her, sometimes quite overdoing it in her desire to make Florence feel necessary and useful, behaving as if she were deaf, blind, and paralysed, sending her for shawls, which she never wore, and asking her to read aloud, though she disliked it intensely and always tried not to listen.

Florence threw her a complacent glance from the other side of the carriage. Mother was having quite a nice little nap. It was a long journey and she'd be very tired by the end of it. One must see that she went to bed early. Old people sometimes didn't realise how tired they were. How fortunate for Mother that she had a daughter to look after her! It was a drain on one's time and energy, but one mustn't grudge it. . . .

Her mind went to Violet who would be joining them to-morrow. ("No, I won't come the same day as you," Violet had said with her unfailing tact. "I'll give you time to get nicely settled down before I butt in.") It was a lucky chance that Violet was able to join them at this time of the year, as normally it would be term time, but she had had a slight operation in the spring and had been given sick leave for the summer term. The thought of Violet sent a warm glow through Florence's heart. She had never analysed the instinct that had made her cling so tenaciously to her friendship with Violet, even through the times when Violet had hurt her so deeply by not answering her letters or not acknowledging her presents. Somehow, the fact that Violet was her friend helped to justify her in her own eyes, and Florence needed constant justification in her own eyes. The friendship between them made her partake to some small degree in Violet's qualities. She couldn't herself be so utterly devoid of charm if Violet—so smart and attractive—was her friend. And, after all, Violet was a very busy woman. She couldn't be expected to answer those long weekly letters that Florence wrote, giving all the news of garden, house, and parish. Once or twice Florence, piqued by her lack of response, had tried to stop writing to her, but it left her life so empty ("My friend, Violet Coniston," was the constant refrain of her conversation) that she had to start again. Everything that happened she stored up in her mind through the week to describe to Violet on Sunday. And Violet's birthday—in April—was one of the high lights of the year. She always gave her a present she had made herself, and, as soon as she had despatched it, began to plan the next. All through the year she looked forward to the week or ten days that Violet generally spent with them in the summer holidays. Of late the friendship had seemed to grow stronger. Violet had begun to reply to her letters more frequently, had been almost enthusiastic over the nightdress-case she had worked for her birthday present, and had accepted her invitation to Merlin Bay by return of post, instead of, as she usually did, leaving it unanswered till all her other holiday plans were settled, treating it obviously as the least important. Of course Florence knew that the reason of the change was Martin, and, curiously, she didn't resent this. Violet's marriage to Martin would bind them together in a yet closer bond of intimacy. "My sister-in-law, Violet," she said to herself with secret satisfaction. It implied a much more durable relationship than that implied by "My friend, Violet."

Martin had met Violet on his last leave five years ago. They had met and parted as casual acquaintances, but the Christmas after he went back Violet sent him a book, and he had written to thank her for it—a letter that breathed loneliness and homesickness in every line. She had written to him again, and a correspondence had sprung up between them that had gradually become more and more intimate. At first Violet used to show his letters to Florence, but lately she had stopped doing this. Florence had mentioned Martin when last they met, and Violet had blushed slightly and changed the subject, but later had said, "Martin's going to try to get a job in England when he's over in the summer, and then—well, then you may be seeing a good deal of me, Florence. Will you be able to bear it?"

"You know I'd love it," Florence had said, blushing furiously in her turn from sheer intensity of feeling.

"After all," Violet had continued, as if in jest, but with an underlying note of seriousness in her voice, "I've given up the best years of my life to making other people happy. I think I deserve a little happiness of my own."

She had refused to say more, but it had been enough to send Florence home dizzy with rapture. Violet was forty-six (just the same age as Martin), but she looked much younger. In spite of her youthful appearance she was strictly honest about her age. That was one of the many things that Florence admired in her.

"I'm forty-six," she would say gaily, "and I'm not a bit ashamed of it. After all, everyone either has been forty-six or, with luck, will be."

Florence glanced at Mrs. Paget, who was still apparently asleep, and wondered if she knew about Violet and Martin.

"Florence darling," Violet had said, "you don't repeat things I tell you to your mother, do you? She's a darling, but people of her generation don't always understand. They've—forgotten. I know I shall get on with her, because I always do get on with people, but—well, till there's really something to tell, I'd rather nothing was said to her."

Florence had, therefore, said nothing to her, though, even so, she couldn't be quite sure that she didn't know. She had a disconcerting way, when you told her things, of having known them all along.

She'd be delighted about it, of course. Any mother would be delighted to have Violet for a daughter-in-law. Visions of happy family gatherings, queened over by Violet, swam before her eyes, and her lips curved into a smile. . . .

Mrs. Paget was letting her eyelids droop to satisfy Florence, but she wasn't asleep.

She had even seen the foolish little smile on Florence's face and knew that she was thinking of Violet. . . . A small boy astride a gate-post, dressed in a pair of knickers and an enormous straw hat, waved a stick in greeting, and she took up her handkerchief to wave back. At once Florence pounced on her with that forced and unconvincing brightness with which one rallies children and invalids.

"There!" she said. "You've had quite a nice little nap, haven't you?"

"Yes, haven't I!" agreed Mrs. Paget.

To herself she was saying: Poor Florence. She ought to have married. . . . She ought to have married that second man who proposed. I've forgotten his name. The one who used to sing "Sailor, Beware" after dinner.

Florence leant forward and picked up the air-cushion from the seat.

"You let it slip down," she said a little reproachfully.

Mrs. Paget looked at it as if seeing it for the first time.

"So I did!" she said. "I'm such a restless sleeper, aren't I?"

Florence pressed the air out and put the cushion back into her case. She was still feeling happy and excited at the prospect of Violet's engagement to Martin. And suddenly another thought struck her. It was beautiful and, somehow, fitting that the engagement should take place at Merlin Bay, where, fifty years ago, her mother had spent her honeymoon.

"You haven't been back there since, have you, Mother?" she said suddenly.

Mrs. Paget was silent for a moment, while something inside her gathered itself into a hard tight ball. From the beginning she had been prepared for Florence's clumsy probings into her reason for coming to Merlin Bay for this summer holiday, but to her relief she had so far been too busy with her preparations and too much excited at the prospect of Violet's visit to think of it. She wondered whether to postpone the issue by pretending to go to sleep again, then decided to get it over.

"Where, dear?" she said, with an air of innocent surprise.

"Merlin Bay. You haven't been back since then, have you?"

"Since when, dear?"

"Since your honeymoon."

The hard tight ball inside Mrs. Paget grew harder and tighter still, but her air of innocent surprise became, if possible, more innocent and more surprised.

"No, dear, now you come to mention it, I suppose I haven't."

Florence sighed. How true it was that old people forgot! Mother had evidently forgotten even that she had spent her honeymoon at Merlin Bay. She had decided to spend this summer holiday there because Pen lived there and she wanted to see the children again. Obviously, till Florence mentioned it, she had quite forgotten that it had been the scene of her own honeymoon. This evidence of old age vaguely comforted Florence, making her feel once more a necessary part of her mother's life. (What *would* she do without me to—well, just to remind her of things, if nothing else?)

She was going to ask some further questions about the place when she saw that Mrs. Paget's lids had drooped over her eyes again. Oh, well, it would do her good to have another little nap. What a pity she'd put the air-cushion away!

Mrs. Paget was back again with Michael in the Merlin Bay of fifty years ago. It had been a small fishing village then, remote and undiscovered by tourists. She and Michael had stayed in a fisherman's cottage. She could see the tiny sitting-room, with the horse-hair sofa (stiff little horse-hairs protruded in places and pricked you when you sat down), the oil-lamp on the red fringed table-cloth, the texts and enlarged family photographs on the wall, the shells on the mantelpiece. . . . The door that led into it from outside was so low that Michael had to stoop to enter, and the ceiling only just cleared his head. She saw it all as plainly as if she had been there yesterday, yet it had the quality of remoteness and unreality that invests a place we have known only in our dreams. Ordinary life, with its complicated pattern of responsibility and duties, had been suspended for these few weeks, and she had lived, as it were, in a vacuum of happiness, adoring Michael and being adored by him. Even then she had known it for the fragile thing it was, had been aware that the breath of ordinary life could quickly shatter it, and so had deliberately savoured it to the utmost, storing up every moment of it in her memory.

Michael had been not only her husband and lover but also her deliverer, rescuing her from a home life that was becoming unbearable. Hardly a day passed on which her father and mother did not quarrel, venomously and passionately, and they each confided in her, trying to win her sympathy and turn her against the other. They had done it since she was a child, and she had hated them for it. Don't, don't, something inside her would cry out, when they began to ply her with their grievances and accusations. Leave me alone. Don't tell me. I don't want to know. It's not fair. . . .

In the end they had made her the chief battleground of their bitterness, contending furiously for her allegiance, hating each other the more on her account. The tragedy was that both of them loved her—with that selfish love that must possess and be possessed, that feeds upon perpetual support and reassurance.

From this nightmare existence Michael had rescued her, sweeping her off to the peace and happiness of Merlin Bay.

"It's heaven to know that they can't come to me, telling tales . . ." she had said.

Michael had looked at her, his grey eyes narrowing, and said, "No, they won't come to you any more. I'll see to that."

The vision of Michael grew clearer in her mind—tall and thin, rather slouching, with keen grey eyes and a narrow humorous mouth. She saw him leaning against the cottage door, looking out to sea, wearing a fisherman's jersey, his hands in his pockets, a pipe in his mouth. Perhaps that was at the root of the lack of real affection for her children, of which she was secretly ashamed—that none of them had grown up like Michael, either in appearance or character. None of them had his gaiety, his quick sense of humour, his sympathy, his vivid unaffected charm. She had longed to find Michael in one of them, and she had conceived a secret, almost unconscious grudge against them as they grew up because she had not been able to. They were good, conscientious, dutiful children, but—none of them was Michael.

Then had come the sudden end of the honeymoon—mysterious, shattering, like a thunderbolt from a clear sky. Even now, after all these years, her heart quickened as she forced her mind to turn to that morning when Michael had gone out carefree, whistling, to return an hour later, his face ashen, his eyes full of fear.

"We shall have to go, Dolly," he had said, his voice little more than a whisper.

She had looked at him in silence, then replied quietly, "Very well. I'll pack at once."

"Listen," he had continued. "I'll tell you what's happened. I——"

And panic had swept over her. He was going to make some confession—she knew that by his face—lay his burden, whatever it was, on her because he wasn't strong enough to bear it himself. It was going to be her father and mother over again. So they had come to her, laying their burdens on her childish shoulders, making ruthless unceasing demands on her sympathy, till she could have killed herself or them.

"Don't," she had cried. "Don't tell me. I don't want to know."

He in his turn had looked at her in silence, and then had said "Very well" and gone to pack his things.

Their departure had been a hurried craven flight and she had never known from what.

After that, things had gone smoothly enough. The rapturous ecstasy of the honeymoon could not be expected to continue, but they had been happy, on the whole, and their love had lasted through the years. Michael had not, of course, proved himself the faultless hero her young imagination had pictured him. She soon glimpsed a strain of weakness in him, but she always ignored it. She was determined to have a husband she could rely on and look up to, and almost by force of suggestion she made him such a husband. Despite her secret strength, she made herself feminine and helpless so that he should protect and cherish her. Through her childhood and girlhood she had had to uphold and reassure her parents against her will, and she was determined that in future if anyone was to be upheld and reassured it should be herself. She sometimes thought that she had made Michael a man by making herself a woman. She had treated him always as if he were the stronger of the two, and in the end he had become the stronger. The strain of weakness in him had vanished. (Just as Pen, she thought, has treated Charles like a fool till she's made him one.)

They had never visited Merlin Bay again or mentioned their sudden unexplained flight from it. Even when Pen went to live there because the doctor said it would be good for the delicate Rosemary, Mrs. Paget had refused all invitations till this year. And this year she had suddenly decided to visit it again. She couldn't have explained why. Ten years ago, when Michael lay dying, he had looked at her and his lips had formed the words "Merlin Bay." She had pressed his hand in answer, thinking that his mind had gone back to the first days of the love that so victoriously survived the ups and downs of their life together. It was only very, very gradually that she had come to realise (she didn't know how) that that had not been his meaning, had come to realise that he wanted her to go to Merlin Bay again. She tried to ignore the knowledge, but the mysterious urge grew stronger, more insistent. The fact that this year would have been the year of their golden wedding if Michael had lived, made it impossible for her to resist any longer. No one thought it strange that she should decide to go there now. Pen lived there, and it was natural that she should want to see the children. It seemed strange that she had not gone before. There wasn't room for them at Pen's house, Sea Meads, so they had booked rooms at Merlin Bay Hotel, which had not existed, of course, when last she had been there.

She glanced at her watch. They would be in Merlin Bay in less than half an hour now. Her heart began to beat more quickly. Something was waiting for her at Merlin Bay. She didn't know what it was yet, but she would know soon—in a day, in a week, perhaps. Certainly, when she passed this spot again at the end of the visit, she would know why Michael had wanted her to go there.

Chapter Two

PEN MARLOWE awoke, looked at her watch, then sank back into her pillows with a sigh of relief. It wasn't time to get up yet. . . . Sunshine flooded the room through the wide open window, and she could hear the gentle breaking of the sea on the shore below. She lay there, enjoying the state of warm semi-consciousness that enwrapped her. She needn't think of anything at all for at least half an hour. . . . But her consciousness became clearer as the mists of sleep faded. . . . It was Wednesday—the day Mother and Florence were coming down. She'd had a letter of six pages from Florence yesterday—all about her household arrangements for the holiday and the preparations she was making for the journey. They would reach Merlin Bay Hotel in time for tea, but Mother must rest for about an hour before she saw anybody. So would Pen and the children come round to the hotel to see her *not* before five at the earliest? Well, that would be all right, because she never got the children's tea over much before five. . . . Florence really was rather ridiculous. She behaved as if Mother were a sort of show and she the showman. It would be nice having Mother here, but it was a pity that everything seemed to be coming together—Mother's visit and Charles's holiday and, of course, there would be Martin and that friend of Florence's as well. She must make them understand quite clearly that she was far too busy looking after her house and children to be able to go about with them or entertain them. When you had six children, ranging from seventeen to five, you couldn't be expected to have much time or energy or even affection to spare outside them. She hadn't seen Martin since his last leave, and then, on the few occasions when they met, they had found very little to talk about. She couldn't pretend to be interested in rubber planting or Malaya, and Martin on his side, naturally enough, couldn't pretend to be interested in the domestic concerns that made up her life. She supposed that that generally happened to brothers and sisters. . . .

What *was* the name of that friend of Florence's? Violet Something-or-other. She remembered that she'd disliked her intensely the only time she'd met her. She always disliked those charming middle-aged unmarried women. There was something so unnatural about them. This Violet Something-or-other was a schoolmistress, but that didn't impress Pen. Pen knew all about schoolmistresses. Just sitting at a desk for a few hours in the morning and looking on at games in the afternoon, and gadding about the Continent five months out of the year and completely misunderstanding and mishandling one's precious children. (Hadn't Miss Clowes kept Rosemary in at "break" only last week for losing her pencil-box, when all the time that little wretch, Lucy Barker, had taken it? Pen still felt hot with indignation when she thought of it.) She'd like them to try *her* job for a day or two—on her feet and hard at it from first thing in the morning to last thing at night. She loved her job—she wouldn't have changed it for any other in the world—but it always irritated her to hear people saying they were hard-worked when they simply didn't know what work was.

When did Charles say he was coming down? The 9th or 10th—she'd forgotten which. She must look up his letter. She'd hoped that he would go abroad for his holiday as he had done last year. . . . Charles travelled in South-east England for a firm of biscuit manufacturers and could seldom get down to Merlin Bay. They had come to live there three years ago because the doctor said that the air would be good for Rosemary's tubercular gland, and somehow the household had settled down into a routine in which Charles had no part. She didn't know what on earth he'd find to do here for a whole month. She was fond of Charles, of course, but she was too busy to have much time or attention for him. His visits unsettled the children, besides giving her a lot of extra work. Strange how much extra work one man *did* make in a house. She wouldn't for a moment let him see that, of course. She'd written a nice affectionate letter to him, saying how delighted she was that he could come down and asking him to bring some of that special liver extract that the doctor had recommended for Rosemary.

She was wide-awake now, lying with delicate brows drawn together, planning, organising. ... Charles on the 9th or 10th, Gordon and Susan over from boarding-school for their half-term next week-end. ... Goodness, she'd forgotten Miss Hinkley, that very much removed cousin of Charles's who always came to them for June. She lived on about ten shillings a week in some back street in Peckham and looked forward all the year to her month with them by the sea. It was Charles's mother who had started the practice of asking her to join them on their summer holiday, and Charles, unnecessarily faithful, as Pen thought, to family tradition, had insisted on continuing it. Each year he sent her the invitation, together with her fare and a little "spending money," as he rather oddly put it.

For a moment Pen wondered whether to write to Miss Hinkley and ask her to postpone her visit, then decided not to. Difficulties always acted on her as a kind of mental tonic, stimulating, invigorating. She loved to meet and overcome them. She gloried in the power that enabled her to meet and overcome them. ... Rosemary could go into Stella's room (though Rosemary, despite her night terrors, hated sharing a bedroom with anyone), Miss Hinkley could have Rosemary's room, and Charles could have the big attic bedroom that covered the whole length of the house and had a glorious view of the bay from the small dormer window. Charles had been a little sulky, when, on coming to Merlin Bay, she had suggested their having separate bedrooms, but he had quite resigned himself to it now. Valerie, the youngest, always slept in Pen's bedroom, and the rooms in this house were so small that there really wasn't space for the three of them. In any case Charles was at home so little that it couldn't make much difference to him. ...

The front door banged, there was the sound of light footsteps on the stairs, then a gush of water from the bathroom taps. That must be Stella. She generally got up first and had a dip in the sea before breakfast.

Stella had been something of a problem. She was seventeen and had left school last term. Pen had looked forward to having a daughter to help her with the house and children, and Stella herself had looked forward to it before she actually left school. After only a few weeks, however, she had become bored and discontented.

"I'm fed up with being at home like this," she had burst out one evening. "I hate house-work and mawling about with the children. I want to *do* something. I'm sick of just messing about in a little place where nothing ever happens."

"Stella!" said Pen reproachfully. "Merlin Bay! You used to *love* it."

"I know I did. It was lovely for holidays. It's different living here. Doing the same things day after day, on and on and on."

Pen could hardly recognise in the sulky young woman the radiant adoring child whose greatest joy had been to "help Mother" in the holidays, who had lived for the day when she could leave school and take her place as lieutenant in the beloved little home.

"Stella," she reminded her gently, "you used to tell me how you'd love living here and helping me when you left school."

"I know I did," said Stella again, with increasing sulkiness. "I thought I would. I can't help it, Mother. I don't *want* to feel like this. It was different just for the holidays. It was a lovely change from school. I thought I'd enjoy it, but I don't. I hate it."

Pen tried not to let the child see how deeply she had hurt her.

"Listen, darling," she had said tenderly. "It isn't what you do or where you do it that matters. It's how you do it. You're doing just as important work helping in the home as if you were—well, a member of Parliament or something like that. We could all of us feel bored and discontented if we let ourselves. It's only a question of self-control and self-discipline. And it's not like my Stella to shirk her duty."

But Stella, usually so responsive to Pen's serious little talks, had only looked at her with that new hard expression on her face.

"I'm not a shirker," she had said, "but I don't think this *is* my duty. I want to be trained for a proper job, not just mess about here."

"What sort of a job?" Pen had said, trying to speak in a tone of loving amusement in order to conceal her secret dismay. It had been so delightful having Stella at home as fellow worker and companion. What on earth had happened to the child?

"I don't know," Stella had said. "I think I'd like to take up domestic economy."

"Well, really, Stella!" Pen had replied, letting her irritation peep out at last. "You've just said you hated house-work."

"I hate messing about with it." ("Messing about," echoed Pen wryly to herself, thinking of her beautifully organised, perfectly managed little home.) "I'd like to learn about it properly—scientifically, I mean—and then get some sort of a real job."

"And what about me, darling? I've so loved having you," said Pen, appealing as a last resort to that loyalty and devotion that had never failed her before. But it failed her now. Stella shrugged and looked away from her.

"You got on all right alone here when I was at school," she said.

Pen felt as if the child had leaned forward and slapped her in the face.

"In any case," she said rather sharply, "we couldn't possibly afford to give you a training in that or anything else. We have five children beside you to bring up."

The set stony look on Stella's face didn't soften.

"I'll ask Father," she said.

At that a wave of anger surged through Pen, taking her by surprise, leaving her breathless and dizzy.

"You'll do nothing of the sort," she said, and added quickly, "I won't have Father worried by you."

"That's not the reason," flashed Stella. "It's because——"

She stopped and the colour flooded her cheeks. Pen's heart beat loudly and unevenly. There was a silence that seemed unending, then Stella muttered "Sorry," and went from the room.

For the next few days she had been very quiet, speaking only when she was spoken to, and then as shortly as possible. After that she had quite suddenly become her old happy self again. Pen couldn't account for the change. Perhaps it was simply that she had realised how ungrateful she had been (Pen was glad to think that she had refrained from actually saying "After all I've done for you . . ."), or might it have something to do with Tim Bevan, whose mother had taken Green Roofs for the summer? Mrs. Bevan was a charming woman, but wholly wrapped up in the care of her half-witted daughter Agnes, and Tim was left to himself a good deal. He had got into the habit of calling to take Stella for a walk in the evening. He was nineteen and was studying for an accountancy examination. Stella, of course, was so pretty that it was natural he should be attracted by her, and perhaps the boy and girl friendship between them was the best thing that could happen just now. It would make Stella more contented at Merlin Bay, and it would give Pen time to think over her tactics should Stella reopen the argument. The wisest plan would be to treat the matter lightly, to appeal with confident tenderness to the loving responsive little girl who must still be there somewhere. ("Darling, I don't want to be selfish, but it means so much to me to have you here.") She wouldn't refuse to consider the question of training, but she would postpone it indefinitely. ("We'll see about it in a year or two. . . .")

She tried not to think of that moment when Stella had begun to say something about her and Charles and then stopped so abruptly. It was probably some quite meaningless piece of childish impertinence that she had bitten back. Certainly, she had nothing to be ashamed of in her relations with Charles. Not only had she never quarrelled with him before the children, but she had never quarrelled with him at all. Very few wives could say that.

She looked at her watch again. It really was time to get up now. Springing out of bed, she went over to Valerie. Valerie was still asleep, lying with her face half hidden in the pillow, showing only a tumble of fair hair and the curve of a smooth rosy cheek. Pen drew up the coverlet, which she had kicked off during the night, and went to the window. Sea Meads stood at the end of a path that wound up from the shore—first over sand-hills covered with coarse grass and convolvulus, then up a slope of firm grassy ground, on which rabbit-burrows afforded convenient footholds, and finally up a short sharp ascent, with large uneven stones for steps between waving bracken, to the garden gate. The garden continued the sharp ascent by steps cut in the untidy little lawn to the front door.

Leaning out of the window, Pen drew in a breath of the fresh salt-laden air. It was going to be a glorious day. The sky was a deep unclouded blue. The sea sparkled in the early morning sunshine. The silver haze on the horizon foretold heat. Mother and Florence would see Merlin Bay at its best.

She turned from the window and took up her dressing-gown, which lay on a chair by her bed, throwing a quick critical glance at herself in the mirror as she did so. She was glad that she had kept the slender figure of her girlhood. No one would think that she had had six children. Her slenderness and the delicate oval of her face, tanned to a honey colour that made her eyes look startlingly blue, gave her a wholly misleading air of fragility. She was wiry, possessed amazing powers of endurance, and had never been ill in her life.

She put on her dressing-gown, combed back her fluffy golden-brown hair, and went on to the landing, pausing outside Stella's room.

"Finished with the bathroom, haven't you, darling?" she called in the bright affectionate tone that she had used to Stella ever since their little disagreement, then listened anxiously for Stella's reply.

"Yes, thanks," called Stella.

Pen heaved a sigh of relief. The voice sounded carefree and happy. Yes, she'd quite got over her small fit of sulks. She had been foolish to think so much of it. Girls of that age were always inclined to be hysterical and neurotic. The little outburst had meant nothing at all.

"Isn't it a marvellous morning?" she went on.

"Marvellous!" sang Stella.

"So glad it's going to be fine for Granny and Aunt Florence."

"Oh, bother! I'd forgotten them," said Stella, but she laughed gaily as she said it.

Pen bathed and dressed, then went to wake Rosemary.

Rosemary's room was at the back of the house, and from her window Pen could see the sloping back garden, trodden almost bare by small sturdy feet, Valerie's wheelbarrow in one corner of the lawn, Rosemary's scooter in another, Roger's engine on the path. Few flowers grew except, erratically, in the small plots assigned to the children. Gordon's rabbit-hutch stood against the wall, and a home-made swing hung somewhat precariously from an old apple-tree, which never bore anything else. Beyond the garden the ground swept up sharply to the top of the hill, where the main road ran.

Rosemary was nine years old—over-sensitive, over-excitable, raised to the highest ecstasy, plunged into the blackest despair, by the veriest trifles. In appearance she resembled Pen, but in her case the look of fragility was not deceptive. She had always been delicate, and three years ago had had an operation for appendicitis that had led to the discovery of the tubercular gland. She hated her delicacy and tried to hide it, making herself do everything that other children did. Pen had need of all her tact to deal with her sometimes. She would come in from school, heavy-eyed with exhaustion, but refusing to give in.

"No, *please*, Mummy, I don't want to go to bed yet. It isn't my bedtime. I want to go out to play with Beryl."

Beryl Egerton was her greatest friend, a sturdy egotistical little girl, a year older than Rosemary, who lived at the top of the hill and went to the same school. Rosemary was proud of the friendship and desperately anxious to keep pace with Beryl, who was physically tireless.

Rosemary woke at the sound of the opening door and sat up in bed. She had the same fluffy hair as Pen, of a soft chestnut shade. Her face was pale and deliciously heart-shaped, with wide-set blue eyes and pointed chin. She was flushed with sleep, her hair rumpled, her pyjama jacket open, showing the small fragile chest.

"Good morning, darling," said Pen. "Time to get up."

She went to the window and drew back the curtains.

"Granny and Aunt Florence are coming to-day," she went on.

Rosemary's expressive little face sparkled eagerly.

"Oh, how lovely!" she said. "I'd forgotten it till you said it, I remembered it last night, but I'd forgotten it this morning."

"They won't be here till after tea," Pen reminded her.

"Oh dear!" said Rosemary. "What a long time to wait!"

She would be worn out by tea-time, of course, thought Pen with a sigh. She had been wild with excitement for days at the thought of Granny and Aunt Florence coming, and they probably wouldn't take much notice of her when they did come. Life was like that for Rosemary, swinging continually from eager anticipation to the bitterness of reality.

"No bad dreams?" asked Pen.

Rosemary's nights were full of secret terrors. Anxiety always descended on her as evening approached—an anxiety that she bravely tried to hide. "I hope I shan't have any *very* bad dreams," she would say, with an unconvincing attempt at cheerfulness, and the unconscious mixture of appeal, resignation, and apprehension in the look she turned on Pen, as she left her for the night, sometimes wrung Pen's heart. She steeled herself to endure the terrors with unchildlike fortitude. There was something poignantly unchildlike, too, in her relief when morning came and made her world safe and familiar again.

"No," she assured Pen, "no *very* bad ones. I woke up once and was frightened because there was a jaguar in that corner behind the wardrobe, and I daren't go to sleep again, case he sprang at me. ... The gorilla was on the wardrobe, too. He's always there at night. I don't mind him so much now."

Useless to explain to Rosemary that such creatures could not possibly invade her bedroom.

"I know," she would say—"I mean, I know in the daytime. I tell myself so in the night, too, but I don't believe myself then."

"Well, get up and dress quickly," said Pen, who knew that it was best not to dwell on Rosemary's nocturnal experiences. "You can wash in my room, then Roger can have the bathroom. I've poured some water out for you. . . . Be as quick as you can."

Roger, aged seven, was the next to be roused. He slept alone in the room he shared with Gordon in the holidays. He was dark and square and stocky—in striking contrast to Rosemary's ethereal slenderness. He was unimaginative, too. His nights held only deep dreamless sleep. He could hear the nursery stories of tortured mermaids, ill-treated children, and cruel stepmothers, which turned the very sunshine black for Rosemary, with impersonal detachment. He was rather slow mentally—no match for Rosemary's leaping intelligence—but he was built on sound athletic lines, a good runner and already something of a cricketer. He was a simple affectionate little boy, and Pen's heart yearned over him as fearfully as it did over Rosemary, for she felt that life could hurt his simplicity as cruelly as it could hurt Rosemary's subtlety.

"Time to get up," she said, throwing back the bed-clothes. "It's a lovely day."

He sat up and rubbed his eyes.

"We're going to practise for the sports this afternoon," he said.

"And Granny and Aunt Florence are coming," she reminded him.

"Oh yes," said Roger without interest.

Roger wasn't interested in people. He didn't reach out to every fresh human contact with tremulous eagerness, as did Rosemary. He accepted people, he was scrupulously polite and just to them, but except for his immediate circle of friends and relations they didn't matter to him. And so he wasn't constantly being rapt up to the heights by their kindness or plunged into the depths by their indifference.

"Be as quick as you can, darling," went on Pen. "See if you can race Rosemary."

Roger swung himself out of bed.

"Rosemary's quicker than me," he said, "but she starts day-dreaming and then I can beat her easily."

"Well, the bathroom's empty, so run along."

Valerie was still asleep when Pen returned to her room. Valerie was the most normal of the six. She was intelligent, but not over-sensitive; sturdy, without Roger's too square build. She was indeed a fairer, thinner edition of Roger, with her round rosy cheeks and straight thick hair.

"Time to get up, darling," said Pen. "Take your things into Stella's room and she'll help you. But try yourself, won't you, darling? Because you're quite a big girl now."

Valerie snuggled down into the bed-clothes and looked up with dancing eyes. Pen obeyed the challenge, tickled her, rolled her over, then swung her out of bed and chased her, laughing with delight, to Stella's room.

Downstairs Dandy was waiting to welcome her with an exuberance of joy that no repetition ever dulled. He behaved each morning as if he were hardly able to believe his eyes, as if he'd never really hoped—at least not till he actually saw her—that she would ever come down and that the day would ever begin.

He was a Dandy Dinmont, given to them by Martin at the end of his last leave, a dog of regular habits and an almost exaggerated respect for tradition, becoming distracted if the family departed by a hair's-breadth from their usual routine. He was an ideal pet for the children, playing with them in a kindly indulgent fashion, letting them pull him about to their hearts' content, but it was Pen whom he really loved. He felt that together he and she ran the house, organised the day, and looked after the children.

Pen had laid the table overnight. There was only the porridge to heat up, the kettle to put on, and the eggs to boil. As she moved about the sunny little kitchen, with blue and white check curtains and tablecloth, the walls half hidden by "nature study" paintings brought home at various times from school by Rosemary or Roger, the window-sill full of wild flowers in jam jars, with, here and there, a saucer of peas on damp flannel, she could hear the children shouting to each other upstairs.

"I'm nearly ready, Rosemary. How far are you?"

"I've only got my frock to put on now."

A peal of laughter came from Stella's room just above, where she was dressing Valerie. The sound gladdened Pen's heart. It was all right. Stella *was* settling down. . . . During those nightmare days when she'd been so sullen and discontented, she'd never shirked her duties in the house, but she hadn't laughed over them.

Rosemary came down first, her short blue cotton frock flying out behind her as her bare sandalled legs lightly skimmed the stairs. She ran into the front room that served as sitting-room and nursery combined and opened the oak chest where she kept her "people"—a heterogeneous collection of dolls and toy animals. Kneeling on the floor, she arranged them in a circle, greeting each in turn. "Did you have a good night, Hetty, darling? . . . *Poor* Wilfred! your arm's nearly off, isn't it? I'll ask Stella to mend it. . . . You *do* look nice in your red coat, Rabbit. . . . Did Kanga help you to dress, little Roo?" Hetty was a doll dressed as a "Beef-eater," whom Rosemary had always insisted on regarding as of the feminine sex, and Kanga a toy kangaroo sent her by Mrs. Paget last Christmas with the baby Roo in its pouch. They were all dressed in an ill-fitting assortment of dolls' clothes, which Rosemary was constantly changing from one to the other.

Roger came down next, slowly, stolidly, putting a foot squarely on each step. Rosemary's knees were always scratched and bruised from tumbles, but Roger looked where he was going and seldom fell. He came into the kitchen where Pen was giving the porridge a final stir.

"Rosemary was ready first," he announced ruefully. "She didn't day-dream."

Then he went down to the bottom of the garden, where his toy bear lived in a little hut he had made with sticks stuck into the ground interlaced with string, an old tin tray forming the roof. Roger didn't care for toys as a rule—the only games he really liked were out-of-doors running-about games—but the toy bear, which he had had on his third birthday, had somehow taken hold on his imagination and assumed a personality of its own. He called it simply "Bear," and loved Rosemary to relate adventures, which, she said, it encountered while he was asleep at night. He carried it into the sitting-room under his arm.

"May Bear have breakfast with your people, Rosemary?" he asked.

Rosemary turned her earnest little face to him.

"Yes, if he'll be very quiet," she said. "Minnie Monkey's got a bad headache."

"Yes, he will be quiet," Roger assured her.

"They're having treacle tart for breakfast. Does he like treacle tart?"

"Yes," said the accommodating Roger. "It's his favourite breakfast."

"Well, who would he like to sit next to?" asked Rosemary in a business-like voice. "Who is he fondest of?"

"Piglet?" said Roger a little uncertainly.

He was never quite sure of his ground in such conversations, and would rather follow Rosemary's lead than initiate any idea of his own. This was evidently all right, however, for Rosemary said, "Yes, Piglet likes him best, too," and, with many admonitions to both not to make a noise because of Minnie Monkey's headache and not to talk with their mouths full, made room for Bear next to Piglet. Roger, squatting on his haunches next to Rosemary, watched the inclusion of Bear into the circle with a faint smile of gratification.

"Did he have any adventures last night, Rosemary?" he asked.

"Yes," said Rosemary, sinking her voice to a mysterious whisper, "he had a *terribly* exciting one. I'll tell it you on the way to school."

Just then Pen called, "Come along, children. Breakfast's ready," and Valerie came downstairs holding Stella's hand, wearing a diminutive pink smock, her rosy face shining, her golden hair brushed smooth. They took their seats round the kitchen table, while Pen and Stella served the porridge and filled the mugs with milk. Dandy bustled about, as if helping to settle them in their places, before he finally addressed himself to the bowl of porridge and milk that the children always insisted on his having with them for breakfast.

"Mummy, may my people have school in the sitting-room this morning?" demanded Rosemary, raising her head from her plate.

"If you leave them somewhere where they aren't in my way," said Pen, who was tying on Valerie's bib.

"I'll leave them on the floor right in the corner by the window," said Rosemary. "Will that be all right?"

"Yes," said Pen, dropping a spoonful of syrup on Valerie's porridge in the criss-cross pattern she liked.

"Can Bear come to your school this morning, Rosemary?" asked Roger.

"Yes, if he'll be good," said Rosemary. "They're going to learn Trig—what was it you used to learn, Stella?"

"Trigonometry."

"Well, they're going to learn that. Rabbit's going to teach them. They're all quite young so they won't have any home-work."

Sometimes Rosemary couldn't resist referring to the fact that she did home-work and Roger didn't.

"We're going to do home-work next term," Roger defended himself. "Mr. Orton said so yesterday."

Mr. Orton was Roger's headmaster—a large, amiable, muscular young man, who was very popular with the whole neighbourhood.

"I'm going to school at half-term, I am," said Valerie from a round milky mouth.

The words caught at Pen's heart, though she knew it was ridiculous. Valerie was her last baby, and her going to school would leave the day horribly empty. She'd have Stella, anyway, she consoled herself. It would be dreadful to have no one. It seemed only yesterday that the whole lot of them had been babies, filling her arms and heart every second of every day. Children left such a dreadful emptiness when they went out into the world. . . . It was foolish, of course, to feel like that. Valerie would only be going to school in the mornings. But always before when one of the children went to school she had had a baby at home to look after. She wouldn't have when Valerie went. . . .

"You don't want to leave Mummy, do you?" she said, trying not to say the words because she knew how silly they were.

Valerie drew her brows together and frowned at her from under her lashes in half-unconscious resentment.

"I do, I do! I want to go to school."

It was absurd to feel so hurt, Pen told herself impatiently. She really must try to be more sensible. But she'd given up every corner of her life to the children, and it was such a desperate wrench when she had to let them go—even for a few hours a day.

Dandy was in the doorway, watching them anxiously.

"Dandy's beginning to fuss already," said Stella. "He tries to get us off earlier every morning. . . . It's not time yet, Dandy, you old idiot!"

Pen looked at her watch.

"It is nearly," she said. "Hurry up, children!"

Rosemary, who had a very small appetite, said her grace, slipped from her chair, and ran into the sitting-room to arrange her school in an unobtrusive corner. They heard her gentle little voice admonishing recalcitrant scholars. "Yes, you *must* learn Trigimy, Wilfred. You'll like it when you've tried it. . . . No, you needn't learn anything, Minnie, 'cause of your headache. . . . Your hands are very dirty, Owl."

In a few minutes she returned, fastening up her school satchel.

"Bear says he knows Trigimy, Roger," she said. "He learnt it all in a bear school before you had him. So he's going to help Rabbit teach it. Roo needn't learn it, 'cause he's so small."

Roger, who was still at the table eating bread and marmalade, smiled a pleased but rather uncertain smile. He loved the sidelights on Bear with which Rosemary was always surprising him, but he never knew how to respond to them.

"Oh," he said, after a slight pause.

Dandy gave an impatient bark from the doorway, and after a short period of scramble and bustle the little cavalcade set off—Dandy trotting in front, then Rosemary and Roger, heads close together as Rosemary told him of Bear's last night's adventure, Pen and Stella at the rear with Valerie between them. The lane wound up to the top of the cliff where the 'buses ran along the main road. Dandy stopped occasionally for them to catch up with him, then set off again with his brisk business-like trot. Rosemary turned suddenly and, seeing Beryl coming behind with the maid whose duty it was to see her into the 'bus, broke off Bear's adventures and flew back to her in wild delight, her satchel flapping against her as she ran. Beryl was a solid, heavy-looking child, beautiful in what Pen thought of as a "barmaidish" fashion, with large blue eyes, rosy cheeks, and sleek golden ringlets. She always wore very short dresses that showed her thick rounded thighs. Pen disliked her intensely and resented her calm acceptance of Rosemary's devotion and quite shameless exploitation of it. The maid, glad to deliver her charge into their care, turned homewards again. Pen stood and waited for the two of them. Rosemary was chattering excitedly, Beryl walking along, stolid and unresponsive. The slightly sneering expression on the rosebud mouth was a natural one and was not directed at Rosemary. She was, indeed, for the present at any rate, fascinated by Rosemary's vivid mercurial personality and by the play of fancy that lent constant enchantment to the everyday world around.

"I do dislike that child," said Pen in a low voice to Stella. "What *does* Rosemary see in her?"

"What does anyone see in anyone?" said Stella.

She was rather pleased with the remark at first, thinking it profound and cynical, and then wasn't quite sure. . . .

Roger dropped behind and plodded along by himself just in front of Rosemary and Beryl but ignoring them. He was somewhat disconcerted to have Bear left stranded on the top of a fir tree with a hyena baying savagely beneath, but he'd have to stay there now till Rosemary could get him safely down. It never occurred to Roger to go on with the story himself, and, even if it had, he couldn't have done it. Rosemary had only invented the hyena this morning. Her heart had sunk somewhat as she invented him (hideous, malevolent, with open baying mouth, red tongue, and gleaming eyes) because she knew that he would now invade her dreams and lurk in the shadows of her bedroom at night, but somehow she couldn't help inventing him.

They had reached the main road and were walking towards the 'bus-stop. Dandy kept turning round as if to hurry them. He'd been terribly put out by their stopping to wait for Beryl. He knew no real peace in the morning till he'd got them safely off.

Mrs. Heath passed them on her bicycle—its carrier laden with exercise-books—and turned round to wave. She taught at Cliff End, Roger's school, and lived at Merlin Bay near the Marlowes. She was a fair, worn-looking woman with kind tired eyes. Her husband had once been headmaster of the school, but he had had a nervous breakdown and since then had devoted himself to his allotment, growing vegetables which he sold to the school and to his neighbours. He was so popular that people sustained the fiction of the nervous breakdown even in their minds, though really they all knew that he had had to give up his post because he drank. Ever since the war he had had periodic bouts of drinking that incapacitated him. Between them he was a cultured, kindly, intelligent man with charming manners.

Mr. Forrester, who also taught at Cliff End School, passed them next on his motor cycle and turned to wave to them. He had a thin sunburnt face and keen grey eyes. He always reminded Pen a little of Gordon. He lived at Faulkland Cove just beyond Merlin Bay.

Dandy had reached the 'bus-stop now and was waiting for them, his small squat body a-quiver with impatience. He could see the 'bus coming in the distance. Once, when they had just missed it, he had run down the road after it, barking furiously. The 'bus stopped at the gate of Cliff End School for Roger and at Maple House School for Beryl and Rosemary. The conductor was an old friend of theirs. He called Roger Tommy Farr and pretended to be frightened of Kanga, whom Rosemary occasionally took to school with her. As they clambered into the 'bus Rosemary remembered Bear and turned to Roger in sudden contrition.

"He'll be all right, Roger," she said breathlessly. "The hyena doesn't get him. A good witch lives in the next tree and she comes out and turns the hyena into a little blackberry bush. He tries to prickle Bear's feet as he climbs down, but he can't even do that."

"Thanks," said Roger, relieved.

They scrambled into their seats and the 'bus moved off. Pen and Stella and Valerie stood and waved till it was out of sight, then turned to walk slowly back home. Valerie, still holding Stella's hand, was singing to herself in a high-pitched, uncertain, childish voice:

> "I had a little nut tree,
> Nothing would it bear
> But a silver nutmeg
> And a golden pear."

Stella joined in with her clear true treble:

> "The King of Spain's daughter
> Came to visit me
> And all for the sake
> Of my little nut tree."

A radiance of happiness flooded Pen's heart. How sweet they all were! How dearly she loved them! Her thought hovered over them in brooding tenderness—Rosemary, now sitting straight and slender in the 'bus, her thin sandalled legs swinging free of the floor, her flower-like face alight with eagerness. . . . Roger, solemn and sturdy in his grey flannel suit, sitting in his usual attitude, a hand on each bare knee. . . . Valerie, soft and round and cuddly, frowning with baby concentration over the song, delighted that Stella was singing with her. . . . Her thoughts soared off to Gordon and Susan at their boarding-schools, enclosing them, too, in a barricade of passionate protective love, so that no harm could get through to hurt them, and finally rested on Stella, who was swinging Valerie's hand and singing:

> "Lavender blue, lavender green,
> When I am king, you shall be queen."

Valerie didn't know the song and skipped with delight as she listened to it.

"Sing it again, Stella," she cried.

It was the culmination of all Pen's joy that Stella was her old happy self again. But suddenly a doubt struck her. Was she her old self again? Wasn't there an undercurrent of excitement that was very different from the old childish serenity? No, no, she assured herself hastily. It was still the little girl Stella, childishly, placidly contented and happy. . . .

They were passing Four Winds—Mr. Ransome's cottage, with the large studio built out at one side. Mr. Ransome spent his life painting water-colours of sunsets over Merlin Bay, which were on sale at a picture shop in Penzance. They were not very good water-colours and not many people bought them, but that didn't matter as Mr. Ransome was quite comfortably off. He enjoyed painting sunsets and being an artist (he wore a beard and a velvet jacket) and didn't much care about anything else. Every June he let Four Winds and went on a Mediterranean cruise.

Stella turned to Pen.

"He's coming on Thursday, Mother," she said.

Something keyed up and eager gave her a sudden look of Rosemary.

"Who, dear?" said Pen.

"Mr. Kemsing, of course," said Stella, as if surprised by the question.

Pen remembered vaguely having heard that Arnold Kemsing, the novelist, had taken the cottage.

"Why does he want a studio?" she said carelessly. "He's a writer, not an artist."

"But he *is* an artist, Mother," said Stella. "He's as wonderful an artist as he is a writer, really, but he only paints when he's on his holidays."

Pen laughed, amused yet faintly irritated by the note of earnestness, almost of reverence, in Stella's voice.

"Darling, where *did* you find out all that about him?" she said.

Chapter Three

THEY had taken up their usual position at the foot of the sand-hills. Pen sat on the gaily striped rug they always brought down with them, her mending basket by her side, darning a stocking of Roger's. Stella had been into the sea and now lay outstretched on her stomach, basking in the sun. The open back of her bathing-costume showed her skin, tanned to a golden brown. Valerie, in a large sun-bonnet and miniature bathing-suit, was digging in the sand near them. Dandy lay at Pen's feet, half asleep. He'd got them all nicely settled with a good deal of trouble and felt that he could now take a well-earned rest.

After seeing the children off, they had returned to the cottage, fed Gordon's rabbits, made the beds, washed up the breakfast things, tidied and dusted the rooms, and set the table for lunch. Mrs. Eastern, one of the local "chars," came to them on three mornings a week but this morning was not one of them. Pen's thoughts still brooded lovingly on the little house they had just left, and again a faint resentment stirred at her heart as she remembered Stella's outburst ("I didn't know how dull it was going to be ... messing about in a little place like this").

Stella rolled over onto her back and lay with her head resting on the rug, shading her eyes from the sun with her hands, and, as Pen watched, her resentment melted into tenderness. How pretty she was, with her slender golden limbs, sweet childish mouth, and the grey-blue eyes fringed with dark lashes!

"Mummy!" called Valerie excitedly. "I'm making a *big* castle."

"Lovely, darling," muttered Pen absently.

Despite her slenderness, Stella looked disconcertingly mature in her bathing-costume, not a child any longer.

She rolled over suddenly onto her side.

"Can I help?" she said. "Throw me a sock or something."

"No, thanks, dear," smiled Pen. "I shall get through them quite easily. . . . Go on cooking."

"Will Granny and Aunt Florence make castles?" asked Valerie.

"Perhaps," said Pen.

Again she thought how glad she'd be when this month was over. Mother, Florence, Charles. . . . She was fond of them, of course, but they would inevitably introduce complications into her ordered life, unsettle the children, upset their routine. She must just get through it as best she could. After all, a month wasn't long. This time four weeks they'd all have come and gone and she'd be back again in the guarded peace of her life with the children. She was glad that Charles had taken up golf. He'd be out at the Crowham links most of the day.

She wondered suddenly what Stella was thinking of, lying there so silent and motionless. . . .

"Penny for your thoughts, Stella," she said.

Stella rolled onto her stomach again.

"Haven't any," she said. "I'm just being a jelly-fish."

Actually she had been thinking of Arnold Kemsing. She had felt wildly excited ever since she heard that he was coming to the Bay, though she had instinctively hidden her excitement from Pen. She had read his latest book during her last term at school, and not only had she completely identified herself with the heroine, but she had fallen passionately in love with the hero. He had been a tall, thin, distinguished-looking man called Sir Peter Messenger, with hair just greying at the temples, beautiful manners, and a noble unselfish character. She had felt that she would rather not marry at all than not marry him. He *must* be somewhere in the world, waiting for her, looking for her. . . . And then she had seen a portrait of Arnold Kemsing in a magazine and read the accompanying article on him. And—he *was* Sir Peter Messenger. He had the same distinguished-looking face and noble unselfish character. Since then life had consisted of a series of day-dreams in which Arnold Kemsing met her in various romantic situations and fell deeply in love with her. It was partly, but not wholly, on this account that she had felt she couldn't go on living in Merlin Bay, helping Mother with the house and the children. She'd have felt that, anyway. She wanted to go out into the world, free and untrammelled, to work and mix with people and *do* things. How *could* Mother think it was enough just to sit at home and wait for something to happen to you? If you did that nothing might ever happen. You might just go on and on and on till you were like Aunt Florence. It was dreadful to think of that. . . . You'd *got* to go out and meet things. Wonderful people like Arnold Kemsing weren't likely to come to a place like Merlin Bay. And then—quite suddenly, when she stopped to speak to Mr. Ransome one evening, as he was painting the sunset from the top of the cliff—she heard that Arnold Kemsing *was* coming to Merlin Bay. At first she couldn't believe it. It *couldn't* be true. A thing as wonderful as that couldn't ever really happen.

"Not—not *the* Arnold Kemsing?" she had stammered.

"Well, yes, if you put it like that," said Mr. Ransome, who didn't read novels and couldn't understand people who did.

"The one who wrote *Starlight*?"

"That, I believe, was his last book," said Mr. Ransome, adding a touch of scarlet to the extreme edge of the sunset. "Have you read it?"

"Yes, of course."

"Why 'of course'?" challenged Mr. Ransome, giving a generous dose of gamboge to the skyline. "What good d'you think it does you stuffing your head with fiction? Read biography or philosophy or poetry if you want to read. Do you far more good."

Stella wasn't listening. How glad she was that she hadn't obeyed the sudden impulse she'd had after that row with Mother to run away to Daddy and ask him to help her find work! She'd nearly done it. She hadn't actually decided not to till this moment. She wouldn't now, of course. . . . It couldn't be just a coincidence that she had felt like that about him and suddenly he should decide to come to Merlin Bay. Their meeting was fated—as was the meeting of all great lovers. Why, out of all places in the world, should he have chosen Merlin Bay if it weren't fated? Something drew him there—? he didn't know what it was, not yet at any rate. She looked into the future and heard him saying (they were middle-aged and he was sitting by her, holding her hand): "Something drew me to Merlin Bay that summer, dearest. I didn't know what it was—till I saw you. I knew then, of course." She had gone home, dazed with happiness. But she had been careful to hide her feelings from Pen, not even telling her that Arnold Kemsing was coming to Merlin Bay till this morning. This belonged to herself and to no one else in the world—not even Mother.

She had counted the days since then. He would be here on Saturday—only three more days now.

Mr. Heath came swinging along the sand, dressed in an old pair of grey flannel trousers and a blue shirt. He had small twinkling eyes, a face that seemed to be smiling even when he was serious, untidy hair, and a friendly boyish manner. It was easy to understand why he had been so popular with the boys when he was headmaster of Cliff End School. He stopped and smiled down at them. Dandy leapt about him in tumultuous welcome.

"Got the kids safely off your hands for the day?" he said.

Pen smiled at him. She couldn't help liking him. No one could help liking him. Every woman who met him had a faint unformulated idea at the back of her mind that she could have kept him straight if she had been his wife.

"Yes," she said. "It seems such a shame to send them to school on a day like this. . . . Mrs. Heath passed us as we were waiting for the 'bus."

"Scattering exercise-books all the way, I suppose?" he grinned. "She never can fix the things right on her carrier. I do it for her when I've time, but I was digging up cabbages for your son's dinner this morning."

The allotment brought in very little money, but he never seemed to feel any embarrassment or compunction at the thought of his wife's having to work for him. Nothing ever seemed to worry him or cloud his easy serene charm.

"He's got the makings of a good cricketer—that young man of yours," he went on. "I was up at the school watching him last Friday. He's steady and plucky and he's got a straight eye."

A rush of pride filled Pen's heart.

"He's terribly keen, of course," she murmured.

He looked down at Stella.

"Nice to see a young woman who browns the right shade," he said approvingly. "They usually turn into one of Ransome's sunsets."

Stella laughed. It wasn't that it was difficult to believe that this kindly genial man was the same as the drunken creature who had terrified her so by lurching into her when she went to the post one night last winter. It was that it was impossible to believe it. . . . Generally he went up to London "on business" when the craving for drink came on him and returned a week or two later, ill and exhausted but with his charm unimpaired. Till she'd actually seen him drunk, Stella had refused to believe the story, and even now she didn't really believe it. . . . People couldn't be as—different as that.

"Still enjoying being a lady of leisure?"

"She's *loving* it," put in Pen quickly; "aren't you, darling? We're having our last day of real leisure for a month, though. My mother and sister are coming down to-day. They're staying at the Bay Hotel, but they'll be with us a good deal, and my brother's joining them on Friday—the one that's home on leave from Malaya this year, you know. Then there's that old cousin of my husband's who generally comes in the summer——"

"Miss Hinkley? I remember."

"Yes. And then my husband comes for his month's holiday. So we shall be having a very busy time from now till the end of the month. We're terribly excited about it."

He twinkled at her, as if he knew how glad she'd be when it was all over.

"I'm sure you are," he said.

Valerie, who adored him, came running up and took his hand.

"Come and look at my castle," she said, pulling him away. "It's a *big* one."

He squatted down by her castle in the sand, and she lent him her wooden spade and watched with pride and interest as he added a row of battlements to the top.

"We can stand there, you see," he explained, "and keep a look-out for our enemies."

"Very tiny we's?" asked Valerie.

"Yes, very tiny. As high as that." He held his hand about three inches from the sand. "Now, we'll make little steps for us to walk up ... like this."

"Are we walking up now?" asked Valerie, tense with excitement.

"Yes."

"Me first?"

"Yes, you first. You've just got to this step. I'm on the one behind."

Pen watched them, thinking of his own child, who had died at the age of eighteen months. Perhaps if the child had lived he would have been different. Odd that one's sympathy went out to him rather than to his wife, though it was he, not she, who was responsible for their misfortunes.

He rose and brushed the sand from his knees.

"Well, I mustn't play any longer," he said. "It's time I went to watch my turnips grow."

Valerie accompanied him to the foot of the rickety steps that led up from the beach to the gate of Cliff Cottage, then ran back to Pen.

"He says his carrots are very proud," she announced importantly, "and won't speak to his turnips. They're proud because of their feather hats. But he likes his turnips best."

Pen began to pack her mending into the basket.

"I ought to go up and begin seeing to the lunch," she said.

But the Bevans were coming along the sands now, Mrs. Bevan looking very small between her tall son and daughter. Her daughter, Agnes, was a large loose-knit girl of eighteen who had not developed beyond childhood. She was not, as many people described her, an "idiot." She was affectionate and sensitive, but utterly without control over mind or body. Her face was heavy and expressionless, her skin coarse and sallow, and she walked with a jerky shambling gait. She adored her mother and wore her out by her perpetual demands. She howled aloud at the slightest hurt or rebuff and when crossed would fly into ungovernable rages in which she was actually dangerous. Only Mrs. Bevan, who loved her with a deep illimitable tenderness, could manage her, and she spent her life managing her, soothing and reassuring her, looking after her physical needs as if she were indeed a child, entertaining her, reading to her, playing with her, coaxing her back into precarious serenity from her onsets of fear and anger, seldom leaving her even for a moment. She was a sweet, pale, ghost-like little woman, dressed now in a grey linen dress and black shady hat. You could see how lovely she must have been before life had stripped her of youth and vitality—of everything but a passionate, protective, all-engrossing, all-enduring love for the daughter whom fate had handicapped so cruelly.

Tim was tall and dark. There was a sulky forbidding expression on his good-looking face. He always felt ashamed of being seen in public with the obviously undeveloped Agnes, but he was devoted to his mother and honestly tried to bear his share of the burden. It was something quite beyond his control that made him unable even to look at Agnes without flinching. He was aware that the greater part of his mother's love was given to her, that, without realising it, she resented his glorious normality, his health and intelligence, almost as though he might have endowed Agnes with them had he wished, and that she bitterly and openly resented his shrinking from Agnes, his inability to respond to her clumsy affection.

He was trying to talk to his mother now as if Agnes were not there, but Mrs. Bevan refused to ignore her and kept speaking to her in a low tender voice she never used to him.

Agnes, wearing a gaily patterned cotton dress (she loved bright colours), radiated an expansive happiness. She was enjoying this walk along the beach with Tim and her mother. Her vapid blue eyes gleamed and her large mouth hung open in a vague tremulous smile. One of the things about her that revolted Tim was that her loose red lips always shone with moisture. She was bare-headed, but her thick, coarse, shingled hair looked dull even in the sunlight.

"Won't you bathe to-day, Mother?" said Tim. "The water's quite warm."

"Perhaps, dear," said Mrs. Bevan evasively. She hated leaving Agnes even to bathe. "Look, darling," she went on, turning to Agnes, "at that ship on the sea right over there."

"Ship on the sea," shouted Agnes excitedly. "Right over there."

Her voice was loud and harsh and she had no more control over it than she had over the rest of her. The sound of it booming noisily and continually in the little cottage rasped Tim's nerves unbearably.

They had reached the spot where Pen sat with Stella and Valerie. Valerie, who was terrified of Agnes, retreated behind Pen as soon as they appeared. The corners of Mrs. Bevan's mouth tightened slightly as she noticed this. Agnes, so sweet and kind, so hungry for affection beneath her uncouth exterior, loved children, and it hurt her mother inexpressibly that they should shrink from her as they invariably did. Apart from that, Mrs. Bevan was herself inclined to avoid children. They roused an intolerable pain in her heart, taking her back to the days when she had struggled so long, so desperately, against the inevitable knowledge ("Just a little slower than other children, perhaps, but—oh, not *that*!").

She stopped and looked down at Pen.

"Isn't it a marvellous day?" she said.

"Lovely," said Pen. She smiled up at Agnes and said, "Well, Agnes, are you quite well?"

The sight of Agnes always sent through Pen's heart a thrill of exultant pride in her own six normal healthy children, and she was always very nice to her.

Agnes beamed with delight at the question.

"Yes, thank you," she shouted. "We went up onto the cliff this morning and I picked some flowers and Mother put them in a vase in the drawing-room."

Pen smiled vaguely. Despite the loudness of her voice, Agnes's words were generally unintelligible except to Mrs. Bevan.

"Quietly, darling," murmured Mrs. Bevan. "Don't shout so."

"And then I paddled," went on Agnes, lowering her voice obediently. She smiled her large, happy, puppyish smile at Stella. "Hallo, Stella!"

"Hallo, Agnes," said Stella uncomfortably.

She never knew what to say to Agnes.

Tim dropped onto the sands by her, and the sulkiness of his expression softened as he watched her sitting there smiling at Agnes, her blue eyes screwed up against the sunshine.

"Has your mother come yet?" went on Mrs. Bevan.

"Not yet," said Pen. "We're expecting her this afternoon. . . . We're going to be dreadfully busy this month because my brother's coming, too, and my husband will be here for his holiday."

Mrs. Bevan sighed. She had had to lose touch with her own friends and relations. Not only did Agnes demand all her time, but also she was subject to violent and uncontrollable fits of jealousy when anyone else's claims seemed to take precedence of hers.

"Can I come and see them?" shouted Agnes.

"Of course, dear."

"Is your mother very old?"

"She's seventy-three."

Mrs. Bevan saw that in another moment Agnes would become over-excited.

"Come along, dear," she said. "We're just going to the end of the bay. . . . Stay with Stella, Tim. We'll be back in a few moments."

They went on down the beach. Val crept out from behind Pen and looked after them, her baby face set and solemn in the frame of the frilled sun-bonnet.

"Don't like her," she said emphatically.

"Hush, Val," said Pen. "It's time for your rest now. Would you like to carry Mummy's work-bag up?"

It always made Val feel happy and important to carry Pen's work-bag, though generally she would stop half-way up the path to gather the scarlet pimpernels that grew there, and leave the work-bag or anything else she happened to be carrying for Pen to collect as she came on behind.

Stella stretched her arms out luxuriously.

"I'm drunk with sunshine," she said.

"You needn't come up yet, darling," said Pen. "There's really nothing to go up for but Val's rest. Come in half an hour. That'll be ample time to help with the lunch."

She wanted Stella to go on being happy and contented . . . basking there in the sunshine and talking to Tim.

"All right," said Stella, lying down again.

"Are you coming with us, Dandy, or staying with Stella?" said Pen.

Dandy, now quite rested from his morning's work, replied by scampering up the cliff path with a tremendous display of energy.

"Call if you want me before half an hour," said Stella sleepily.

"Very well. Come along, Val."

When the Marlowes wanted to summon any member of the family from the beach, they would stand at the end of the little garden that overlooked the bay and give a call rather like a peewit's cry. Most of the families in the bay had similar private summonses.

"That's Mrs. Egerton calling Beryl," people would say, when Mrs. Egerton's cry, reminiscent of the Volga boat song, rang out from the cliff.

They climbed up the short steep path, then disappeared among the waving bracken at the top.

Tim sat with his arms clasping his knees. His striped sports shirt, open at the neck, showed his lean brown chest. His thin arms were sinewy and hairy.

"Don't you think she looks rotten to-day?" he said gloomily.

"Who?"

"Mother. Agnes wouldn't let her sleep last night. Agnes doesn't need much sleep and when she can't sleep she makes Mother read to her. She was reading to her nearly all last night."

"What a shame!" said Stella perfunctorily.

Always before it had been Stella, with the interest of the normal in the abnormal, who had wanted to discuss Agnes, and Tim who had avoided the subject, but now she felt suddenly resentful towards him for telling her his troubles. She didn't want to have to feel sorry for people, unhappy about them; she wanted to be left alone with her dream, a dream in which there was only love and unclouded happiness, in which there were no Mrs. Bevans or Agneses struggling unequally against fate.

Tim, however, seemed satisfied by the crumb of sympathy her words threw him.

"I told you about Sunday, didn't I?" he went on, digging his bare sandalled feet more deeply into the sand.

"Yes."

On Sunday Agnes had flown into a rage and thrown every book she could lay hands on across the room. One had caught Mrs. Bevan on the forehead, raising a bruise.

"She does her hair so that you don't see it, but the cover cut right through her skin. She'll kill her one of these days if I don't kill her first."

"*Tim!*" said Stella, shaken out of her dream.

"Oh, I don't mean I really shall," said Tim with increasing gloom. "I haven't got the guts. But when I read of people killing people like Agnes I understand, and I wish I had the guts. I hate her so much that sometimes I can hardly bear it. . . . You see"—his frowning gaze was fixed on the distance—"it isn't only that she's wearing Mother out, it's that she comes between Mother and me. Mother doesn't know it, but she can't quite forgive me for being like other people while Agnes isn't. And she can't forgive me for hating Agnes. I can't help hating her. . . . I don't wonder Father cleared out."

Stella sat up, her face set and stern.

"He hadn't any right to leave her," she said in a tone of youthful asperity. "If he'd loved her he'd have stayed with her."

"The trouble was he did love her," said Tim slowly. "He loved her so much that he couldn't bear to watch it any more. I suppose"—thoughtfully—"it was like standing by and watching a wild animal mauling someone you love. She's so strong that she really hurts Mother when she's angry or excited. He stood it as long as he could and then he said that, if she wouldn't agree either to send her away to an institution or get a proper attendant for her, he'd go."

"Well, why didn't she, then? I think it was mean of her not to."

"She *did* try," said Tim, rising hotly to his mother's defence. "I mean, she got an attendant for her, but Agnes cried all the time and got so much worse that she sent the attendant away again. It was after that that Father left her. He said he'd rather have no home at all than a home like that. Of course, it *was* awful for him. Agnes loves people and parties and that sort of thing, and she raised hell if she couldn't be with them when people came to lunch or tea. And Mother never will see how bad she is. She keeps trying to persuade herself that she's getting better."

"Where is your father?"

"He lives at his club in London."

"Do they see each other?"

"No, they decided not to. You see, it isn't as if they didn't get on—apart from Agnes. If it weren't for Agnes they'd be perfectly happy together."

"It's dreadful . . ." said Stella.

Then, with the egotism of youth, her thoughts flew off to her dreams again. There would be no cloud like this to mar her happiness. If she had children, they would be perfect—clever, beautiful, enchanting. She wasn't really keen on children, though. She had too much of them at home. Perhaps she'd just have one child—the attractive amusing type of child people had in books and that you so seldom found in real life. Children in books never seemed to cry or get into tempers or want their noses wiped.

Tim had rolled over on the sand and was lying looking at her, his chin propped on his hands.

"You are pretty, Stella," he said simply. "I love the way your lashes curl on your cheeks, when you look down. . . . People don't often have fair hair and dark eyelashes, do they?"

"Don't they?" said Stella.

Ordinarily she would have been annoyed and embarrassed by his praises. She hated "soppiness." But now she drank it in eagerly. Surely, if Tim thought her pretty—*he* would, too.

Chapter Four

FLORENCE and Violet walked slowly along the cliff towards the hotel. Violet had arrived yesterday, and Florence was still in a flutter of excitement and pleasure. Violet, as always, seemed to bring a breath of the great world with her. As soon as Florence saw her stepping down from the railway carriage in a smart new costume of pale grey, with a red hat worn at a fashionable angle, she began somehow at once to feel smarter and more important herself. And Violet had so much to tell her. Violet lived in London and was a member of a well-known woman's club and went to cocktail parties and knew a lot of interesting important people. Gwynne Beauchamp, the famous woman writer of historical novels, was one of her greatest friends. The name ran through Violet's conversation like a thread. "Then I met Gwynne for tea. ..." "Gwynne and I went to a concert. ..." "Gwynne told me all about the new book she was working on. ..." She always waited for Florence to ask what its subject was (Florence reverently read all Gwynne's books because of her friendship with Violet) before she said, "Well, of course, it's quite confidential. I'm afraid I mustn't tell anyone, even you, dear. It's not fair to Gwynne or her publisher. Gwynne likes to discuss her work with me, but she wouldn't do it if I chattered about it to outsiders."

"Of course," agreed Florence, humbly accepting this description of herself as an "outsider."

It was easy to gather from Violet's conversation how popular she was with both staff and pupils at the school in Kensington where she taught, and yet she never allowed this to make her conceited. She had a deprecating, almost whimsical attitude to it.

"I said to her, 'You're the tenth girl who's asked me, my dear, and with the best will in the world I can't sit next to ten girls at the concert.' "

The rest of the staff was, it seemed, peculiarly inadequate and inefficient ("I put it as nicely as I could. I said, 'You only need to be firm. Kind and friendly but *firm*. I never have any difficulty about discipline myself. I never have had since I began to teach' "). The headmistress in particular appeared to be so lacking in every quality necessary to her position that it was difficult to understand how she had attained it. According to Violet, she needed her constantly at hand to advise and support.

"Of course, it's not easy for me," said Violet. "I take the responsibility for the muddles she makes and give her the credit when I manage to keep things going smoothly."

"It's so unselfish of you, Violet," said Florence fervently.

Violet waved her unselfishness aside.

"Oh no, not really. It's just that I *am* like that. It's the work that matters to me, not any personal credit. Though, as a matter of fact, she does appreciate it. Only the other day she said . . ."

Florence drank in eagerly a eulogy of Violet, expressed in a style of speech curiously akin to Violet's own, then said, "What *will* she do without you this term?"

Violet smiled and shrugged.

"Heaven knows, my dear. . . . To make things worse, she's plain and dresses badly, and girls *are* so sensitive to that sort of thing."

Florence's glance went admiringly to the oval, regular-featured face and the neatly waved dark hair, flecked with grey, beneath the white hat, then travelled down the freshly laundered, well-fitting dress of blue and white washing silk . . . and her heart swelled with thankfulness at having such a friend.

"Violet," she said, "do tell me——"

Violet stopped abruptly, gazing out over the sea, and laid her hand on Florence's arm in a gesture of command.

"Hush, dear," she said.

Florence hushed obediently and stood looking at Violet with deepening admiration. Violet's mouth was slightly open and her face was twisted into a sort of anguished smile. Then she drew a deep breath and turned to Florence.

"You know, dear, suddenly it all—*gripped* me. The loveliness of it. The light over the sea. That golden sweep of the sands and the green cliff. I know it sounds silly, but a sight like that is *food* to something in me. . . . I think that if I had to choose between life without beauty and death I'd choose death."

Florence preserved a respectful silence. She liked a nice view herself, but she knew that her feeling was not to be compared with Violet's. Violet was quoting poetry now in a deep tremulous voice:

"A thing of beauty is a joy for ever:
Its loveliness increases, it will never
Pass into nothingness: but still will keep
A bower quiet for me and a sleep
Full of sweet dreams and health and quiet breathing.

"Do you know where it comes from?" she went on, speaking in the light brave tone of one who has just controlled some almost uncontrollable emotion.

"No," said Florence.

"You ought to read more, Flo, darling," said Violet in affectionate reproach. "I make it a rule to read a few lines of good poetry every day. It helps to keep one on the heights. It's so easy to slip down without noticing. . . ." She put her arm through Florence's and her voice became gay and whimsical. "I shall have to be your schoolma'am and set you so much to read a day and see that you do it."

This new intimate tone of Violet's made Florence feel quite bewildered. Bewildered, but very, very happy. Generally Violet was rather short and impatient with her. She felt so grateful that she decided to try to read a piece of poetry every day in order to be a little nearer the heights where Violet lived. She'd never cared much for poetry since the days when she'd had to learn "The Wreck of the Hesperus" and the one that began "At Flores in the Azores," but she'd make a real effort.

"In about two hours now Martin will be here, won't he?" said Violet.

"Yes," agreed Florence, counting conscientiously.

"Let's sit down a moment," said Violet.

There was something very serious to her voice. Florence obeyed, composing her face to suit Violet's new tone. They sat down on the short green grass among the bracken and sea pinks and looked over the expanse of the bay. Florence remained silent in case Violet was satisfying her hunger for beauty and didn't want to be disturbed.

"I gave you a hint as to how things are between Martin and me, didn't I?" said Violet at last.

"Yes," murmured Florence.

"Of course," said Violet dreamily, "we've not actually met very often, I know. . . . That doesn't matter. I mean, it's the mind that matters, and our minds have gradually been drawing closer together ever since he went away. I think that letters *do* sometimes bring two reserved people together more quickly than ordinary intercourse. My feelings, you know, dear, are very deep. I may seem light-hearted, perhaps even shallow, on the surface——"

"Oh no, you don't, Vi," said Florence loyally. "You never seem that. I've often said to Mother——"

"But underneath," interpolated Violet, raising her voice slightly to show Florence that contradiction was unnecessary, "I have, as I said, very deep feelings. I can't—change. I can't take up people and drop them. When I give my friendship I give it for ever. I remember Gwynne once saying that loyalty is the keynote of my character. It's nothing to do with me, of course," she added modestly. "It's just—that I *am* like that."

Florence, though deeply appreciative of Violet's character, wished that she would get back to Martin. She longed to know something a little more definite. As if reading her thought, Violet got back to Martin.

"Well, my feeling for Martin has grown slowly and is deeply rooted like all my feelings. Martin and I mean a great deal to each other. In his last letter I gathered that he wants us to mean all that a man and woman can mean to each other."

49

"Oh, *Vi!*" breathed Florence. "Has he proposed?"

Violet smiled faintly.

"Martin wouldn't do anything quite so crude as to propose by letter when he was going to see me in a few weeks' time. But his last letter—well, it left no room for doubt."

Florence hoped that Violet would show her Martin's last letter, or at least tell her what he'd said in it, but Violet evidently wasn't going to do that, so after waiting for a few minutes she murmured:

"It will be lovely for us to have you in the family, Vi."

Violet turned her eyes dreamily towards the horizon.

"I've had to think about it very seriously. It's not an easy decision. I've always looked on my teaching as a sort of social service. I know that I mean a lot to these girls. . . . When I had my operation in April several of them said that they'd cried themselves to sleep for nights. . . . I know that I help them, that I open out new worlds to them—it would be false modesty to pretend that I didn't—and so, in a way, I feel that I should be deserting my post, because so few teachers really understand girls, but"—she smiled again, a deprecating, rueful little smile—"after all, I've given them the best years of my life. I deserve a little happiness of my own. Of course, this is all in the strictest confidence, Flo. Martin may have changed his mind. He may have met someone he likes better on the way home."

Anxiety and distress flashed into Florence's face at the idea, then vanished as she saw that Violet was smiling confidently. She was only joking, of course. Martin couldn't possibly have met anyone he liked better on the way home.

"And now, dear," went on Violet brightly, "here I am talking about myself! I don't often do that, do I?" (Violet had not once stopped talking about herself since her arrival yesterday, but Florence was too loyal to let that thought even enter her mind.) "Tell me about yourself. Are you as busy as usual?"

Florence felt grateful to Violet for that. Usually when Florence told her how busy she was she would say, "You ought to try my life for a change, my dear. Then you'd know what it is to be busy."

"Yes, I really am," said Florence. "It's lovely to come away for a rest. Of course, with Mother getting so old, she needs me now all the time. And there's the house to see to. And the garden. And the work I do in the parish. . . ."

"I know," said Violet sympathetically. "I think it's wonderful of you to get through all you do."

The rush of gratitude brought a sudden lump to Florence's throat and made her speechless for a moment. Then she said, "Of course, it's nothing, *nothing*, to what you have to do."

"Oh, I don't know," said Violet. "At least I have definite hours."

Of course it was just kindness that made Violet say that. Violet had often told her that, what with corrections and preparation and having to have the girls to tea and take them out to concerts and picture galleries in order to influence them for good, her work was never finished. The rush of gratitude engulfed Florence's spirit again, and she felt how lovely it was going to be to have Violet as a sister-in-law.

Violet looked at her watch.

"We'd better be walking on now," she said. "We mustn't keep your mother waiting for tea."

They walked down the path that led from the cliffs to the lower end of the bay. They could see Pen's house, Sea Meads, quite clearly, with a row of washing hung out in the back garden and a brightly coloured ball in the middle of the trampled lawn. A little flag flew from the roof of Bear's hut, fixed there by Rosemary, because, she said, he was the top of the school.

Florence, who made great play in her garden at home, pottering about with a trowel, scissors, a pair of gardening gloves, and a rush hat trimmed with raffia, couldn't understand how Pen could bear to see her garden in such a state. Things grew very well in Merlin Bay, and, if she'd only get it properly set out and forbid the children to go on the lawn and flower-beds, she could have quite a show. Gardens were always classified in Florence's mind as "quite a show" or "not much of a show." She'd taken Violet to see Pen yesterday afternoon, but the visit hadn't been a success. Florence really did think that Pen might have put herself out a bit more to receive a visitor of Violet's standing—a B.A., second mistress of quite an important London school, and a friend of people like Gwynne Beauchamp. When Violet mentioned Gwynne Beauchamp, Pen said that she'd never heard of her, which was ridiculous, because everyone had heard of Gwynne Beauchamp. If she hadn't, it was a thing to be ashamed of, not to boast of, as she seemed to be doing. Of course, it was unfortunate that they arrived just as the children were sitting down to tea, but Florence didn't think that was any excuse for Pen's offhand manner. She *did* have the grace to ask them to have some tea, but there obviously wasn't any room for them at the table, and anyway they'd just had it at the hotel. The children were sitting at the kitchen table, too, and, though Violet was very tactful, saying what a pretty kitchen it was and how she loved meals in a kitchen, Florence had felt quite ashamed. Stella was out with Tim Somebody-or-other, and Pen was flying about all the time, cutting bread and butter and pouring out milk and fetching things and answering the door, and more than once had interrupted Violet in the middle of a sentence to say something to one of the children and hadn't even apologised or asked her to go on with it afterwards. It wasn't the kind of thing that Violet was accustomed to. Even the children hadn't seemed as impressed by her as they should have been. They hardly stopped to listen to what she said before they went on talking to each other again. When Florence thought of the snapshots she'd seen of Violet with girls crowding round her on the playing-field, simply hanging on her words, it made her feel again (though she tried not to) that Pen's children were just a little unnatural. Once when Violet said to Roger (so sweetly that Florence was quite touched), "Would you like to come for a walk with me sometime, dear, while I'm down here and we'll teach each other the names of the wild flowers?" and Roger just said, "No, thank you," she'd looked really put out for a moment or two. Pen, of course, ought to have made him apologise and insisted on his going, but she didn't. She just took no notice. It might have been better if Stella had been at home. On the other hand, it might have been worse, because Stella was at the age when most girls adored Violet, and it would have been so dreadful if she hadn't done.

Violet was very nice about it on the way home, and said what a relief it was to be with children who didn't expect you to be "giving out" all the time, but Florence could tell that really she'd have preferred to be giving out.

"I've always thought that Pen brings them up badly," said Florence. "I think she ought to train them to be more pleased to see people."

Violet laughed.

"You do say funny things, darling," she said, but the "darling" showed that she approved of Florence's attitude. "I remember Gwynne once saying," she went on, "that a child's mind is a mirror of the minds around it. . . . You've never met Gwynne, have you, dear?"

"No," said Florence.

She had never been allowed to meet any of Violet's intellectual friends, and she'd never resented this because she knew that she wasn't intellectual and never could be.

"You must meet her one of these days," said Violet graciously.

Florence tried to say something that would adequately express the emotion she felt but could only say, "Oh, *Violet*!"

The thought that as Violet's sister-in-law she might actually take her part in the full absorbing life that at present she only knew from Violet's accounts of it, sent a thrill of delight through her. She would make a real effort from now on to read the less interesting parts of the newspaper—leading articles and the bits about music and art exhibitions. She could never be worthy of Violet, of course, but she must at any rate try to be.

"I think I told you that Martin said he'd like to get work in England, if possible, didn't I?" said Violet.

"Yes," said Florence, deciding to turn on to the duller parts of the wireless programmes, too—talks and readings and politics.

"If he still wants that when he comes home," went on Violet, "I think that perhaps my uncle could find him something. He's in touch with quite a lot of business firms. It would have to be a good post, of course. . . ."

"Oh, Violet!" said Florence, her heart full to bursting point. "Won't it be *lovely*!"

*

Mrs. Paget sat by the window in the lounge of the Merlin Bay Hotel, looking out onto the beach. The hotel—a long rambling building, painted white, which had been built the year after Mrs. Paget spent her honeymoon there—was in the centre of the bay, where the cliffs from either side sloped down almost to sea-level. Its front door opened onto a narrow lane, which came down from the main road, encircled the bay, then rejoined the main road again. At the back was a small garden, enclosed by a hedge of veronica, in which was a tennis court, a rockery smothered in gazania, one or two palms, and a not very secure garden seat. From it a small green gate led straight onto the beach. There was nothing up-to-date about the Merlin Bay Hotel. The lounge in which Mrs. Paget sat was furnished like an old-fashioned drawing-room, with chintz-covered chairs and lace curtains at the windows, while the dining-room contained the largest sideboard Mrs. Paget had ever seen, and over it a stuffed fish of proportionate size in a glass case between two Landseer engravings. There was a bar, but it was small and dark and a little musty. It did not cater for the "road house" public. The clientele of the hotel consisted chiefly of children and parents, retired couples, and middle-aged maiden ladies. Even the board on the main road, "Merlin Bay Hotel, First Turn on the Right," was by now so weather-beaten that it was almost indecipherable. One glance at it told "bright young things" rushing past in sports cars that there would be no chromium or plate glass or darkie barman, and they rushed on somewhere else. The keynote of the hotel was not smartness but solid comfort—deep mattresses in ugly but immaculately clean bedrooms, with "toilet sets" on the dressing-table and crochet mats on the washstands, and tender, perfectly cooked joints beneath the Landseer engravings.

Mrs. Paget had been down to the old village and found the cottage where she and Michael had spent their honeymoon. It had been turned into a shop, which sold tobacco and sweets and a jumble of toy boats, spades, walking-sticks, oranges, and beach shoes, but it had not really been altered. The doorway was still so low that Michael would have had to stoop to enter it, and you still had to go down a step into the dark little front room that

54

was now the shop. She could almost see Michael leaning against the doorway, his hands in his pockets, his pipe in his mouth, looking out to sea. . . . She had bought some sweets for Pen's children and walked back to the hotel slowly, dreamily, the strange sense of anticipation deepening at her heart. She had thought that perhaps when she actually got here she would find that she had come down on a fool's errand, obeyed a whim of the moment as inconstant as a will-o'-the-wisp. Like those ridiculous women who call themselves psychic and follow the "guidance" of every fleeting impulse. But that hadn't happened. The knowledge that she had come here for some specific purpose had grown stronger as soon as she set foot in the place. A new sweet delight pervaded her, almost as if she were in love with Michael again. It wasn't excitement. It was too calm, too serene, for that. She had come here because Michael had wanted her to come—she still didn't know why. Something was going to happen to her here—she still didn't know what. And she had no desire to hasten the knowledge. It was coming surely, inevitably, towards her. At exactly the right moment—not a second before or after—it would reveal itself. Meantime, this deep sense of happiness filled her spirit—a sense of happiness that she had not known since her youth. She had indeed almost forgotten that it existed, so long had she lived without any stirring of the depths. She even wanted to postpone the knowledge as far as possible, so that she might extract the utmost savour from this soul-sweetening delight.

Pen and the children had come to see her on the evening of her arrival and again yesterday. They were dears—especially Rosemary—but somehow, like everything else around her now, they seemed not quite real. Except Stella. Stella was real and vital, and about her Mrs. Paget glimpsed something of the same secret exaltation that dwelt in her own spirit. She was too old for it to show, but it shone unmistakably in Stella, enhancing her loveliness, informing her youth with a kind of radiance, making her seem poignantly defenceless and vulnerable. Whatever her love was, it would probably bring her unhappiness (one's first love generally did), and she wouldn't realise that the unhappiness was just as precious as the happiness. Poor Florence, who had not known either—enwrapped in the barrenness of her friendship with Violet. Sometimes Mrs. Paget felt a little remorseful about Florence, as if it were her fault that she was like that, as if she had bequeathed to her in an exaggerated, distorted form the fear of responsibility that had made her shrink so from her parents' confidences and even refuse—in this place fifty years ago—to listen to Michael's. . . .

Pen certainly had inherited nothing of it. Not as far as the children were concerned, anyway. She had been amused by the mother-hen airs that Pen had put on yesterday. Pen adored being the mother of six children and had looked for a moment quite sulky when Mrs. Paget mentioned an aunt who had had sixteen. All the same, she was making a great mistake about Charles. Children didn't make up for a husband, though they seemed to when they were little. Sooner or later Pen would find herself left high and dry. Inevitably as they grew up she would lose her children, and if she hadn't Charles to turn to she would be a very lonely woman. Moreover, children didn't really like being absorbed in the way that Pen absorbed hers. Something in them instinctively resented it and tried to outwit it. . . . It wasn't her business, however. She hadn't come here to poke her fingers into Pen's pies. A faintly mischievous smile flickered across her face as she pictured the meeting between Violet Coniston and Pen—Pen showing off as the happy wife and mother, Violet showing off as the successful professional woman. How they'd hate each other! But Pen would score. . . . They all knew that Violet had been trying to get married for years. And she was probably going to succeed. Martin, homesick, lonely, starved for companionship, hungry for romance, would fall into her lap like an over-ripe plum. Conscientiously she tried to feel towards Martin as a mother ought to feel towards her son, but again her innate honesty made her face the fact that they were strangers. He had left her as a boy. He had come back a man, his character formed by experiences in which she had no share and of which she had no knowledge. She knew nothing of his background or of his friends, very little of his tastes. They had nothing in common but the memories of his childhood. Odd to think of that trusting, adoring little boy who had once looked to her for everything, whose whole world she had formed. Probably hundreds and thousands of mothers all the world over stood in that relation to their sons, were bewildered and secretly dismayed by strangers who had once been those trusting, adoring little boys.

Florence and Violet were coming in now, opening the wooden gate that led from the beach to the garden. How ridiculous Florence looked, with her hat on one side and that languishing sentimental expression on her face! Florence's admiration of Violet had always irritated Mrs. Paget. Perhaps it's maternal jealousy on my part, she thought suddenly, and was amused and interested by the idea.

George, the old waiter (who out of season was boots and hall porter as well), brought in the tea and almost immediately Florence and Violet entered.

"Had a nice rest?" said Violet, smiling brightly at Mrs. Paget.

"Yes, thank you," said Mrs. Paget. "Did you have a nice walk?"

"Lovely. It's a fascinating little place, isn't it?"

"Isn't it!" agreed Mrs. Paget. "Did you call to see Pen?"

"Yes," said Violet rather shortly.

"Attractive children, aren't they?" said Mrs. Paget.

"Y-yes," said Violet.

"It's a wonderful place for wild flowers, Mother," put in Florence. "Vi's simply wonderful. She knows them all."

"Oh, only the more common ones," laughed Violet, her good-humour restored.

"Will you pour out, Florence dear?" said Mrs. Paget.

She hated to see Florence fumbling about among the tea-cups, but she wanted to make up for having called her ridiculous, even in her thoughts.

Florence beamed with pleasure and glanced at Violet, hoping that Violet noticed this proof of Mother's dependence on her.

"We've met quite a number of the locals," said Violet, with the amused air of a giant among pygmies. "There was a couple in the garden of a bungalow called Cliff Cottage—a charming young man and a woman who looked old enough to be his mother but who was obviously his wife. Such an old hag! I felt so sorry for him. Why *do* men marry women like that? One can only suppose she had money."

"They're the Heaths," said Mrs. Paget quietly. "Actually she's younger than he is and she hadn't any money but was very pretty."

Violet looked a little put out, and Florence glanced reproachfully at her mother. It was really extraordinary the way Mother always knew everything about everybody. She was afraid that Violet would think her a dreadful gossip.

"How *do* you know that, Mother?" she said.

"Oh, I just talk to people," said Mrs. Paget, trying not to feel irritated by the way Florence was splashing the milk into the cups. "George told me quite a lot."

Florence looked nervously and apologetically at Violet. Violet would never be guilty of the vulgarity of gossiping with a servant. It wasn't the sort of thing that one openly admitted doing, anyway. Violet smiled at her kindly as if to show that she didn't mind.

"I think it's so interesting to know about other people," she said, "but I'm afraid I'm always too busy myself to find out."

"Did you see anyone else?" asked Mrs. Paget, taking her cup of tea from Florence and pouring the slops carefully back from the saucer into the cup. (Florence could never pour out tea without slopping half of it into the saucers.)

"Yes, we saw a dreadful girl," said Florence. "She looked like one of those mental cases. Terribly excited about something and shouting at the top of her voice. The woman who was with her could hardly get her along."

An expression of fastidious disgust came over Violet's chiselled features.

"I think it's horrible that people like that should be allowed out," she said. "I felt quite upset by it."

"Some people have to live with her, you know," Mrs. Paget reminded them. "It's even worse for them."

"I know," said Violet, letting a shudder expressive of acute sensitiveness pass over her frame. "I couldn't, I just couldn't." She glanced at her watch. "Martin's train gets in quite soon now, doesn't it? I think I'll go up and change."

Mrs. Paget smiled wryly to herself. There was half an hour before she need have got ready. Going to put on all her war paint. Poor Martin! There wasn't much chance for him. Or was there? She'd probably overdo things. . . .

Florence nibbled happily at a piece of shortcake. Perhaps this time to-morrow Martin and Violet would be engaged. She'd have liked to tell Mother about it, now that it was so near, but, after all, it wasn't her secret. It was Violet's. . . .

Violet didn't come down till the last minute. She wore a brown coat over a brown-and-white silk dress, and an extremely becoming hat. (She's bought it specially, thought Mrs. Paget. Must have cost a pretty penny, too. She's taking no chances. . . .) She had arranged her hair in a mass of small curls round her head instead of in its usual bun. Her cheeks were delicately rouged, her eyes darkened. She looked a little self-conscious as she met Mrs. Paget's eye.

"Come on, Flo dear," she said brightly. "It's time we started."

Martin Paget watched the green countryside flash past the carriage window. He was in a state of nervous tension, excited and depressed by turn. He had looked forward eagerly to this visit to England, building extravagant hopes on it, making extravagant plans for it, and so far it had proved a bitter disappointment. He had, he found, dropped out of everything. . . . It hadn't been so bad on his last leave five years ago. He had lost touch with a good many of his old friends, of course, even then, but there had still been Barrow and Franklin, the two chief friends of his boyhood. They had welcomed him, gone about with him, and "reminisced" with him by the hour, reviving old jokes, old memories. The three of them had toured Scotland together in a second-hand car. In spite of a few disappointments he had enjoyed his last leave, and it had never occurred to him that Barrow's marriage and Franklin's engagement would have made so much difference.

Barrow had turned into a uxorious husband and doting father, and, though polite and hospitable, had plainly no use for him. In

Franklin's eyes only his fiancée now existed, and he was, in addition, buried deep in prospective in-laws. He sent hasty and perfunctory excuses. "Sorry, old man, next week no use at all. Going to stay with Sally's people. Might manage a week-end later." But he never did manage a week-end. Martin trailed about, looking up other old friends, only to find that the years had separated him from them irrevocably. Once the old memories (very dim and far away and unreal now) were disposed of, there was nothing left to talk about. Their lives were full of interests in which he had no part. They asked him about his work in Malaya but were obviously bored when he told them about it. A nightmare sensation of unwantedness had taken possession of him. He had felt himself an exile in Malaya and looked on England as his home, but he felt even more of an exile here than he had felt abroad. He went to the country village where he had spent his childhood (his mother and Florence had moved from it when his father died) and found that it had been "developed" into a small town, with a network of streets and shops and little villas and garages. There was hardly a single feature that he could recognise. London itself had changed, too. It was busier, more cosmopolitan, more full of people rushing about on their own business with no time to spare for anyone or anything else. He was coming to Merlin Bay with something of the same hurt bewilderment at his heart as had been there, once, when he was a child and the other children had ignored him at a party to which he had been looking forward excitedly for weeks.

His mind turned with increasing apprehension to the thought of Violet. Would she disappoint him like everything else? Her letters had been kind, but it might have been the casual meaningless kindness of a good-natured woman. He wanted more than that. During these last few weeks he had been made to feel as if he were a ghost, haunting other men's firesides. He wanted to be a real man with a fireside of his own. He remembered that when he last came home on leave he had vaguely hoped to meet someone with whom he could fall in love, but it hadn't happened. That was five years ago. He was older now. He was forty-six. If it didn't happen this time it would probably never happen. It was more than a romantic hope now. It was a desperate resolve. After all, it was only the ordinary lot of man that he wanted—a wife and home. He was tired of the feeling of exile with which he had lived so long. There had always been the difficulty of taking a woman out to Malaya, of course, but with luck he might get a job in England. He had said so to Violet in his last letter. He had said rather a lot to Violet in his last letter. But he'd meant every word of it. The friendship that had grown so slowly and surely between them in the last five years had become the most precious thing in his life. He was ready to fall in love with her, and she, he felt sure, was ready to fall in love with him. Odd that he could hardly remember what she looked like. He had known of her for years, of course, as Florence's friend, and had avoided meeting her because she was coloured in his thoughts by that something of the ludicrous that belonged to Florence and all her doings. It wasn't till that last meeting just before he went back to Malaya that she had suddenly ceased to be an appendage of Florence and become herself—kind, charming, sympathetic. And from that point, through the letters that had arrived regularly each fortnight, she had become more and more real, more and more glamorous and desirable and necessary to him. She had sent him a photograph of herself about six months ago in which she looked amazingly young and beautiful. Of course, he reasoned with himself, she couldn't really look *quite* like that—he didn't even want her to look quite like that—but he had put her photograph on his bedroom mantelpiece and spent a good deal of time studying it. He wondered suddenly what she was feeling now, whether she remembered him at all clearly. On an impulse he rose and rearranged his cases on the rack in order to glance at himself in the mirror. God knew he wasn't much to look at—swarthy, with deeply furrowed cheeks, a scar across one temple, and crooked teeth (they'd made him a bar to wear as a child, but he always took it out). He needn't worry about that, though. It wasn't as if she'd never seen him before. . . . He leant out of the window. St. Ives Bay. . . . He must be very near Penzance now. Would Mother come to meet him, he wondered. She was such a darling. There was something mischievous and elfin-like lurking always behind her serenity. She must need all her patience, living with Florence. Nice to see Pen again, too. Roger had been a baby on his last leave and Valerie not yet born. They hadn't moved to Merlin Bay then, either. Martin took a vicarious pride in Pen's family and felt a secret envy of Charles, with his comfortable home, capable little wife, and six bonny children. But it was no use trying to think of Mother or Florence or Pen. He couldn't really think of anyone but Violet. . . .

The train was slowing down at Penzance station. He looked out of the carriage window. There they were, Florence as dowdy and dishevelled as ever, and Violet—no, she didn't look *quite* as young and beautiful as she had done in the photograph, he was relieved to see. But she looked pretty enough as she stood there by Florence, smiling a welcome. He stepped down onto the platform, his heart beating violently, and took her hand in a long firm grip.

Chapter Five

ROSEMARY darted up and down stairs, a white-hot flame of excitement.

"How many of them can I take, Mummy? I *must* take Roo. He's been looking forward to it all week. *And* Minnie Monkey. *And* Kanga. They'd be *terribly* disappointed if they couldn't go."

"Not more than three, darling," called Pen from the bedroom.

Rosemary stopped and considered, her small figure tense and quivering.

"Can two little ones count as one big one?" she said.

Pen laughed.

"Very well. But not more than two. I mean, you mustn't take six little ones and count them three."

"No, I won't," promised Rosemary. "I'll take Roo and Wilfred for the two little ones and Minnie Monkey and Kanga to look after Roo. ... Hetty's been *hoping* she could come," she added tentatively.

"Well, tell her she can't."

"All right," said Rosemary resignedly.

"And you mustn't expect anyone else to carry them for you."

"Of *course* not," said Rosemary, shocked by the idea, forgetting how often she had set off for walks laden with her "people," half of which Pen had had to carry home.

It was the children's half-term and Stella's birthday. Gordon and Susan had arrived from school for the week-end last night, and the morning had been a whirl of excitement, with Stella's birthday presents and the preparation for the afternoon's picnic. Besides the family—including Mrs. Paget, Florence, Martin, and Violet—Mrs.

Egerton and Beryl and the Bevans had been invited. Pen would have liked to ask Tim and his mother without Agnes, but Mrs. Bevan, usually so gentle, became hotly indignant when anyone tried to exclude Agnes from an invitation.

"She *enjoys* things so, and it's so unkind of people to want to deprive her of a little pleasure. I know she's—excitable, but she's always quite good when I'm with her."

So Agnes had had to be invited and Valerie urged to conquer her fear.

"She can't help looking like that and talking like that, Val darling," said Pen, "and she's very kind, really. She wouldn't dream of hurting you. Try to think of her as a princess under a spell."

"Like the Beast?" said Valerie with interest.

"Yes, like the Beast."

"All right, I'll try," said Valerie.

Stella was in her bedroom, standing in front of the looking-glass, damping her curls with setting lotion. On the bed were ranged her birthday presents—the book-mark worked in cross stitch from Valerie, the china cat from Roger, the handkerchief with a bunch of violets embroidered in the corner from Rosemary, the book token from Gordon and Susan, the peach-coloured slip from Pen, the handbag that had arrived from Charles by the morning's post, the gay silk triangle from a school friend, and a dreadful little bead purse, worn and frowsty, from Miss Hinkley.

It wasn't the thought of her birthday, however, that made her eyes so bright with excitement as she sprinkled the setting lotion recklessly over her fair shining hair, or even the thought of the picnic this afternoon. It was the knowledge that Arnold Kemsing was coming to Four Winds to-day. Old Crump, the agent, had told her so definitely when she met him yesterday by the post office.

"Gettin' all the summer lot in good an' fine now," he had said, with a self-congratulatory grin. "Mr. Kemsing's comin' along to-morrow. Bringin' his tackle an' all."

Old Crump saw to the letting of all the holiday cottages in Merlin Bay, did the odd jobs and spasmodically tidied the gardens. He had a hatchet face in a frame of white whiskers and was always immensely amused by the "goings on" of the summer visitors, whom he looked on as a species of performing animal.

She had put on a new dress of printed shantung and was going to tie the silk triangle (whose colourings exactly matched it) round her hair, but it would be all spoilt if her hair wouldn't go right. She must look her best to-day—to-day of all days. It was strange how one generally seemed to look one's best when there was nobody to see one, and when it mattered terribly what one looked like everything went wrong. To-day—the day that mattered more than any other day in her whole life—a spot was coming on her chin and her hair was awful. Perhaps she'd put too much setting lotion on it. . . .

There was a knock at the door and Susan entered. Susan was tall for her twelve years, and the white linen school tunic with the red belt emphasised her thin coltish figure. There was about her something of Rosemary's flame-like eagerness but nothing of the dancing excitement that characterised Rosemary. In Susan the flame glowed deep down beneath a covering of shyness and reserve.

She stood inside the door and looked at Stella across the room. She had large dark eyes, bobbed dark hair, and a pale narrow face.

"You *do* look nice, Stella," she said.

The tribute, convincing in its childish ingenuousness, banished the slight irritation that her interruption had caused Stella.

"I can't get my hair right," she complained.

"I think it's lovely," said Susan, coming into the room and sitting on the bed. "I shouldn't do anything else to it."

"All right, I won't," said Stella, who had been wondering what else she *could* do to it.

She tied the silk triangle carefully over it.

"Earwig sent you her love," said Susan.

"Oh, did she?" said Stella, thinking of the lank spectacled Earwig, now in the Upper Sixth, who had been one of her friends at St. Julian's. Those days—of confidential talks, heart-stirring battles on the playing-field, and arm-in-arm promenades in the garden—seemed very far away. Now that she stood on the threshold of her great romance she couldn't be expected to take much interest in people like Earwig, but she added politely, "Well, give her mine."

"She's got terribly uppish since she was made a prefect," said Susan.

"Has she?" said Stella, becoming interested despite herself. "How?"

"Oh, bossy and throwing her weight about and that sort of thing."

"Yes, she would," conceded Stella judicially. "You could always see that she had it in her."

"I wish you hadn't left," said Susan. "It's rotten without you."

"Nonsense!" said Stella in a brisk elder-sister tone, but secretly much flattered. "You ought to learn to stand on your own feet."

"I know," said Susan. "I am trying. I think I'm better than I was. . . . But somehow having you there made things easier."

Stella was examining her face anxiously in the mirror.

"Can you see a spot on my chin?" she said. Susan got up from the bed and inspected it conscientiously.

"No."

"I can feel it," said Stella, drawing her finger over the smooth skin. "I suppose it's just not showing yet. It'll probably look awful by tea-time."

Susan went over to the window and sat on the low wooden seat, drawing up her long bare legs.

"What's Uncle Martin like?" she said. "I hardly remember him."

"He's rather"—Stella considered for a moment, then went on—"like Charles the Second, but not so attractive."

Susan looked a trifle taken aback.

"I thought Charles the Second was a bad man," she said.

Stella, who was now tidying her room by the simple process of bundling everything into the nearest drawer, stopped to gaze into the distance with an expression of deep worldly wisdom.

"That's not so simple as it seems at your age, Sue," she said.

"I suppose not," said Susan humbly.

"I believe he's almost engaged to Miss Coniston," went on Stella. "That friend of Aunt Florence, you know, who's staying with them."

"Is she nice?" said Susan.

"No, but she tries so hard to be that it's rather pathetic."

Susan laughed, then looked out again over the sunlit bay. There was a short silence before she said: "Oh Stella, you are lucky to be living at home. I sometimes can't bear it when I think that I've got to live through five more years of school. Isn't it lovely being here all the time with Mummy and the children and no hateful term looming in front of you?"

Stella, intent on searching for a clean handkerchief in an extremely untidy drawer, made no reply.

Susan continued: "I did hope that Daddy's holiday would have begun by now. I'm terribly sorry he's not here this week-end."

"Mother isn't," said Stella with a short laugh, finding a handkerchief and slipping it up the elastic leg-band of her knickers.

Susan turned wide startled eyes on her.

"Why? What do you mean?"

Stella had returned to the looking-glass and was powdering her petal-like skin.

"Mother's jealous of us with Daddy," she said carelessly. "Didn't you know that?"

"Oh, *no*, Stella! I don't believe it."

"I didn't once. Then—I remember—I went for a long walk with Daddy one afternoon and Mother was alone at home and she sulked all evening about it. . . . She's always quite kind to Daddy, but she hasn't really much use for him, you know."

"Stella!"

Stella turned, and, at the look on Susan's face, compunction pierced her youthful hardness.

"You silly kid!" she said. "I was only teasing you."

The black mist that had suddenly shut out the sun cleared away from before Susan's eyes. It wasn't that she was specially devoted to Daddy, but Daddy's and Mummy's devotion to each other was a necessary part of the universe. To doubt it would be to lose all sense of security, to feel quicksand instead of solid earth beneath one's feet.

"You are a wretch, Stell," she said, with a little breathless laugh.

Stella glanced critically round the room, took her dressing-gown from the floor and hung it behind the door, then gathered up everything else that was lying about and threw it into the wardrobe.

"Come on," she said; "we've got to pack the picnic baskets. It was all Mummy could do to stop Miss Hinkley packing the whole lot this morning and staggering up the cliff with them."

Miss Hinkley had arrived the day before, wearing a long black coat and black silk dress, both of which hung about her in voluminous folds.

Miss Hinkley's wardrobe was regularly supplied to her by one of the numerous charities that cater for reduced gentlewomen, but the subscribers who so kindly sent their cast-off garments for distribution among their less fortunate sisters all seemed to be of much heavier build than Miss Hinkley. Occasionally she had tried "taking them in," but she was not a good needlewoman, and the results were not successful. She was a tiny mouse-like woman and there was always a faintly musty smell about her that may have originated from the subscribers' garments or may have been due to the somewhat inadequate facilities for washing provided by the cramped and sunless bed-sitting-room in which she lived. Her sallow, somewhat grimy-looking face was a network of wrinkles, but, despite her eighty years, her thick wiry hair was still predominantly black. She had been a poor relation all her life and had brought it to a fine art. She was humble and deprecating in manner, and could melt into the background so effectively that it was difficult to realise she was there at all. And yet beneath her humility ran a vein of grim tenacity, an instinctive determination not to be quite engulfed by fate. She lived, as it were, on the very fringe of life—her food a bare sufficiency, her clothes always made for and worn out by somebody else before they reached her—but to that fringe she clung with limpet-like endurance. This holiday with Charles's family at Merlin Bay was the high-light of her life. If Charles had not written to invite her at the usual time she would have written herself in her thin spidery writing on her cheap tissue-paper-like notepaper as if taking for granted that they were expecting her as usual. She would have got here somehow, even if she had had to come uninvited, so that they would be forced either to take her in themselves or find room for her elsewhere. People were always being surprised by the unexpected persistence of the grey little shadow with the cringing manners. As soon as she arrived at Sea Meads a silent contest began between her and Pen. Miss Hinkley's idea of being a poor relation on holiday had always included "helping." One "helped" and so in a way paid for one's board and lodging. One did the shopping and made the beds and dusted the rooms and looked after the children and sat on the more uncomfortable chairs and pretended one didn't like the choicer titbits of food so that there would be more of them for the family. Miss Hinkley's pride and sense of fitness insisted that this should be so, and she was disconcerted and secretly aggrieved by Pen's refusal to let her do anything in the house or for the children.

"Of course not, Miss Hinkley," Pen would say briskly, when Miss Hinkley demanded dishcloth or duster. "I shouldn't dream of letting you help."

It would have annoyed Miss Hinkley if she had let things annoy her, because she knew that Pen knew that she really *wanted* to help. She felt that it was partly showing off—as if Pen meant her to see that there was no single chink in her armour of efficiency through which Miss Hinkley and her duster could creep—and partly a determination that Miss Hinkley should not work off any of her feeling of indebtedness in that way, should not be allowed to flatter herself by the delusion that in this holiday arrangement she gave as good as she got. On the contrary, Pen's attitude implied, she gave nothing and got everything. There was an added edge to Pen's firmness where the children were concerned.

"No, of course, Miss Hinkley, there's *nothing* you can do for them. They're used to looking after themselves, and, anyway, they're out of doors all day long."

"My dear," she said to Stella, "she actually asked if she could bath Valerie. As if I'd let that dirty old creature *touch* her!"

Stella had laughed and said, "She's not really dirty," and Pen had replied, "Well, if she's clean, she's only *just*."

Pen, however, couldn't stop her working off something of her sense of obligation by taking the uncomfortable chairs and always choosing the less exciting pudding, and she got a certain small satisfaction from this.

She had made a desperate effort to "help" over the picnic, and had had a prolonged argument with Pen after breakfast as to whether she should spend the morning carrying things up to the spot chosen for the picnic in readiness for the afternoon.

"I should enjoy doing it," she kept saying.

"It's absurd, Miss Hinkley," Pen had said at last impatiently. "There are the five children—not counting Val—and Martin and Florence and Miss Coniston as well as the hotel car that Mother's bringing. We can manage it perfectly in the one journey."

So Miss Hinkley had contented herself with cutting the bread for sandwiches, and even then Pen had to turn her head away in order not to see the brown, wrinkled, claw-like hand (*surely* they were dirty!) clutching the loaf.

They were just packing the picnic baskets when Stella and Susan came downstairs.

"Can we help?" said Stella.

"Of course you can," said Pen.

She thought that Stella needn't have spent quite so long titivating when there was so much to do downstairs. Still—one mustn't be cross on her birthday and she did look very sweet. For Tim's benefit, she supposed. The rest of them were just family and hardly accounted for the good half-hour she'd taken over it.

"Will you pack the fruit in the little suitcase, Stella? It's over there. You might put some of the cakes in, too. I think there's room. And, Sue darling, go into the garden and make sure that the boys are ready. Rosemary's just gone to fetch Beryl. I'll get Val up from her nap."

Sue went out into the garden to Gordon and Roger. Roger held Bear tightly under his arm, trying to make him look as inconspicuous as possible. He wanted to take Bear to the picnic because Rosemary was taking some of her "people" and had impressed upon him that their pleasure would be spoilt if Bear were not there too, but he felt ashamed of carrying a toy about with him under Gordon's superior eye. In spite of Rosemary's uncanny humanising of Bear, the fact remained that he *was* a toy. Gordon, however, was ignoring the dumpy figure squeezed under Roger's arm and engaging him in a flatteringly man-to-man conversation.

"How's old man Orton getting on?" he asked.

"He's all right," said Roger, carefully imitating Gordon's casual tone. "He got in an awful bait the other morning in Arithmetic. Nearly knocked Moston's head off—then told him he was sorry."

"That was a mistake," said Gordon judicially.

As Roger wasn't sure whether the mistake lay in nearly knocking Moston's head off or saying he was sorry, he made no comment.

"He's not a patch on old Heath," went on Gordon.

Gordon had been at Cliff End School when Mr. Heath was headmaster and had left after Mr. Orton's first term.

Instinctive loyalty stirred at Roger's heart, and, carefully preserving the detached supercilious note of the conversation, he said, "Oh, he's not too bad really. . . ."

"Old Ma Orton's not much good, anyway, is she?" said Gordon.

"Well," admitted Roger, "she's"—he searched for the expression he had heard applied to her and brought it out at last with an air of modest triumph—"a bit second-rate."

"You bet she is!" said Gordon. "Now Ma Heath was a decent sort."

"Yes, she's *jolly* decent," agreed Roger, allowing a regrettable note of enthusiasm to mar his detachment.

"Is Mr. Forrester still your form master?"

"Yes."

"He's all right," admitted Gordon.

"Oh yes, he's all right," agreed Roger, with admirable nonchalance.

Susan came out suddenly from the kitchen door and stood screwing up her eyes in the sunshine.

"Mummy wants to know if you're both ready," she said.

"I am," said Gordon, putting his hands in his pockets.

"So am I," said Roger, trying to imitate Gordon's gesture in spite of the presence of Bear under his arm.

In imagination he had jumped seven years and was looking down from an immense height upon a small Cliff Endite and saying in a tone of aloof amusement, "Well, how's old man Orton?"

Susan looked at Gordon shyly, but with earnest questioning in her dark eyes. Before they went away to school Gordon and Susan had been inseparable. They had lived in a world of their own, to which no one else had the key. Stella, as the eldest, had always been Mother's confidante and right hand, with a lieutenant's authority over the little band. Rosemary and Roger were friends and allies, and Val, as the baby, completed the circle by belonging specially to Mother on the one side, as Stella did on the other. Between Gordon and Susan there had always been a special bond of sympathy. The private world they had invented and which had been for so many years more real to them than the world around them, was a world peopled chiefly by animals. The reading of *The Kingdom that Was* and its sequel *The Second Leopard* had suggested it in the first place, and, though the main characters were still those of that story, they had enlarged and developed it till it would have filled innumerable volumes.

But this secret world depended for its very existence upon Gordon. Together they had evolved it, built it up, agreed upon every detail of it, and Susan knew that if ever it ceased to be real to Gordon it would cease to be real to her. And then—she dared not even let herself think of the emptiness of life without it.

They had decided not to carry on the game by letters, and at the end of each term a nightmare fear assailed Susan lest Gordon should have tired of it, and come to despise it as childish. He was so much older, more grown-up, more practical, than she.

The night before she came home this half-term she had prayed that Gordon might still be "playing the Kingdom," as she put it, and she still didn't know whether he was or not. They had not yet been alone together, and, in any case, when first she and Gordon met after an absence she always felt shy and ill-at-ease with him. He meant so much more to her than anyone else in the world. ("I shall never marry," she sometimes said to herself, "because I couldn't possibly love anyone more than I love Gordon.")

Her eyes now searched his face, longing for some reassurance, but before either of them could say anything, Rosemary and Beryl came tumbling in at the gate, and at the same time Dandy hurled himself out of the house, barking excitedly.

"Oh, look at Dandy!" laughed Rosemary. "He thinks it's *his* half-term, too."

"*Him!*" said Roger bitterly. "His life's *all* half-term."

Pen came out holding Valerie's hand—Valerie clean and fresh and clear-eyed after her nap, wearing a crisp clean cotton frock printed all over with tiny flowers, and a sunbonnet to match.

"Now, children, I want each of you to carry something . . . Hello, Beryl. Is your mother coming?"

Beside Rosemary's lithe dancing figure Beryl looked heavier and more solid than ever.

She turned upon Pen a sideways glance from between the fat sleek ringlets and answered in the fat sleek voice that matched the ringlets so perfectly, "She's not quite ready yet, Mrs. Marlowe. And she said, please do you mind us bringing Carry?"

"Carry?" said Pen.

"Carry Peters. I forgot about the picnic and asked her to tea, so Mother says, please can she come, too."

"Yes, of course," said Pen in a curt tone, fiercely indignant on Rosemary's behalf. (Fancy *forgetting* it, when Rosemary had been looking forward to it for weeks!)

She glanced at Rosemary to see if she minded, but Rosemary was too full of excitement at Beryl's presence to have room for any other feeling. She was hopping round and round on one leg, like a small sprite.

"What *does* she see in that hateful child?" Pen asked herself for the hundredth time.

But, though she disliked Beryl, she was very anxious that Beryl should be nice to Rosemary. She knew how terribly Rosemary could suffer when people she loved weren't nice to her.

Chapter Six

THEY lay or sat in sun-steeped drowsiness on the grassy plateau where they had had tea. It was on the further arm of the bay at the highest point, where the cliff rose sheer from the water. Far below them the sea gently lapped the foot, while landwards a slope of bracken, waving grass, and sea-pinks ran up to the main road, which was hidden from sight by a hedge and steep bank.

Blue sky, blue sea, white cliffs, green slopes starred by wild flowers, all bathed in the golden sunshine of a cloudless summer afternoon.

The children had been forbidden to go nearer the cliff-edge than a certain point, but the cliff-edge did not in any case attract them. They preferred to play on the grassy slopes, picking flowers and clambering over the big rocks that projected here and there out of the ground.

Martin and Violet had climbed a small hill that crowned the cliff-top like a miniature kopje and were sitting there in the shade of a jagged boulder.

Mrs. Paget reclined in the deck-chair which she had brought with her in the hotel car, gazing out to sea and pretending to be asleep. Florence sat at her feet on a mackintosh (because with grass you can never be quite sure), knitting a dish-cloth and trying to conquer a feeling of depression that was stealing over her. She had put on her navy-blue coat and skirt and felt much too hot in it, and sitting on the ground always made her back ache.

Tim and Stella had wandered out of sight in one direction, and Susan and Gordon in another. Roger and Valerie were picking sea-pinks on the slopes. Rosemary, Beryl, and Carry had gone up to the farm—from which they had had to fetch extra supplies of milk—to return the empty milk-can.

Miss Hinkley, hot on the scent of a possible opportunity of "helping," had attached herself to Mrs. Bevan and Agnes and was making daisy-chains for Agnes, who plunged about, pulling up daisies with large clumsy fingers, her face moist with perspiration and beaming with delight. She already wore several chains on her head, round her neck, and round each wrist.

Mrs. Bevan sat by, watching them with her sweet strained smile, ready to interfere at once if Agnes should show any signs of the "over-excitement" that could assume such disastrous forms.

Pen was sitting next Mrs. Egerton, knitting a pullover for Roger in his school colours of grey and red. The remains of the tea were still on the table-cloth because everybody had been too lazy to clear them away.

Bear, Kanga, Roo, Minnie Monkey, and Wilfred were seated on the cloth among the remains, each at a plate on which Rosemary had spread some cake crumbs.

"Shall I help you pack up the things now?" said Mrs. Egerton.

She was a large, stupid, good-natured woman, who must have looked exactly like Beryl when she was a little girl. Her eyes were still round and blue, her hair sleekly blonde, but the chubbiness of her childhood had degenerated into an unwieldiness of build that was emphasised by her obviously home-made shorts.

"Oh no, we needn't bother yet," said Pen, yielding to the languor of content that steals over one when an occasion for which one has made careful preparation is successfully over. Everyone had obviously enjoyed the tea (especially the little cocoanut cakes she'd baked last night) and they had all made much of Stella, in whose honour it was. Pen was so anxious for Stella to be happy, and she seemed radiant with happiness this afternoon. . . .

The three children came running down the field from the farm. Their voices cut sharply through the sleepy air. Rosemary arrived at the stile first and flew over like a piece of thistledown. Beryl and Carry followed more slowly. Beryl stood on the top of the stile and shouted, "Hello, everybody!" She wore a short blue frock that was just the colour of her eyes.

"How sweet Beryl looks!" said Pen insincerely, watching Rosemary's elfin figure leaping down the slope towards her.

"Yes, doesn't she!" said Mrs. Egerton, and, though Pen waited for it, made no comment on Rosemary in return.

Pen felt as outraged as if she had deliberately cheated in a game.

"It's funny that she's the eldest in the form and Rosemary the youngest, isn't it?" she said casually.

"Yes, isn't it!" said Mrs. Egerton, still obtusely placid.

Rosemary danced up to them.

"We've had a lovely time!" she said breathlessly. "I went into the field behind the farm all by myself, and a horse came galloping up to me and I was very nearly frightened, but I said 'Pax' to it, and it seemed to understand and went away again."

Beryl and Carry came slowly towards the group. Carry's black fringe was cut just above her eyes, giving her the air of a Japanese doll. She was polite and well-behaved, but to Pen's critical eyes she had the air of a child who "knew more than she should." Pen had always discouraged her visits to Sea Meads, and had been sorry when she was moved down into Rosemary's form at school.

Mrs. Egerton seized upon Beryl, took a small comb from her hand-bag and began to repair the ravages that time had wrought upon the ringlets, combing them one by one round her finger, then letting them spring back to their full length. Rosemary watched the process, fascinated.

"Now don't run about and get too hot, darling," said Mrs. Egerton, releasing the last smooth corkscrew. "It's so bad for you."

"Let's play Hide-and-seek," said Rosemary. "Come on. . . . Come on, Roger and Val. We're going to play Hide-and-seek."

Agnes had become excited by the sight of the three children running down the hill.

"Me, too," she shouted. "Me play, too!"

"Couldn't she play with them?" pleaded Miss Hinkley.

Mrs. Bevan shook her head.

"She might hurt them. She wouldn't mean to, of course. . . ."

Agnes's face darkened.

"Me play, too," she shouted again. "Me play, too!"

"Come for a little walk with me instead, Agnes," said Miss Hinkley brightly, "and I'll tell you a story."

The scowl left Agnes's face.

"A fairy story?" she said.

"Yes, a fairy story," said Miss Hinkley.

"All right," said Agnes, quite forgetting about the game.

Miss Hinkley felt pleased and flattered by the little triumph. She had been secretly somewhat hurt by the young Marlowes' attitude to her. They were quite polite, but they obviously didn't want to listen to her fairy stories or let her join in their games.

"You choose what it shall be about, dear," she said, "and we'll go for a little walk along the cliff while I tell you." She turned to Mrs. Bevan. "That will be all right, won't it?"

Mrs. Bevan was touched. It wasn't often that people went out of their way to be nice to Agnes.

"How kind of you!" she said. "But you'll stay where I can see her—won't you?—because——"

"Oh yes, we'll do that," said Miss Hinkley. "We want to be able to see Mother, don't we, Agnes?"

"Yes," agreed Agnes happily.

The two walked off together—Miss Hinkley with her little mincing steps, Agnes lumbering along and towering over her companion. There was a look, almost of complacency, on Miss Hinkley's wrinkled old face. At last she was "helping," earning, in however indirect a way and to whatever slight degree, that comfortable bed and those well-cooked ample meals that Pen provided for her at Sea Meads. Her self-respect returned to her with a rush.

"About the sea," she said, taking up Agnes's suggestion. (How sensible the child was, after all!) "Yes, dear . . . I'll tell you one about the sea. Once on a time . . ."

Mrs. Bevan, who had got up to assist in the pacifying of Agnes, sat down by Florence, with a faint sigh of weariness, and relaxed as far as she ever allowed herself to relax, for her eyes never left Miss Hinkley and Agnes for more than a few seconds, and she was braced always to spring to her feet and fly to Agnes at the least sign of "over-excitement."

"What are you knitting?" she asked Florence, and Florence told her all about the dish-cloths and the Sale of Work and how busy she was at home from morning to night. She enlarged on it even more than usual because she'd had a sort of nightmare last night (it *must* have been a nightmare, of course), from which she'd awakened with a dreadful feeling that it wouldn't make any difference to anyone if she weren't there at all. She knew that it was absurd—Mother for instance, depended on her every minute of every day—but she couldn't get rid of the feeling, as she'd have been able to at home, by weeding the rockery or doing the flowers or checking the tradesmen's books again. Time always hung a little heavy on one's hands when one was away from home.

"So that a little rest like this," she ended, "is a real *oasis* to me."

"I'm sure it is," said Mrs. Bevan, taking her watchful gaze from Agnes for a fleeting moment to show that she was really interested in what Florence was saying.

Violet's rather high-pitched voice rang out from the hillock where she was sitting with Martin, and Florence turned to look at them.

The intoxicating promise of intimate friendship that Violet had held out to her yesterday had been left, as it were, in mid-air. Since Martin's arrival Violet's manner had been withdrawn and impersonal. It was natural, of course, thought Florence with a sigh, that only Martin should now exist for her. Strange to think of Violet married. . . . Come to that, strange to think of anyone married. They went on doing just the same things they'd done before, shopping and sewing and going to the pictures and talking about their neighbours, and all the time *that* was happening to them. Dozens of Florence's contemporaries had entered the married state and emerged from the experience apparently just the same as they had been before, except that one knew they couldn't be *quite* the same. Watching them with their newly acquired husbands, Florence could never repress a shrinking curiosity of which she was ashamed. . . .

Mrs. Bevan's eyes followed Florence's to the grassy eminence where Martin sat, pipe in mouth, his arms clasping his knees, Violet stretched gracefully on the grass beside him.

"He's so nice, your brother, isn't he?" she said. "And I do so admire Miss Coniston. So clever and good-looking."

To Mrs. Bevan, living in a kind of hermetically sealed cell alone with Agnes, the free denizens of the outside world who passed and re-passed the window of her prison seemed to be of superlative beauty and intelligence.

"Yes, isn't she!" said Florence, and, lowering her voice reverently, added, "she's a friend of Gwynne Beauchamp's. . . ." Then she proceeded to obey the rules of the game that Mrs. Egerton had just broken so egregiously and added, "I think your Tim's such a dear."

"Yes . . ." agreed Mrs. Bevan, her blue eyes troubled and unhappy.

She had had a dreadful scene with Tim last night. He had been setting off for a walk, when Agnes had suddenly demanded to go with him. Agnes's admiration of Tim was pathetic. She was delighted when he showed her the slightest attention and seldom flew into a rage with him, however great the provocation.

"Please," she had begged with tears in her eyes. "Please, Tim."

"No," Tim had said shortly, going into the hall.

Mrs. Bevan had followed him.

"Tim, do take her," she pleaded. "You needn't stay out long. Just a little walk on the cliff and back. She'll be quite good."

And Tim, usually so amenable, had swung round on her angrily.

"No, I won't," he had said hotly. "I just can't look at her or touch her. It makes me sick. I *hate* her, I tell you. . . . That's why I'm going out, because I can't bear to see her or hear her indoors a moment longer. . . ."

"Tim, how *can* you!" burst out Mrs. Bevan. "You have everything and she has nothing. She——"

He interrupted her: "You mean she has everything and I've nothing. You'd see me cut into little pieces if it would help her. You love her so much that there's nothing left over for me. There never has been. I've always known it. Even when I was a child I knew it. She's spoilt everything for me. All my life you've—almost hated me for being ordinary, when she's like that. As if I'd taken more than my share. As if I could help it. . . . I've loved you terribly, always, and you've never loved me at all——"

"Tim, don't!"

"I must. I must tell you what I feel about it. I've bottled it up for so long. I didn't want you to know how hateful I was, because I didn't want you to think badly of me, but you don't think of me at all, so it doesn't matter. You don't care that I've never been able to have any friends, that I've never had a real home. I don't wonder Father couldn't stand it. I——"

He stopped short, aghast at what he had said. She went white and looked at him in silence, an odd terror and pleading in her eyes. Then he turned on his heel and went out, his heart full of shame and misery, and did not return till after she was in bed.

This morning both had been embarrassed and self-conscious, each avoiding the other's eye, and Agnes, who was curiously sensitive to the atmosphere, had been stormy and intractable.

"It's—it's hard lines on Tim, of course, having Agnes," went on Mrs. Bevan slowly. She had not faltered for a moment in her resolve to give her whole life to Agnes, but she couldn't help feeling sorry about Tim. Was he going to fail her—as Simon had failed her?

"I do think this place is doing Agnes good," she added. "I'm sure she's a little better since we came here."

"I'm so glad," said Florence. "It's doing Mother good, too. Look, she's asleep now. It's the air."

Mrs. Paget was not, of course, asleep, but she was keeping her eyes half shut because she wanted to be left alone with her thoughts. . . . As she went about the little village, memories, dead for years, sprang suddenly to life. She had forgotten till she saw the low stile leading to the path across the fields how Michael and she had sat there one evening, and how he had told her that he had lain awake all the night before he proposed to her, rehearsing his proposal, sitting up in bed in his night-shirt with dishevelled hair pleading and protesting into the darkness. She had laughed helplessly at his description and at the stilted form in which he finally decided to put his proposal. "And then, when I came to the point, I forgot what I'd meant to say and just said—What did I say?" They discovered then that actually he had not proposed at all, had just kissed her and said, "Darling, let's get married soon," so, to make up for it, he proposed in extravagant language on one knee in front of the stile, while she doubled up with laughter, and a cow watched him sardonically over her shoulder.

Then there was the evening when a cask of wine was washed up onto the beach, and she and Michael sat on the rocks and watched the villagers fill every available bottle, jug, and even tin with it and scurry away. Michael tasted it and said it was sour and vinegary. Even the seagulls, standing motionless on the wet sand in the evening, made her think of Michael. Their attitudes of ponderous reverie used to amuse him so. She was just thinking of that when Stella and Tim came up the cliff hand in hand. Tim had told Stella about the row he had had with his mother last night, and Stella had been sympathetic, if a little *distraite*. To his timid clumsy compliments, however, she had been unexpectedly encouraging, seeming to want to be assured over and over again that she really was pretty. Terribly pretty. Prettier than anyone else he'd ever seen. . . .

Tim threw his mother a shy questioning look, and she smiled in reply and held out a hand to him as if asking him to join her. He sat by her, playing mechanically with Florence's ball of dish-cloth cotton, which lay on the grass, near him, relieved by the reconciliation but heavy hearted none the less. Nothing was really changed. He could almost find it in him to admire his father for the courage that had enabled him to break loose from it all. He would never be able to. . . .

"Thank you, Tim," said Florence shortly, taking the ball of dish-cloth cotton from him. (She really couldn't bear to watch him mangling it any longer.)

"Sorry," muttered Tim.

He changed his position so that Agnes should be out of his line of view, and saw the old look of reproach flash over his mother's face as she noticed the movement.

Stella had flung herself down at Mrs. Paget's feet.

"Hello, Granny."

Mrs. Paget was obliged to wake up at that.

"Hello, dear."

"Has this place changed much since you were here before?"

"Let me see," said Mrs. Paget, "when was that?"

"On your honeymoon, of course."

"So it was," said Mrs. Paget.

She looked across at Pen, who was sitting, her eyes fixed on space, her knitting-needles motionless, and said, "Twopence for your thoughts, Pen."

Pen started. She had been thinking about Roger and wondering whether he wanted a dose. He was a bit puffy under the eyes. He'd reached the stage when he resented being questioned about intimate physical matters but hadn't enough sense to look after himself properly. They all went through that stage, and it was rather a difficult one.

"Oh, just nothing," she said.

"Thought you might be thinking of Charles's visit," said Mrs. Paget a little maliciously. "When does he come?"

"Tuesday," said Pen shortly. Then, meeting her mother's eye, she flushed slightly and added, "I'm looking forward to it terribly."

Stella holla'd to Martin on his kopje, "Hello, Uncle Martin! You *are* being lazy."

Martin waved his pipe.

"Yes, aren't we!" he called.

He had suggested joining the others several times, but each time Violet had demurred. So he sat there—miserably ill-at-ease. This whole business of Violet had developed into a sort of nightmare. He couldn't go on with it, and yet he didn't know how to get out of it. ... He had honestly thought that he was in love with her when he came to Merlin Bay. He *had* been in love with the woman he had built up for himself out of her letters. For the first few hours after their meeting he had still imagined himself to be in love with her—she was good-looking, cultured, and intelligent—then a sort of dreariness had descended on his spirit as her colossal egotism and complacency gradually made itself felt. He looked at her now as she sat there, her fine eyes gazing out to sea, a rather forced smile on her well-shaped lips, dressed, unlike Florence, in wholly suitable picnic clothes, and panic gripped him as he tried to remember exactly what he had said in that last letter and in the letter immediately preceding it. How far had he actually committed himself? Could he—in decency to her and himself—draw back now? She obviously took for granted that they were on the point of becoming engaged. So did all the others, leaving them tactfully together, watching them indulgently, speculatively. Violet had at first clearly enjoyed this state of things. She had been brightly, archly possessive, assuming that he was merely waiting till a decent interval had elapsed before he proposed to her. Then, as time went on and his manner grew more constrained, something of her carefree assurance left her. She became, if possible, brighter and more animated than ever, but a tense anxiety now underlay the brightness. She stopped being arch and elusive and began to try to make things easy for him. She gave him openings—openings so obvious that it would have been impossible for him to mistake them. Still he remained silent. There was acute discomfort now in their intercourse, but she persevered, with feverish unremitting gaiety, displaying her charm, her culture, her pre-eminent fitness to be his wife. He realised that she had built everything on the certainty that he was going to propose to her. He felt ashamed of himself, sorry for her, desperately unhappy.

"Don't you adore this sort of weather?" she was saying. "Don't you feel on a day like this that we're part of it all—that really we *are* the sea and the sky and the grass and the rocks? I love that bit in Traherne's *Centuries of Meditation*, 'You can never enjoy the world aright, till the sea itself floweth in your veins, till you are clothed with the heavens and crowned with the stars.' "

He nodded, gazing out to sea. She seemed to have a quotation for everything at her fingers' ends. She had already quoted Chaucer, Donne and Herrick to him since lunch. It caused him the same sort of embarrassment that he used to feel in his young days when people recited in public.

"I read that first, I remember," she went on, "when I was spending a summer vacation with Gwynne. We had an angelic little cottage in the Cotswolds, and Gwynne wrote all day and I did the house-work and cooking. Gwynne said she'd never had such delicious food in her life. She gave me an imitation *cordon bleu* as a joke the last evening. We were miles away from anywhere, but I've never minded being alone. I've never wanted people and excitement. . . . Just to be alone with someone I'm fond of. . . ."

On the surface she was talking lightly, disjointedly, flitting from subject to subject, but in reality she was crying her wares shamelessly, stridently, pleading with him to propose to her, to let her go down to them and tell them that she was engaged to him. And suddenly he thought: After all, what have I against her except that she's self-centred and garrulous, and is there a woman in the world who isn't both? I mustn't drop the substance for the shadow. The woman I imagined from her letters doesn't exist, or, if she does, wouldn't look at me, and Violet's straightforward and capable and intelligent and—most important of all—she's prepared to take me. I shall be all sorts of a cad if I let her down after those letters. And—if I don't propose, I shall be cursing myself for a fool when I get back. At least she's better than that hellish loneliness. She won't be quite like this, either, when we're married. She's only like this because she's keyed up and on edge—waiting. Marriage steadies a woman and tones her down. My God! What do I want? I'm ugly and dull and unattractive. I'm lucky to have any woman on earth willing to marry me—let alone a woman like Violet. I expect every man gets cold feet like this just before he proposes.

He turned to her, relieved to have made up his mind. "Violet . . ." he began.

But at that moment Dandy came bounding up the hill, followed by Valerie and Roger. Valerie was scrambling up on short fat legs, her round face pink with heat and exertion, her fair hair clinging to her forehead, her sun-bonnet hanging down her back.

"Do come and play Rounders with us, Uncle Martin," she panted.

"Yes, come on, Uncle Martin," said Roger. "We're tired of Hide-and-seek. We're going to play Rounders."

"Don't go, Martin," said Violet breathlessly.

She looked at Valerie, and the cold hard fury in her eyes frightened the child so that she flung herself against Martin, hiding her face on his shoulder. Violet recovered almost at once and drew Roger to her with a tender maternal gesture that made him squirm indignantly away.

Martin had got up and swung Valerie onto his shoulder.

"Come on," he said cheerfully. "We must do our duty."

He couldn't help feeling glad of the respite. After all, there was plenty of time. . . .

They went slowly down the hill. Violet's only comfort was a consciousness of the pleasing domestic picture they must be affording the onlookers—Martin carrying Val pick-a-back and she holding determinedly to Roger's hand.

"Come on, Uncle Martin," said Roger again when they reached the level ground.

"Are you coming?" said Martin to Violet, uncomfortably aware that the children had not asked her.

"No, thanks," said Violet.

She looked for a moment old and haggard, but by the time she reached the group on the cliff edge she had recovered her usual poise. Her expression was gay and carefree and even a trifle mischievous.

"Poor old Martin!" she said as she sat down by Florence. "Those children have simply dragged him away by main force. He made every excuse he could think of, but they *wouldn't* let him off. . . . I was ruthless. I said, 'No children, I'm *not* coming to play with you, but I'll lend you Uncle Martin for a little.' "

Martin, half-way up the grassy slope, turned, and she waved to him in airy possessive fashion. He waved back. . . .

Mrs. Paget looked at her keenly. He hasn't asked her yet, she thought. And surprised herself by a sudden pang of pity.

Martin, with the two children clinging about him, reached the spot where Rosemary, Beryl, and Carry were waiting for him. Rosemary stood some distance from the other two. All the sparkle had gone from her face, leaving it strangely dead and still. Beryl and Carry had seemed to avoid her when they went to the farm with the milk-can, giving her a dreadful little feeling of hurt loneliness, but since then they had all played Hide-and-seek together and she had quite forgotten it. Now, when Roger and Val went to ask Uncle Martin to play Rounders with them, she had run eagerly to join the other two, but they had turned their backs on her in obvious dismissal, walking away from her, whispering and giggling together. She had stood watching them, silent and motionless, while the winged happiness in her dropped like a shot bird.

But now Uncle Martin was coming up with Val and Roger. He mustn't guess what she felt like. So she began to hop about on one leg, imitating her ordinary happy self.

"Come on, Uncle Martin," she called, in a voice that sounded a little shrill and unsteady. "Come on and play with us."

Gordon and Susan walked slowly back from Bramber Cove. A radiant happiness possessed Susan. Gordon hadn't stopped caring about the Kingdom. . . .

When he said, "Let's walk over to Bramber Cove," she had set off with him, her heart heavy with apprehension. Suppose he just began talking about ordinary things. . . . She wouldn't dare to mention it if he didn't. . . . But as soon as they were out of earshot of the others he had turned to her, serious, frowning, and said, "Fela's on the march now, you know. We've got to make our plans quickly."

Her spirit, freed of that weight of apprehension, seemed to soar into the air. It was all right. He hadn't stopped. Going about the ordinary world of school, in the classroom and on the playing-field (in both of which he acquitted himself with credit), his real life was still—like hers—in the Kingdom.

"Mopa said that Siluana's getting his army ready," she said.

"I know," said Gordon, "but it isn't ready yet and Fela's is."

"The roans and sables and gorillas and rhinos are joining Siluana's."

"Yes, but the jackals and baboons and cheetahs are Fela's, and they move so much more quickly. We've got to hold them up. What can you do with the Little Animals to help?"

"We had a meeting last night," said Susan, "and Rut said he'd take the badgers and rabbits and moles to burrow near to the surface so that the ground would give way when they walked on it. He said it would make them slower. The rabbits would make false paths so that they'd get lost, and the mice said they'd go and nibble at them in the night so that they wouldn't sleep."

Gordon chuckled.

"Of course," deprecatingly, "we can't do much *harm*. We can only worry them."

"I know," Gordon agreed, "but I think that jolly good. I'm trying to drill the men, but there's such a few of them and they're so scared of Fela that it's not going to be easy."

They had scrambled down the cliff into Bramber Cove, and, sitting on a large boulder, Gordon took an envelope and pencil from his pocket and began to draw the map of the Kingdom.

"Let's get it quite clear, because the next week's going to be terribly important. ... Here's Big Animal Land ... here's Little Animal Land ... here's the Leopard's cave ... there are the grazing grounds ... here's Monkey Kopje. ... There are the men's caves and there is the river. ..." His pencil moved busily. "... Buffalo Ford ... the desert ... the forest. ..."

Susan sat by him watching, lost to everything else in the world.

They walked back slowly, discussing their plans, till they reached the point on the cliff from which they could see the others, and then by tacit consent they began to talk of everyday things.

The path led past Miss Hinkley and Agnes. Agnes was still listening enraptured to Miss Hinkley's story. She greeted Gordon and Susan excitedly, torn between her desire to talk to them and her desire to hear the end of the story. Her moist lips shone in the sunlight.

"Do stay, do stay," she shouted. "Do stay and listen ..." and to Miss Hinkley, "Do go on ... do go on."

Miss Hinkley smiled complacently. It was lovely to feel that she was such a success with dear Agnes. ... It gave her a sense of slightly malicious triumph towards Pen, who had so obviously not wanted her to "help."

"So he jumped into the sea."

"Right into the sea?" said Agnes excitedly.

"Yes, dear. Right into the sea." Gordon and Susan walked on, and Agnes was too much engrossed to notice them. "Right into the sea. The merman had said, 'You must jump in at the new moon and I'll show you my palace.' "

"And did he? Did he?"

"Yes, dear. She went in with a splash just as you or I would have done, and she sank down at once, but the sea didn't make her wet at all, and there was the merman waiting for her at the door of his golden palace. And he took her in to a lovely feast and there were all the things she liked best. . . ."

"Cream?" shouted Agnes, with gleaming eyes.

"Yes, dear, lots of cream."

"And doughnuts?"

"Yes, dear. Hundreds of doughnuts."

Agnes's lips were dribbling slightly as they always did when she was in the grip of any strong emotion.

"And chocolates?" she yelled.

Mrs. Bevan threw them an anxious glance.

"Yes, dear," said Miss Hinkley soothingly. "Boxes and boxes of chocolates."

"And wasn't she sick?"

"No, dear, of course not."

Susan and Gordon went on to join the others. The children were still playing Rounders with Martin. Dandy was racing about after the ball and running away with it whenever he got the chance. The picnic was outside the usual household routine, therefore he took no responsibility for it and could enjoy himself whole-heartedly. The other grown-ups were still sitting together on the grass talking. As they approached, Violet's high-pitched laugh rang out.

"I wish she wasn't here," said Gordon. "She spoils it."

"Aunt Florence says she's terribly clever," said Susan.

"I dare say," admitted Gordon. "They're generally conceited."

Susan threw herself down by Pen, and Gordon went to stand near the cliff edge, hands in pockets. Pen smiled down lovingly at Susan. How lanky she looked in that straight belted dress—and what a mess she'd got it in! How sweet and serious she looked, too, with her dark eyes and the pale skin that never seemed to tan in the sun!

"Had a nice walk, darling?" she asked.

"Lovely," said Susan.

"Do you and Gordon still play the Kingdom game?" went on Pen casually.

Something inside Susan went cold and tight. It was dreadful that Mother knew about the Kingdom at all (she'd known about it, of course, when they first read the books, before it had become something more real and important than ordinary life), but that she should mention it like this casually in front of everyone as if it were on the same level as Rosemary's "people" was terrible.

"Of course not," she said on a quick intake of breath.

She was horrified by the untruth but doggedly determined to sustain it. It would spoil the Kingdom for ever if Mother knew about it. She'd even try to join in it and make up things about it herself, as she had done at first. . . .

Pen stretched lazily and began to put her mending back into the bag.

"It's time we went back now," she said briskly. "Help me pack the baskets, Sue darling. Children! Time we went back."

They packed the picnic baskets and went down the steep cliff towards the centre of the bay. At the gate of Sea Meads Mrs. Paget and Florence said good-bye to Pen and the children and set off towards the hotel. Violet hovered behind, obviously waiting for Martin. Panic again descended on him, and he made great play of carrying in the baskets and helping Pen with the children.

Suddenly Roger stood still in the middle of the garden path, his face tragic.

"I've forgotten to give in my arithmetic book to Mrs. Heath," he said. "I've just remembered."

"Oh, what *does* it matter, dear?" said Pen impatiently. She was tired and a little cross. And worried about Rosemary. There were dark shadows round the child's eyes and that patch of dead white round her mouth that spelt utter exhaustion. It was through running about in the sun all afternoon, of course. . . .

"It *does* matter," Roger was saying. His face was flushed and dirty and streaked with perspiration. His tone threatened tears. "I'll get an order mark and I promised Mr. Forrester not to get any next week."

"Well, it's too late now, anyway," said Pen.

"It isn't. If you'll let me take it to her now, I know she'll count it," pleaded Roger, "even if she's done the others."

"Of *course* you can't take it now, Roger," said Pen. "It's after your bed-time."

Martin, aware of Violet still waiting for him, seized the opportunity.

"Where is it?" he said. "Can I take it?"

"Oh, Martin, that's awfully good of you," said Pen.

"Oh, thanks *awfully*, Uncle Martin," said Roger, his flushed smeared face radiant with relief.

"It's just up the road, Martin. We passed it coming down. It's called Cliff Cottage."

Martin went down to the gate.

"Don't wait for me," he said to Violet. "I'm just going to give Pen a hand with things and then take along an exercise-book for Roger."

Violet turned without speaking and followed Mrs. Paget and Florence.

Chapter Seven

STELLA went swiftly down the lane towards Four Winds. Though small, it lay at the more exclusive end of the bay among the houses whose gardens, gay with flowers, bordered the lane with aristocratic trustfulness, without fence or hedges. She had expected that it would be difficult to shake Tim off after the picnic but it hadn't been. Agnes was tired and still a little over-excited. "She jumped right into the sea," she kept telling them, "and she didn't even get wet, and the merman met her and took her into the palace, and she had doughnuts and cream and chocolates and red jelly and iced cakes and plum pudding and roast chicken, and she ate them all and she wasn't sick. She jumped right into the sea." She told them the story over and over again in her loud harsh voice, the words jumbled up together so unintelligibly that even Mrs. Bevan could hardly understand her.

"You'll help me with her, won't you, Tim dear?" Mrs. Bevan had said, and Tim, on whose spirit the memory of last night's scene had weighed heavily all day, responded with eagerness.

"Of course I will . . ." he said, taking Agnes's arm to guide her over the rough grass.

"Time to go home, Agnes," he said kindly.

She was wildly delighted by his attention and began to tell him the story again.

"It had to be the new moon," she shouted. "She ate it all and wasn't sick."

Mrs. Bevan was thanking Miss Hinkley for helping with Agnes.

"It's so *kind* of you," she said. "Not many people take the trouble. . . ."

Miss Hinkley glowed with pride and hoped that Pen was listening.

"I think she's a dear," she said happily, "and really quite intelligent." Then, feeling that perhaps this was going too far, added, "I mean, she does understand."

"Yes," agreed Mrs. Bevan fervently. "She *does* understand. . . ."

Stella helped to carry the baskets to the house, ran upstairs to rearrange the silk triangle and powder her face, then slipped out of the side door and along the lane towards Four Winds.

Pen, who had taken off the dress she had worn for the picnic and was putting on an overall, watched her from her bedroom window and stifled a sense of aggrievement. Really, she might have stayed to help with the children. But, after all, it was her birthday and, most important of all, she did seem to be settling down happily at last. One mustn't expect too much of her. . . . She went to the bathroom, tied a rubber apron round her waist, turned on the taps, and went down to fetch Valerie. Valerie, hot and tired and cross, was quarrelling with Roger in the garden and began to cry when Pen said that it was bed-time.

"Your turn next, Roger," said Pen. "Do *stop* it, Valerie."

Roger seemed to have got dirtier than ever since coming in and looked as if he, too, were going to be difficult when his turn came.

Rosemary was sitting on the bench just outside the back door, emptying the sand from her sandals, too much occupied in the process, apparently, even to notice Dandy, who was jumping about trying to worry them. He enjoyed worrying sandals and Rosemary's just fitted his mouth. The children always sat on that bench to empty the sand from their shoes, and there were little heaps of it all round. Sand, of course, was everywhere—in the kitchen, sitting-room, and bedrooms, and generally Pen was proud of taking it in her stride, of making as little trouble of it as most women would make of dusting a mantelpiece. But this evening she felt tired and unaccountably depressed, and the prospect of the sand-strewn rooms seemed the last straw. It'll be lovely when I've got them all to bed and can have a little peace, she thought. But even then, of course, there was the washing to do. They needed clean things every day in this hot weather. It really *was* inconsiderate of Stella to have gone off and left her with everything. Valerie was still crying, on a shrill monotonous note, and Pen felt a momentary sympathy with women who work off their irritation with their children by slapping them. But she only said, "Hush, Val. Don't be such a baby." It wasn't the child's fault, of course. She was just over-tired. . . .

In the bathroom she sat down with Valerie on her knee, pulled off the soiled crumpled little garments, and threw them onto the floor. She noticed with a sigh that even the fair tousled hair was full of sand.

Miss Hinkley, encouraged by her success with Agnes, opened the door and peeped in.

"Can I help at all?" she said.

Pen, remembering suddenly that she loved being busy from morning to night, became almost aggressively bright and cheerful.

"No, thank you, Miss Hinkley. There's nothing I can't manage quite easily."

Miss Hinkley smiled at Valerie, sitting rosy and naked on Pen's knee, and made a silly clicking noise as if she were a baby. It rather annoyed Pen that Valerie stopped crying and smiled back.

Stella slowed her pace on approaching Four Winds. She meant just to go quickly past the house and then home again. A swift sidelong glance as she passed would show her, perhaps, open windows or some other sign of habitation. She only wanted to know whether he'd come or not. She didn't expect actually to meet him to-day. Now that the meeting was imminent and possible, indeed, shyness had seized her and she wanted to postpone it. She wouldn't know what to say or do. In all her dreams of the meeting she had been self-possessed and assured. Now she felt awkward and schoolgirlish and afraid. She decided not to look at the house till she'd reached the gate. Her heart began to beat more quickly, but she kept her eyes determinedly in front of her till she got to the gate, then——

He was in the garden working a pump-handle up and down with a rather comic air of bewilderment. There was a pail beneath the pump but no water came from it. It was so funny that she forgot all about being grown-up and assured. She even forgot the dreams of romance she had woven around him. She gave a sudden peal of childish laughter and said:

"That pump doesn't work."

He looked up at her and started.

"What?" he said.

"It doesn't work," she repeated. "Mr. Ransome bought it at a sale because he thought it was picturesque, but it doesn't work. It isn't fastened to anything."

He stood mopping his brow with a gaily coloured handkerchief and smiling at her ruefully. He wore a pair of beautifully cut grey-flannel trousers and a striped sports shirt with very short sleeves and a navy-blue scarf tucked into it at the neck. He was fully as handsome and distinguished-looking as he had been in the picture.

"My God, what a priceless fool the man must be!" he said.

"He is," said Stella.

She was still laughing. She couldn't think how handsome he was and how wonderful it was that she'd actually met him. She could only think how funny he'd looked trying to get water out of Mr. Ransome's sham pump.

"I thought I must have struck a drought or something," he said. "I say, you aren't pulling my leg, are you?"

"No, honest injun," Stella assured him. "He bought it last year. It's just *put* there."

"No, but listen." He came down to the gate. "It distinctly says something about a pump, and I can't get a drop of water indoors."

He had taken a letter from his pocket and was turning its pages.

"That's one of old Crump's letters, isn't it?" said Stella, leaning over the gate. "Aren't they heavenly? How many words has he spelt wrongly?"

"All of them," said Mr. Kemsing, "but he excels in 'convenience' and 'amenities.' "

"He's only just discovered 'amenities,' " explained Stella. "He thinks it another word for view."

"Oh, that explains it. It did read rather oddly. Now about this pump." He turned the pages again, "He distinctly mentions a pump. . . ."

"But that's indoors," explained Stella. "It's in the kitchen. It fills the cistern. I'll come and show you."

"You angel straight from Heaven!" he said fervently. "I was just on the point of bursting into tears. It was like one of those dreams where you go on and on and on and nothing happens. I felt that in another minute I should have found myself in a tram-car in my vest and pants. They generally end like that."

Stella's fresh young laughter rang out again. He had opened the gate for her and they went together up the little path to the open back door. In the kitchen she showed him a small pump-handle near the sink.

"Good Lord!" he said. "I thought that was a mangle. Well, I'd better start on it. I can't get a drop from the taps."

"But the cistern can't be empty," said Stella. "They *wouldn't* have left it empty. I expect the water's just turned off." She stood on tip-toe and turned a small tap high up on the water pipe. "Yes, it was just turned off."

"Where did you leave your broomstick?" he asked.

"Oh, it's just like ours," she laughed. "The tap, I mean."

She turned on the tap over the sink and a flow of water gushed out. "It's all right now."

"I'm not quite sure of you," he said. "I'm keeping my fingers crossed. . . . Anyway, let's have tea now. Or do you only eat—

Eye of newt and toe of frog,
Wool of bat and tongue of dog?"

"Adder's fork and blind-worm's sting,
Lizard's leg and howlet's wing,"

she added, glad that she'd "done" *Macbeth* her last term at school and could remember the quotation. Then she added a little uncertainly, "I ought to go now."

"Nonsense! You must have tea."

"I've had it."

"Then you must have some more. You can't possibly go, anyway. I shall probably get tied up in the gas taps next and you'll have to disentangle me."

"Oh, the gas is quite straightforward. I'll light it now while you fill the kettle."

In a few minutes he had carried the tray into the studio—tea, bread-and-butter, and some biscuits.

"You see I'm really a very capable housewife—or should one say house-husband?" he said. "I've forgotten nothing. I've even got some salt somewhere in case of need. You mustn't judge me entirely by the pump."

"No, I won't," she assured him. "And you've made the tea beautifully."

"Women can't make tea," he said. "I always insist on making the tea whenever I get the chance. I've lost the friendship of innumerable women by insisting on making the tea. Somehow—I don't know why—a woman looks on it as a womanly prerogative. I like to pour out, too. I've lost another lot of them over that."

Stella was wandering about the studio.

"He's hung up three more sunsets since I was here last," she said.

He looked at the walls.

"Good Lord, are they sunsets? I thought they were still-life studies of ham and eggs."

"No, they're sunsets," she laughed. "He takes them to a shop in Penzance. Aunt Florence bought one there this morning. She thinks it's beautiful."

"Well, that tells us all we want to know about Aunt Florence, doesn't it?"

"Yes, she *is* just like that. . . ."

"Come and have some tea, you restless child!"

She sat down and took a cup of tea from him.

Looking at his tall well-proportioned figure and handsome face—grey hair brushed smoothly back, grey humorous eyes, perfectly moulded mouth and chin—shyness overwhelmed her.

Shyness and a terrible feeling of having wasted a glorious opportunity. Fate had allowed her to meet him on the very first evening of his visit, and not only to meet him, but actually to come to the studio and have tea with him and—she'd behaved as Susan or Rosemary might have behaved. Where was the fancied assurance with which she had meant to meet him? He was probably thinking of her as a child. The laughter died out of her eyes and a prim self-consciousness took its place.

"I do so admire your books, Mr. Kemsing," she said in her grown-up voice.

A look of boredom came into his face. "Never mind that," he said shortly. He stirred his tea. "Tell me about yourself. Where do you live?"

"We live at Sea Meads. We've all been for a picnic on the cliffs this afternoon because it was my birthday."

She bit her lip. She oughtn't to have told him that it was her birthday, of course.

"Splendid! How old?"

"Eighteen."

"Still more splendid! I must give you a present. Take a sunset. Choose any you like from the wall."

"They're Mr. Ransome's."

"He'd never miss one or two. I expect he's got boxes of them stored away upstairs."

"Yes, he has. He showed me them once."

"There you are! I'll give you the whole lot."

She laughed again, but a little ruefully. How lovely it would have been if he'd given her one of his books with her name written in and "With the author's compliments"!

She wished he hadn't been so short with her when she mentioned his books. She wanted to talk about them, to let him know that she understood, that she wasn't really a child. She wanted to tell him how deeply she had sympathised with Moina in *Devil's Guerdon*, how she had adored Gervaise in *Puppet's Dance*, and how she had loathed Sir Peter's wife in *Starlight*.

"Have another biscuit?" he said, passing her a plate.

There was one of the sugary kind she liked, but she refused the temptation to take it.

"No, thank you," she said, and felt glad that she'd had such a large tea up on the cliff, so that she could display the sort of appetite people always had on the stage and in the pictures.

"Cigarette?"

He produced his case. His hands were long and thin and beautifully shaped.

"No, thank you," she said, making a mental resolution to buy some cigarettes and practise smoking in private.

"May I?"

He lit a cigarette and threw the match into the fireplace. She made another effort to get onto the right footing with him.

"You're going to paint here, aren't you?"

He nodded.

"I think it's wonderful of you to write *and* paint."

He smiled at her quizzically through his cigarette smoke.

"It's much more wonderful to be eighteen."

She glowered at him from under her lashes like a sulky child. It was *mean* of him to treat her as if she weren't grown-up. His voice became kind and serious as if he guessed that he had offended her.

"I'm not teasing you," he said. "Honestly, I'd give everything I possess at this moment to be eighteen again."

"But—why?" she said, puzzled.

"You'll know when you're my age," he said. "Youth's the most glorious thing in the world, but its tragedy is that the people who have it never value it. I suppose you're longing to be twenty-eight, thirty-eight, forty-eight?"

"Well—not forty-eight," she said.

He laughed.

"There you are!" he said.

"Mavis was eighteen, wasn't she," said Stella, "when she first met Sir Peter?"

"Was she?" he said carelessly. "I never read my own books. . . .

And I'm much more interested in real people. You've told me nothing about yourself yet. What's your name?"

"Stella."

He nodded approvingly.

"Quite right. I think I'd almost have guessed it. . . . Now tell me about the others."

She told him, her eyes roaming round the room to see if he had put any of his personal belongings there. Yes, a pile of new books on the table by the window . . . an open attaché-case, overflowing with papers, on the floor by the fireplace . . . a framed photograph on the bureau. . . . She stopped in the middle of telling him how old Roger was. His eyes followed hers.

"That's my wife," he said.

She was silent. Somehow she'd never even considered the possibility of his having a wife. It was a shock. It took her a little time to adjust herself to it.

"She looks very beautiful," she said.

"She is very beautiful," said Mr. Kemsing.

She glanced at him, but he was intent on lighting another cigarette, and his face was quite expressionless.

"She's in Scotland at present," he added.

She looked at the photograph again.

The face was beautiful, but, she thought, hard and cruel. Gwenlian, Sir Peter's wife, had been like that in *Starlight*. It was Mavis whom he had loved, who had comforted and upheld him through all his wife's unkindness. At the end his wife had been killed in a railway accident and he had married Mavis. . . . It complicated matters, of course. But love—real love—triumphed over every obstacle. Divorce wasn't as satisfactory as a railway accident, but it was quite possible. There had been several girls at school whose parents were divorced, and no one seemed to mind about it. And, even if they did, people who really loved each other wouldn't care. . . .

She stood up uncertainly.

"I ought to go now . . ." she said.

She'd had a nagging sense of guilt at the bottom of her mind throughout the interview. It had been mean of her to leave Mother to put the children to bed and tidy everything up alone. Susan was too dreamy to be much use. . . . Still, it was her birthday, and it was the day, too, on which her real grown-up life had begun. Strange to think how sure she'd been she would fall in love with him, and that she *had* fallen in love with him. It sent a thrill through her just to look at him. He stubbed the end of his cigarette on his plate and rose from the settee.

"Must you?" he said. "Well, thanks for coming to my rescue. Tell me where you live again, so that I can fetch you if I need any more taps tamed. You've got quite a way with taps, haven't you?"

"I don't think there are any more. You won't want to turn the gas off, will you? I live at Sea Meads. It's just along the lane, a bit lower down."

He looked at her, appraising the radiance and freshness of her youth through narrowed eyes. She was adorably pretty. He longed to try to transfer that indefinable sheen and sparkle of youth to canvas.

"May I paint you?" he said suddenly.

She flushed with pleasure.

"Oh—do you really want to?"

"Of course. Ransome's evidently got a patent out for sunsets, so I must try something else."

"I'd love it."

"No, you wouldn't. It would be a dreadful nuisance. Coming every day and just sitting still. . . . You'd hate it."

"I wouldn't," she protested.

"Well, let's make a bargain. Come as long as it amuses you, and the moment you get bored say so and we'll stop. Do you agree?"

"Yes. I'll never get bored."

"Won't you, young woman! You wait and see. . . . But we're going rather fast, aren't we? I must get the parents' consent."

"There's only Mummy. I mean, there *is* Daddy, but he's hardly ever here and no one asks him about things. . . . I'm sure Mummy will let me."

"I'll come along to-morrow, then. Sea Meads, isn't it?"

"Yes . . . and she'll help you about tradespeople and things. They put on the prices *terribly* with summer visitors. You've got to be on your guard."

He looked at the stern young face with twinkling eyes.

"I will be," he assured her gravely.

"They'll try to charge you *double* the proper price."

"I'll halve every account they send me."

She saw that he was laughing at her and smiled uncertainly.

"But they do ... especially the butcher."

They went out into the little garden, past the ornamental pump, and down to the little gate. He opened it for her.

"I hope they let you sit for me," he said. He was already studying her with a professional intentness.

"I'm sure they will," said Stella, feeling slightly nervous under his scrutiny. "Anyway, we'll see you on the beach. You do bathe, don't you?"

"Rather! I shall start getting rid of my contemptible town whiteness first thing to-morrow."

"Well ... good-bye."

"Good-bye, and thank you."

She left him leaning his bare arms (they were quite brown) along the top of the gate. His very superior watch-wristlet glittered in the sun. His greying hair was very smooth and tidy. He was dressed just like everyone else, but he looked much smarter. Perhaps smart wasn't the word. Well-groomed. Yes, that was it. Well-groomed. All the men in his novels were well-groomed. Well-groomed and immaculately tailored. His beautiful grey trousers were in a different world from Tim's shapeless bags. She turned on an impulse to look back. He was still leaning over the gate. He waved to her, then went slowly into the house, his hands in his pockets.

She walked home in a kind of dream. It had happened. She'd met him and fallen in love with him as she'd known she would. Was he in love with her? Anxiously her mind went over the interview—his desire to paint her, his long close scrutiny of her, the firm clasp of his hand when he said good-bye. *Surely* he was. ... She wished that she'd acquitted herself better—shown herself more grown-up and assured, more as she'd been in those many imaginary conversations with him. . . . It would be dreadful if he thought of her as a child.

She remembered his wife—so cold and hard and cruel. How he must have suffered! But he wouldn't suffer any longer. She was going to make up to him for everything. . . .

Chapter Eight

MARTIN made his way slowly towards Cliff Cottage. He had undertaken the errand solely in order to postpone further conversation with Violet. He still didn't know whether to be glad or sorry that Valerie had interrupted his proposal. Certainly at the time he had grasped at the interruption instinctively. But it was, of course, only a postponement. He would probably propose to her that evening. They would jog along together all right. He would get used to the things in her that irritated him now. It was absurd to expect perfection. He was far enough from it himself. And, after all, anything was better than loneliness. It got a man down so. . . .

Cliff Cottage. Here it was. He screwed up his courage to introduce himself and explain his errand. He was naturally shy, and his years in the East had intensified his shyness. Sometimes the prospect of the most ordinary social occasion would cause him agonies of apprehension. Marriage with Violet would be good for him, he assured himself. She had any amount of social poise.

He opened the gate and looked round uncertainly. A man was sitting in a deck-chair on the small lawn, smoking a cigarette, his hands behind his head. There was about him a disarming air of friendliness, of carefree good fellowship. One felt that he liked everybody and that it would have been churlish of anyone not to like him.

Martin entered and, holding out the exercise-book, spoke rather stiffly.

"I'm Martin Paget. My nephew Roger asked me to give this to Mrs. Heath with his apologies for its being late."

The man took the cigarette out of his mouth and grinned.

"Little devils, aren't they? They want well kicking—every one of them. Never remember anything till a few hours too late. Not a bad kid, Roger, all the same, is he?"

He rose from his chair, a tall lanky figure, and hitched up his trousers.

"Have a pew. I'll call Jessica."

He took a deck-chair that was leaning against the house, set it up in one quick deft movement, and went to the open door.

"Jessica!" he called.

A woman came to the door. She wore a green linen smock overall, and her bare legs ended in workmanlike brown leather sandals. She was thin and worn-looking, with high cheek bones and two deep lines between her eyes. Her soft greyish hair fell untidily about her face. She pushed it back as she stepped into the sunlight.

"This is Mr. Paget," said the man cheerfully. "He's brought young Roger's arithmetic book. If you've finished the others, don't do it. Why should the little beggar send it round two days late and get away with it?"

Embarrassment engulfed Martin. It had never occurred to him till this minute that he might be giving her unnecessary trouble. He flushed hotly, and put the exercise-book back into his pocket.

"No, please, don't," he said. "I hadn't realised . . ."

She came forward, holding out her hand for the book and smiling a little lop-sided smile that was oddly reassuring.

"It's quite all right. I hadn't started them. I wasn't going to do them till after supper. Come and sit down."

"I oughtn't to keep you if you're busy . . ." said Martin, aware to his great surprise that his usual instinct of flight had deserted him and that he wanted to stay.

"Oh, I was just coming out in any case," she said. "I've been cutting onions for a salad and I need an airing. Brian, darling, get another chair."

But Brian had spread himself out on the grass, so Martin sat down in the deck-chair next Jessica's.

She looked at him with eyes that were brown flecked with golden lights.

"So you're Uncle Martin," she said. "I've heard of you from Roger, of course."

They talked about Roger and the children and Pen and the picnic ("We saw you all go by." . . . "How pretty Stella looked!" . . . "Isn't Rosemary a pet!"), about his mother and Florence (they didn't mention Violet) and Merlin Bay and its inhabitants.

"Don't say you haven't seen one of Ransome's sunsets!" laughed Brian.

"Florence bought one in Penzance, I think," said Martin uncertainly.

"They're pretty ghastly, aren't they?"

"Are they?" said Martin, still more uncertainly. He'd taken for granted that they were good. "I don't know much about art."

Jessica smiled her lop-sided motherly smile at him.

"Arnold Kemsing's taken his studio for this month. He was to have arrived to-day."

"Arnold Kemsing?" said Martin, his sense of inadequacy deepening. Wherever he went people referred familiarly to names he'd never heard before. It made him feel like the inhabitant of a desert island.

"Best seller," said Brian shortly. "Can't read his stuff myself." He rose to his feet. "I'll just run up to the allotment and make sure I locked the gate. I rather think I didn't. Tramps do the devil of a lot of damage if you forget."

His wife looked at him anxiously.

"Don't be late for supper, dear."

"Back on the tick," he said with exaggerated heartiness.

He waved to them both and went out of the gate, whistling cheerfully.

A curious sense of peace had descended on Martin, a sensation as if light and air were suddenly penetrating the dark places of his spirit. It was a sensation that he had never experienced in his life before. He felt none of the awkwardness and shyness that generally afflicted him in the presence of strangers. She wasn't a stranger. He'd known her all his life.

"I ought to offer you a drink," she said, "but I'm afraid we've nothing in the house—not even sherry."

(Brian had said, "For God's sake, Jess, don't have any of the stuff where I can get hold of it," and since then she'd never had any of it at all.)

She looked at him again with the little crooked smile that spoke somehow of courage rather than mirth.

"How do you like Merlin Bay?"

"Very much."

His inarticulateness didn't matter. Words meant nothing at all.

"You're having quite a family muster here."

"Aren't we! And Charles comes on Tuesday—my brother-in-law."

"Oh yes. I don't think I've ever met him. He's been here occasionally, of course, but we've always been away."

She watched Brian's figure disappear round the bend of the cliff. He wasn't going in the direction of the allotment, after all. Something had told her he wouldn't. He was going to catch the 'bus on the main road and go into Helston or Penzance. He was always careful not to drink at the village pub. She suspected that he'd been to Helston this morning. He'd gone off directly after breakfast and come back for lunch in that mood of hilarity that she knew and feared. He had been restless for a few days now, with a bright glancing secret restlessness that always preceded one of his "attacks." It was nearly two months since the last one. . . . He would come back to-night, not drunk or even tipsy, but with everything about him pitched to an unnaturally high key, his usual quiet sociability transformed to garrulity and a too frequent laughter. It would be no use questioning him. He wouldn't get angry. He never got angry. He would laugh at her, reassure her, even disclaim all knowledge of what she meant ("You're potty, darling. I just ran into Helston to get some tobacco and stretch my legs.").

And all the time he would have decided to give in to it, to let it have its way with him. She would get up to-morrow, perhaps, and find a note from him saying that he had gone into Penzance to catch the early London train. That was always his last impulse of self-protection—to go away from Merlin Bay, where everyone knew him. She had begged him not to. She suffered torments at the thought of him in London, sleeping in doss-houses, sodden, incapable. But he told her it was better than that both of them should lose their jobs. She blamed herself bitterly for this state of things. Surely she ought somehow to be able to "keep him straight." She tried hard and he assured her that she could do no more than she did, but it seemed that all she could do was to receive him tenderly, compassionately, when he returned to her in the end, drained of vitality, penitent and docile as a child, to be restored to health and sanity. She knew that once the violence of the attack had worn itself out he had no thought but of getting back to her. And yet—surely she ought to be able to help him to fight it. The trouble was that once the temptation was on him he didn't want to fight it. He loathed himself afterwards, but as soon as the craving began he longed only to yield.

She turned her anxious eyes to Martin.

"Where is it you work? Mrs. Marlowe did tell me, but names of places mean so little by themselves, don't they?"

He found himself describing the day's work to her—how he got up at five in the grey heat mist, held a roll-call of coolies, superintended the tapping of the rubber trees, checked the latex returns. . . .

"It's terribly monotonous, of course. The same routine day after day. . . ."

He told her how the grey mist yielded gradually to a brazen heat that seemed to drain the colour from everything ("We have to change two or three times a day"), and of the uncanny hush of midday, when the heat was at its height. "The storms are terrific. The grass seems to grow green as you watch it and in a few minutes everything's just a lake."

He described his bungalow, with its large open verandah.

"No chimneys, of course. You never see a chimney out there. . . . Where I am, it's miles away from good roads or railway or a town, and the jungle's always trying to come back. You have to keep weeding all the time. There's something—terrifying about it."

He had never talked like that before—freely, confidently, without the note of apology that the perfunctory interest of his questioners generally induced. It wasn't that he'd lowered his defences. His defences had melted clean away. Everything in him that had been shut up tightly in the dark seemed to open itself to the warmth and brightness of her sympathy.

She looked tired and worn, he thought, and he longed to comfort her. He loved her far more than if she'd been young and beautiful. He loved the brave little lop-sided smile, the anxious eyes, even the two lines between her eyes and the soft greying hair. He noticed how loose her wedding ring was on her thin finger. She didn't seem to be outside him at all. She seemed to be, in some strange way, inside his heart, sending this new life-giving current through his soul and body.

He got up to go at last, awkwardly, clumsily.

"Come and see us again some time," she said. "Brian loves talking about foreign places."

He was aware of the anxiety that underlay her pleasant sympathetic small talk, aware too that it was connected in some way with her husband. He hadn't heard the local gossip and was puzzled. Obviously they got on all right. . . . He'd have given anything in the world to help her. How silly and trite it sounded, but he would gladly have died for her. . . . He thought of Violet. She didn't even exist. The woman he'd imagined for himself from her letters didn't exist either. They were trivial and unreal, too trivial and unreal to cause any emotion at all in him, even compunction.

She went to the gate with him.

"If you pass Sea Meads, tell Roger it's all right about the book."

At the gate she looked anxiously up and down the road, but no one was in sight.

Chapter Nine

"SHALL I take your deck-chair down onto the sands, Mother?" said Florence.

"Very well, dear," said Mrs. Paget, turning over the page of her newspaper.

They were sitting in the lounge after breakfast. The hotel was rapidly filling up, and most of the chairs were now occupied by guests in various forms of seaside costume. Florence had been particularly outraged by a very stout lady in very short shorts who sat at the next table and made constant overtures of friendliness, to which Mrs. Paget, despite all Florence's remonstrances, persisted in responding. ("If only she wouldn't!" wailed Florence to Violet. "It lets us down so. . . .)

"Such a pity to waste any of this lovely day," said the stout lady, who was sitting near them, waiting an opportunity to join in their conversation.

"Isn't it!" agreed Mrs. Paget pleasantly, laying aside her newspaper.

"I expect Pen will be coming down with the children when she's seen off Gordon and Susan," went on Florence, trying to give the conversation a personal turn in order to keep the stout lady out of it. "The others have a holiday to-day, as well."

"I think it such a mistake to let children go home for half-term," put in Violet. "It quite demoralises them."

"Yes, home has a very bad influence," smiled Mrs. Paget.

Florence glanced at her reproachfully. It was really too bad, the way Mother kept chipping Violet. Violet knew everything there was to know about children, and was used to being treated with respect. Why, only that morning she had had a letter from a girl who was very unhappy at home, because her mother didn't understand her. She'd read it to them at breakfast and said, "Poor child! The trouble is that half these mothers are subconsciously jealous of their daughters." Mrs. Paget had muttered, "Stuff and nonsense!" and, though Florence had coughed as hard as she could to drown the words, she was sure that Violet had heard, because she went very stiff and dignified all at once.

It had been rather an uncomfortable breakfast altogether. For one thing Martin hadn't been there. He had got up and had an early breakfast before any of them were about and left a message that he was going out for a walk. They had seen practically nothing of him since the picnic on Saturday. He had spent all Sunday at Pen's with the children and yesterday he had been for a long tramp, taking sandwiches with him and not coming back till evening.

Violet had offered to accompany him, but he had seemed not to hear her. He had been dreamy and absent-minded and at the same time restless and keyed up. Violet, too, had been unlike herself. ... It was natural, of course, thought Florence with a sigh. They were in love with each other, and love did make people a bit queer just at first till they'd settled down to it. She wondered if Martin had Spoken (she'd been sure that he was Speaking on the hill-top the afternoon of the picnic, but she had waited in vain for Violet's confidences). Perhaps he had, and they weren't telling people yet. Or perhaps he was nervous and was putting it off, just as one always put off Speaking to the tradespeople. Violet had been very quiet and short in her manner yesterday while Martin was out, and in the evening, when Florence, longing to know at what stage the affair was, had gone to her bedroom in hope of a talk, had not answered her knock.

This morning, however, her manner was bright, almost gay. She had laughed over her letters at breakfast (she'd had a most amusing one from Gwynne, as well as the one from the girl whose mother didn't understand her) and had teased Florence about the precise way in which she took off the top of her egg.

"It's a perfect and complete circle, darling. How *do* you do it?"

Florence was inclining more and more to the belief that Martin had Spoken. . . .

Mrs. Paget put her paper aside and went to the window. The weather seemed to be settling down into a prolonged "fine spell." The sky was still cloudless, the sea a shimmery silver blue.

"Yes, we must certainly go out," she said, giving the stout lady a smile.

"We'd better leave a message for Martin, hadn't we?" said Violet, "telling him where we are."

They left a message with George and went down the garden and out of the little gate that led onto the sands. Florence carried her work-bag and the deck-chair, and Violet a rug, an attaché-case (she always seemed to have innumerable letters to write), and an anthology of modern verse. She wore a pair of well-fitting navy-blue slacks and a sports blouse. Florence was still in the navy-blue costume. Somehow it seemed the safest thing to put on in the morning, as one could never be quite sure how the day would turn out. If it got too hot, of course, she could slip off the coat. She had quite a summery blouse on underneath.

They went to the foot of the sandhills in the middle of the bay, where the path led down from Sea Meads, and there they settled themselves—Mrs. Paget in the deck-chair, Florence and Violet on the rug. Florence took out her knitting, Violet opened her anthology of modern verse, assuming a rapt expression and keeping on hand, as it were, a start of surprise and radiant smile of welcome should Martin appear. Mrs. Paget lay back in her chair, watching the other people on the beach and occasionally making comments on them.

"Those two girls in blue bathing costumes were here yesterday, too. They come by 'bus from Penzance. They're shop girls and they're staying at home for their fortnight's holiday and taking day excursions. Very sensible, I think. . . . That child's had mastoid. They've got rooms in the village. He's shockingly spoilt, but, as his mother says, what can you do with a delicate child? . . . That man has a fish-shop in Peckham. He's from that camp at Bramber Cove. It's the first time he's had a holiday like this. He's always gone to Margate before."

Florence set her lips and knitted vigorously. There Mother was again! And it was always such common people she knew about. She never seemed to know about the really interesting ones who lived in the big houses at the further end of the bay. What *would* Vi think—Vi, who was so fastidious and refined and had friends like Gwynne Beauchamp? It was a good thing that she was reading the anthology of modern verse and not listening. . . .

Violet wasn't listening, but neither was she reading the anthology of modern verse. She was thinking of Martin. He had begun to propose to her on Saturday at the picnic, but Valerie had interrupted him, then later his shyness had kept him from approaching her again. It was obvious that he wanted to propose, but he was afraid to put his fate to the test. She must let him know somehow that she was willing to accept him. Most women probably had to help their lovers out. It was merely a Victorian convention that the man had to do the asking. One couldn't expect a shy and nervous man like Martin to risk a refusal in cold blood. He had obviously decided to postpone his proposal till he felt more sure of her. Well, it was up to her to make him more sure. She threw a faintly irritated glance at Florence. If Florence had been different she might have helped, but she was such a fool that she could never take a hint, or if she did would make a hopeless mess of things. After all, didn't Bernard Shaw say that it was the woman's place to choose the man she wanted and secure him? And she wanted Martin, wanted him to-day in a way she hadn't wanted him before. It wasn't only that he had so nearly proposed to her. It was something that had happened to her as she sat by him on the hillock, on the afternoon of the picnic. Desire. . . . It had always seemed such a meaningless word when she read of it in books, but suddenly she knew what it meant—not with her mind, but with her restless hungry body. She had lain awake all the night after the picnic at the mercy of forces she had never known before. The feverish torment had now left her, and she felt faintly shocked at the memory of it, but she was none the less determined to come to grips with Martin. It would be so easy. Just a few words. She tried to say them to herself, "Martin, you shy old darling, I know how you feel . . ." Or something like that. . . . Her heart hammered in her chest as she imagined herself saying them . . . but she must. Apart from the emotion that had so suddenly and so completely mastered her, she couldn't face the possibility of going back at the end of this holiday not engaged to him. She'd counted on it. She'd taken it for granted ever since he had begun to write those friendly affectionate letters to her. She'd been a fool not to clinch matters then, not to write back in a strain that would have left him no loophole for escape. She couldn't go back to teaching again. She pretended to like it but she didn't really. She wasn't as popular and successful as she tried to make people believe. She had a few admirers, of course, and she cultivated them zealously, flattering and favouring them, but she knew, though she never acknowledged it to herself, that the majority of the staff and girls disliked her. She couldn't endure the thought of going on teaching till she was old. . . . She'd do anything rather than that. ("Martin, you shy old darling, I know what you feel about me. . . .") Her thoughts went back over her life. She was always faintly surprised that she had not married, that no one had even proposed to her. Girls with far fewer pretensions to good looks and intelligence got married every day. She had always comforted herself by the reflection that men liked stupid women and that anyway she had no use for "that sort of thing"—but suddenly she knew that she had. She wanted Martin, wanted him in "that sort of way." She was upon the hill-top again with him in the sunshine, seeing the pin points of perspiration on his brow, the blue veins that stood out on his brown hands, catching the faint smell of soap and tobacco that came from him and feeling again the blood pulsing through her veins as his bare arm touched hers by accident. She wanted him and she was going to have him. ("Martin, dear, don't beat about the bush any longer. You needn't ask and I needn't answer. We understand each other. . . .")

She kept her eyes religiously on the anthology of modern verse, remembering occasionally to turn a page in case Florence was watching her, but there was a mist in front of her eyes and her heart was beating so loudly that she thought the other two must hear it. He shouldn't escape her. . . .

Suddenly the four children, Rosemary, Roger, Beryl, and Valerie, came tumbling noisily down the steep sandy path, followed by Dandy. Roger turned head over heels in the sand as soon as he reached the bottom of the path.

"Oh, Roger, your hair!" moaned Pen, who came down behind them with Martin. ("He's brought a body-guard, wise man!" thought Mrs. Paget.)

"I called for Pen on my way back," explained Martin. "I thought I might help her carry a few things."

He set down a beach bag bulging with towels and bathing-suits.

Pen's fine cloudy hair shaded her delicate forehead. Her eyes, faintly anxious as ever, followed the children, who had kicked off their sandals and were running barefoot over the sand.

Martin, the hard shell round his heart softened by his new love, felt a sudden unaccustomed rush of affection for her. She was such a good sort, old Pen!

"What a day!" she said, sitting down by Mrs. Paget's chair. "I've just got Gordon and Susan off, and Charles is coming this evening."

"No peace for the wicked," put in Florence pleasantly (she had slipped off the navy-blue coat, revealing a very frilly crumpled white blouse), but no one took any notice of her.

Pen opened the mending bag she had brought with her and took out a cotton dress of Valerie's.

"Just *look* at it," she said, holding it up. "It was too long last summer, and now I shall have to put on a false hem. I'd no idea how she'd grown till I came to take out her last summer frocks."

In spirit she was bracing herself up for Charles's visit. She mustn't let him see how much extra trouble his coming gave her in the busiest month of the year. She felt a familiar glow of satisfaction, as she contemplated herself—perfect wife to Charles, perfect mother to the children. She couldn't help thinking how much better a place the world would be if all women were like her. . . .

"Where's Miss Hinkley?" said Mrs. Paget.

"She's out with Agnes," answered Pen, with a little laugh that was not quite free from annoyance. "Mrs. Bevan came for her immediately after breakfast. Agnes has taken a ridiculous fancy to her and wanted her to tell her a fairy story again. It's too bad when it's the poor old thing's holiday."

"I imagine she likes it," said Mrs. Paget drily.

"Oh, well, if she does . . ." shrugged Pen. "But, honestly, when one goes all out to give her a good holiday and a real rest, one feels it hardly fair of her to spend it playing nursemaid to Agnes Bevan."

Roger had run off to the end of the bay, where the cliffs rose sheer from a tumble of rocks, to join a boy who lived on the main road and was in the same form at Cliff End School. Together they clambered over the rocks, shouting loudly and unintelligibly to each other.

Valerie, in miniature butcher-blue smock and knickers and white sun-hat, was already at work on a castle, digging with frantic energy, her bare dimpled legs planted firmly apart, her small face set and frowning, the minute wooden spade throwing up cascades of golden sand in all directions.

"Mind you eyes, darling," cautioned Pen.

Rosemary had been delighted when Beryl came to ask if she would play with her that morning (Carry, it seemed, had gone into Penzance with her mother to buy a pair of shoes). She couldn't have meant anything on Saturday at the picnic. Darling, beautiful, wonderful Beryl! She arranged the selection of her "people" she had brought with her in a row at the foot of the sandhills, then danced off happily to Beryl, who stood, sleek and solid, holding her spade.

"What shall we play at?" said Beryl.

"You choose, Beryl."

"All right," said Beryl. "Let's make a throne for me and then let's play I'm a queen and you're my slave."

They made a little heap of sand, and Beryl sat down on it, arranging her ringlets over her shoulders and putting her stalwart knees together.

"Now," she said, with obvious satisfaction, "I'm a queen and you're my slave. You've got to do everything I tell you."

"All right," agreed Rosemary, dancing eagerly around her.

"First of all go and find me twelve pebbles just the same size."

Rosemary darted off to the rocky end of the bay to look for the pebbles.

Dandy stood panting and looking about him. He felt the heat and was wondering what he could do that wouldn't be too energetic. Finally he decided to go and guard Rosemary's "people." There was a gollywog among them for whom he cherished a deep dislike and whom he always suspected of moving when not watched.

He went to them and lay down just opposite the gollywog, with his head on his paws, occasionally opening one eye or cocking one ear or growling softly to show him that he wasn't asleep.

Martin sat looking over the golden expanse of sand. A thin line of seaweed marked the point where the tide had turned. Between the edge of the sea and the horizon a streak of green cut through the blue expanse. Idly he wondered what the explanation was. He had noticed it on the afternoon of the picnic and had nearly commented on it to Violet, but had stopped himself in time, remembering that she would probably have some lengthy and apposite quotation about it.

Florence was gazing admiringly at Beryl, who sat, pink and blonde and shining, waiting for Rosemary to return with the pebbles.

"She's a beautiful child, isn't she?" she murmured to Pen.

"Do you think so?" replied Pen coldly. "I think she's like a blancmange. And those short frocks she wears are disgusting."

She had moved her position slightly so that she shouldn't see the child ordering Rosemary about, but she was as indignantly aware of it as if she were watching every movement.

Rosemary had brought the pebbles, had been made to present them on her knees, and had been sent off to find "twenty tiny shells."

Pen broke off a thread of cotton impatiently.

"Only a blancmange is more healthy-looking," she added.

"Oh, but I think she looks the picture of health," expostulated Florence.

Martin was lifting up the sand in handfuls and letting it drop down. "Sand beetles" settled on his hand and arm, hopped off again, or opened tiny yellow wings to fly away.

"They're awfully bad just here," said Pen. "We call it Beetle Corner. They bite sometimes."

"Where did you go for your walk this morning, Martin?" said Violet brightly.

She gave him, as she spoke, an intimate smile that was meant to convey her message to him ("After all, there's no need of words. We understand each other"), but a blind seemed to close down over his face as he met her eyes.

"I went inland," he said. "Through the woods towards Beesley."

"There's a little stream in the wood with ferns growing by the side of it," said Mrs. Paget, dreamily, "and at Beesley there's a tiny thatched cottage where you can get tea."

She had worn a leghorn hat trimmed with black velvet ribbon and a smart little dress of pink alpaca draped stylishly over her bustle. Going through the wood she had taken off her hat and let the breeze blow through her hair. They had sat down on a little hillock of moss, and Michael had told her again how dear she was and how much he loved her.

Martin smiled at her. She looked so sweet, sitting there in her neat grey cotton dress, her silver hair shining under her shady black hat, her blue eyes gazing dreamily over a gap of fifty years. Her memories must be placid enough, like the memories of most of the women of her generation. A happy marriage and a sheltered life. . . . What would his memories be when he was as old as that? His heart beat unevenly at the thought.

"The little stream's still there," he said, "but at Beesley every other cottage has a notice out with 'Cornish Teas' on now, and there's an enormous Tudor Road House."

"I hear Arnold Kemsing's staying here," said Violet suddenly. "Gwynne knows him. She and he were both speakers at a Literary Luncheon last month."

"He wants to paint Stella," said Pen. "I quite forgot to tell you. He came round on Sunday to ask if he might. Stella saw him trying to work that old pump that Mr. Ransome bought and explained to him that the real pump was indoors. He's so charming. . . . She's gone for the first sitting this morning. He wanted her in the dress she wore at the picnic with that handkerchief round her head. She was pressing the dress out before breakfast."

"I hope it won't make her conceited," said Florence rather grimly.

She thought that Stella really might have paid a little more attention to her since they'd come down. And to Violet. Violet had gone out of her way to be nice to her, and she hadn't responded. Girls of Stella's age usually adored Violet. It was so annoying of Stella not to. . . .

Pen tossed her chin in the aggressive way she always did when any of her flock was attacked.

"Conceited?" she said. "Of course it won't. Stella hasn't an atom of conceit in her. She's absolutely unspoilt. Why, the only thing she cares about is being at home with me and the children. She was longing for it all the time she was at school."

"Now run round my throne ten times," shouted Beryl, in her husky sleepy voice, "then hop to the rocks and back."

"I thought he wrote books," said Martin.

("I can't read his stuff," the man had said, and at the memory of those smiling eyes and pleasant indolent mouth a spasm of hatred seized him.)

"Oh, he explained that," said Pen. "He's an artist as well, but his painting's a sort of hobby. He only lets himself paint when he's on holiday. Writing's his real job. But he paints awfully well. . . . Wouldn't it be lovely if Stella's portrait were in the Academy?"

"We'd all go up to London to see it," said Florence, already a little excited at the prospect. Perhaps Gwynne would ask them to lunch at her club. . . .

"Is there still a funny little church with a lych-gate, Martin?" said Mrs. Paget.

"Yes, that's still there," said Martin. "Just outside the village."

She nodded, satisfied, and saw Michael looking at it, his handsome face alight with pleasure, and saying, "It's made for us. Let's get married all over again."

They had gone into it, and, while Michael was looking at the brasses, she had slipped into a pew and prayed that their love might not die. . . . And the next morning had come their hurried flight from—she didn't know what. But her prayer had been answered. Their love had not died. . . . A dreamy smile curved the wrinkled lips beneath the shady black hat.

"Well, perhaps not the Academy exactly," said Pen, "but I believe he does have exhibitions of his work."

Val came up to them, hot and panting.

"Look at my castle," she said proudly, pointing with her spade. She had made a little heap of sand, patted it smooth, and decorated it with the convolvulus flowers that grew on the sandhills.

"Lovely, darling," said Pen.

"Lovely, darling," echoed Violet, and added, "perhaps a trifle rococo," thus giving Martin simultaneous displays of motherly tenderness, humour, and culture.

"Can I have my swimming suit on and paddle, Mummy?" said Val, ignoring Violet.

Pen took the tiny swimming suit out of her bag and slipped off the cotton frock and knickers. Val stood for a moment, straight and sturdy—brown dimpled arms and legs, white body, rosy face, and fair tousled hair—before the suit was slipped on.

She patted her stomach and looked at them proudly.

"I'm a *big* girl," she said.

The suit was a red one with an anchor embroidered in white on the chest.

Mrs. Paget smiled at her.

"Aren't you smart!" she said.

"I knitted it," said Pen. "It's rather sweet, isn't it?"

"I'm going to school to-morrow," said Valerie.

"Will you like that?" said Violet in her good-with-children voice.

Val lowered her head and looked at her under thick curling lashes.

"Yes," she said.

Pen sighed.

"I'm afraid she won't," she said. "She's such a Mummy's baby. It's only for the morning, but I don't know what we're going to do without each other." She looked at Valerie. "Mummy will cry, won't she?"

"No," laughed Valerie.

Martin was smiling at them, and Violet was watching him, her eyes dwelling covertly on the deeply furrowed cheeks, the open chest, the bare brown arms. . . . As she looked at him that strange sensation of melting weakness swept over her again. She knew at last what love was. She had never known before, and she would never know again. . . . It was her one chance, her last chance. There surged through her a savage primitive lust of possession. He was hers. . . . He shouldn't escape her. . . .

"Are you going to bathe, Martin?" she said.

"Not just yet," he replied.

Roger came running along from the rocks to join them.

"Oh, Roger! You're soaked," said Pen, with no real surprise or annoyance because it happened so often. "Go up on the sandhills and put your bathing suit on."

"It'll dry in the sun, Mummy," Roger reassured her. He sat down by them. "Miss Hinkley's along there with Agnes, and Agnes is making her tell her the same tale over and over again. All about someone who jumped into the sea and a merman met her and gave her a feast. And she keeps asking if she had doughnuts and chocolates and things. . . . She keeps going on and on."

"*Poor* Agnes!" said Pen. "You mustn't laugh at her, Roger."

"I know. I didn't," said Roger. "I just smiled a little, but not where they could see me."

He ran back to the road to join his friend.

"I think he's tall for his age, don't you, Martin?" said Pen.

Martin nodded absently. He was wondering if he could escape them and go to Cliff Cottage. He *must* see her again. He couldn't really believe that this had happened to him. He knew and loved every line of her face, every movement and gesture and expression . . . the sudden lop-sided smile, the quick alert turn of her head . . . the sweetness and soundness and gallant courage of her. He saw her again coming out into the garden, her eyes screwed up against the sun. The picture would be there in his heart till he died. He had guessed that she was unhappy, though at the time he didn't know the reason, and when he went back to Pen's she told him the whole story. He had returned to the hotel, his heart wrung by pity, and late that night he had gone down to the cottage again, afraid that the man might have come back drunk and that she might be in danger. Everything had been peaceful, however, the little house silent and in darkness. He had hung about with the idea of staying there all night in case she should need him, then, realising how crazy it was, had returned to the hotel to lie awake racked in turn by misery and delight. He had not seen her since, though he made a point of passing the house on all his walks, hoping to catch, at any rate, a glimpse of her. It was three days now since their meeting. Suddenly he couldn't bear to go on any longer without seeing her. He rose abruptly to his feet.

"I think I'll just go—"

He stopped. Violet, too, was rising as if to accompany him, and the thought of her company when his heart was full of this miracle was a sacrilege.

"—and see what Val's doing," he ended and walked down to where Valerie stood, her bare feet planted in the surf, watching the water ripple round them.

Violet sank back again (for Valerie was well within earshot of them all) and began to talk with slightly raised voice.

"I couldn't help laughing when she said her name was Dorothy Mately. 'My dear,' I said, 'don't you know what happened to *her*? Have you never read Bunyan's *Life and Death of Mr. Badman*?'"

It appeared from Florence's constrained laugh and the silence of the others that they hadn't either, so Violet passed on to a series of anecdotes all conspicuously redounding to her credit.

"I know she hated me and had told the most shameless lies about me, but when I got the chance of doing her a good turn, I did it. I didn't really want to, but I just couldn't help it. ... I *am* like that. ..."

The sound of her voice in the distance irritated Martin as the droning of a mosquito might have done.

Rosemary and Beryl were still playing Queen and Slave. Rosemary had just had to run to the corner of the bay and back before Beryl counted a hundred. The familiar signs of over-fatigue were already appearing—the dead pallor round the small sensitive mouth, the flushed cheek-bones, the faint hollows round the blue eyes. . . . Pen couldn't bear it any longer.

"Come and sit down in the shade, Rosemary," she called. "You mustn't run about in the sun any longer."

Beryl got down from her throne.

"I've had enough, anyway," she said, in her slow fat voice. "I'm going home."

"May I come with you?" said Rosemary. "Mummy, may I go with her?"

Pen tried to resist the pleading in her eyes.

"What are you going to do, Beryl?" she asked.

"Dunno."

"I'll read to you, Beryl," said Rosemary. "That's not running about, Mummy."

Beryl was too lazy to read herself, but she sometimes enjoyed being read to. She didn't like the fairy stories that Rosemary loved so. She liked school stories, in which she always saw herself as the pretty popular heroine.

"*Queen of the Upper Third*?" she stipulated.

"Yes," agreed Rosemary, who found the story boring but loved doing anything for Beryl.

"I don't care what you do," said Pen, "as long as you sit quietly in the shade. If you do that you can go to Beryl's for half an hour."

"We'll sit in the hammock," promised Beryl, "and Mummy will let us have some lemonade. Come on!"

Rosemary collected Owl and Wilfred from her little row of "people." Dandy, feeling rested and considering the gollywog sufficiently cowed, had trotted off to join Roger and his friend, who were practising a three-legged race in preparation for the school sports.

"Val," she called, "will you look after my other people till I come back?"

"Yes," promised Val, proud to be left in charge, "I'll look after them."

Rosemary and Beryl raced up the cliff path together. Pen sighed and returned to her sewing.

Martin and Valerie went to sit by Rosemary's "people."

"I'm looking after them, aren't I?" said Val importantly.

Violet was watching them narrowly as she talked to Florence, ready to leap to her feet and join him if Martin set off for a walk.

"Let's play a pretend game," suggested Valerie. "Let's pretend we're ladies and gentlemen. I'll be Mr. Sainsbury. What will you be?"

Martin considered.

"I'll be Mrs. Grieg," he said at last.

"You start talking," said Valerie.

"How are you to-day, Mr. Sainsbury?" asked Martin.

"Very well, thank you."

"How are your wife and children?"

"They're dead," said Valerie cheerfully.

"Oh," said Martin, taken aback. "I'm sorry. How did that happen?"

"They ate the stones off the rockery yesterday," said Valerie, still more cheerfully, pouring handfuls of sand over her brown chubby knees. "I told them not to, but they would do it and they've all died. All ten of them," she ended, looking up at him with a beaming smile.

"Good heavens!" said Martin.

A battered rag doll at the end of the row of "people" fell over sideways. Valerie replaced it carefully.

"That's Poppy," she said. "She's always ill. She has sixteen colds every day and"—her face grew solemn as she lowered her voice impressively—"she doesn't know about God."

"How's that?" enquired Martin, with interest.

"Well, she was ill in bed with one of her colds when Rosemary told the others about God, and Rosemary's never had time to tell her by herself, so she doesn't know." Valerie gazed at the unsightly object with morbid fascination. "She doesn't say any prayers at all." She turned to Martin. "How long prayers do you say? I say them so long." She held her hands a few inches apart. "And Rosemary says them so long." She widened the gap. "And Sue so long. . . ." She widened it again. "I expect you do them so long." She widened her small arms to their fullest extent.

("Look at Val telling a fishing story," said Violet, with a shrill laugh.)

"Well . . ." began Martin, but she burst in again, her small round rosy face aglow with laughter.

"I don't tell Mummy, but I have such fun with God. Sometimes in my prayers I say things like, 'Please bless shells and seaweed,' just to make Him laugh." She grew serious for a moment. "He does laugh, doesn't He?"

"I'm sure He does," said Martin.

She chuckled. With its beaming smile and the golden hair standing untidily up all round it, her face looked like a baby sun.

"I've got something for to-night that I'm sure will make Him laugh."

"What's that?" said Martin.

She shook her head.

"I shan't tell you. He'd hear and I don't want Him to know till to-night."

Mrs. Paget got up. She wanted to go to the little house where she and Michael had stayed—to look at it again, to imagine Michael standing at the doorway, his hands in his pockets, his pipe in his mouth, gazing out over the sea.

"I'll just go back to the hotel," she said vaguely.

"Yes, dear," said Florence, getting up. "I'm sure you need a rest before lunch."

"I don't want you to come, Florence," said Mrs. Paget, but Florence insisted on taking her to the gate and standing there till she had disappeared indoors. Then she went back to rejoin the others.

Mrs. Paget walked through the hall of the hotel and out of the front door and along the lane to the other end of the bay where the cottages were. Just as she had passed Four Winds, Stella and

Arnold Kemsing came out of the door and walked down to the gate. Stella's eyes were starry, her cheeks softly flushed.

"That's my grandmother," she said, looking after the small slight upright figure.

"Taking the morning constitutional?" said Arnold Kemsing. "Isn't it ghastly to think that we shall all come to it—the morning constitutional and the afternoon nap the high-lights of the day?"

Stella laughed rather unsteadily.

"I can't imagine *you* old."

He smiled down at her, stirred by her youth and loveliness, aware that she was in love with him and that he would do well to leave her alone.

"And I can't imagine you . . ."

Mrs. Paget was slightly dismayed to find that a man was standing at the little door just as Michael used to stand, his hands in his pockets, a pipe in his mouth, gazing out to sea. His head was turned away from her. She hesitated, then decided to go into the shop and buy some more sweets for the children.

He turned round as she stepped forward, and her heart leapt wildly.

"*Michael!*" she said.

He took his pipe out of his mouth and looked at her, puzzled.

"Yes, my name is Michael," he said. "Michael Forrester."

She looked at him, struggling to get her breath. It *was* Michael—the narrow clean-cut face, the grey kindly eyes, the firm beautiful mouth. But she saw that he was a much older man than Michael had been—then.

"I say. . . . You'd better sit down. Half a sec."

He vanished into the little shop and reappeared a few moments later carrying a glass of water and a wooden chair. She was leaning against the wall, fighting the wave of faintness that had swept over her.

"Here . . . sit down and drink this."

She sat down and drank the water obediently. Still puzzled, he watched the strange old lady, who had appeared suddenly from nowhere, called him by his name, and then proceeded to faint on him.

She handed him back the glass and smiled. The colour had returned to her face.

"I'm so sorry," she said. "What must you think of me? It was just—you're so exactly like someone I once knew that it gave me a shock."

"You said my name."

"He was called Michael, too. Just for a moment I thought—" She took herself in hand and spoke in a brisk business-like tone. "I'm Mrs. Paget and I'm staying at the Merlin Bay Hotel. Perhaps you know my daughter—Mrs. Marlowe of Sea Meads?"

"You're young Roger's Granny," he said with a friendly grin. "Of *course* I know all about you, then. He's been chattering about your coming for weeks. I'm on the staff of Cliff End School, so I know the young blighter well."

She rose.

"You've been so kind. I mustn't trouble you any longer." She glanced at her watch. "I must be getting back to the hotel. . . ."

"Let me come with you."

"No. Honestly," she smiled, "I'd rather go alone."

"But we must see each other again," he persisted. "I want to know about my double. And I want my wife to meet you. You'd like each other, I know. I live over at Faulkland Cove. Could you come to tea?"

"I'd love to . . ." she said.

That strange dreamy feeling was closing round her again. His voice, his gestures, his smile, everything about him was Michael's. . . .

"To-morrow?"

"Yes. . . . I could come to-morrow."

"I'll call for you. You don't mind a side-car, do you?"

"I'd love it. I've never been in one before."

"You needn't be nervous. It's *very* luxurious—all side-screens and wind-screens and cushions and things."

"It sounds magnificent."

"Well—to-morrow, then. Are you sure you're all right?"

"Quite, thanks. Good-bye."

"Good-bye."

She turned at the bend of the road. He was still standing there, watching her. He raised his hand in a gesture that was as familiar to her as her own face.

Chapter Ten

CHARLES MARLOWE stepped down from the train onto Penzance Station and looked about him. He was a thick-set shaggy sort of man, vaguely suggestive of a sheep dog, and had a slightly unkempt appearance, due partly to his clumsy build, and partly to his habit of forgetting to have his hair cut. He looked the sort of man who needed mothering, and that was what had first attracted Pen to him. Then he had turned out not to need mothering, after all. . . .

Yes, there was Pen hurrying down the platform to meet him. None of the children were with her. . . . The sight of her slender figure, with its air of almost childish fragility caught at his heart unexpectedly, though he had been hardening himself against her all the way down.

She came up to him and raised her face for his kiss.

"Well, my darling . . ." she said.

Her tone was affectionate enough, but it chilled him. So she would have greeted Valerie or Rosemary—with that bright welcoming smile and tender motherly voice. (I believe she sees the whole world as a sort of nursery and herself the nurse, he thought ruefully.) It wasn't exactly affected, but there was a note of conscientious determination in its brightness, as if she were thinking: Whatever my trials and difficulties, the children mustn't guess them.

"This *is* nice," she said, tucking her arm through his. "I *have* been looking forward to it."

He walked down the platform with her, feeling like a small boy coming home from school. He conquered an ironic impulse to ask if his rabbits were all right.

"Hello!" he said. "A car. . . ."

"It's the hotel car," she explained. "Mother insisted on my having it to meet you. It goes on her bill, of course. Come along," she laughed, "let's be grand while we can."

The chauffeur took his bag and he got in beside Pen. She chattered gaily to him, pouring out all the family news.

"I told you that Martin was here—didn't I?—and Violet Coniston, that friend of Florence's, so we're a real family coach. . . . Gordon and Sue were over for the week-end—their half term, you know. They were so well and jolly. They only went back this morning. And Roger's practising hard for the sports, and Val's going to school next week. Just for the mornings, of course. I'm afraid she'll be terribly home-sick at first, but I suppose she's got to start some time."

He knew that bright artless manner of hers. It was her armour. You couldn't break through it. But he'd come down this time determined to break through it, to have things out with her once and for all. He was undecided whether to deliver his ultimatum at the beginning or end of his holiday, but he was determined to deliver it, to batter down her defence of gay detachment and make her face reality. He'd tried before, and she'd eluded him time after time. It was extraordinary how effective her method was, how helpless it made one feel, but he was going to come to grips with her at last.

"How's Rosemary?" he said suddenly.

Rosemary, of course, had been her excuse for coming to this outlandish place, which could never be home to him, where he could be, at best, an occasional visitor. She had heard some tale of special healing properties in the Cornish air, and whisked the whole family off before he realised what she was doing. But he'd been consulting doctors himself and had chapter and verse for everything. He'd barred *that* way of escape, anyhow.

She looked at him warily, as if she half glimpsed what was in his mind.

"*Much* better since we came down here," she said with exaggerated heartiness. "All of them are. It suits us all much better than Dulwich."

He said nothing and for a moment she, too, was silent, as if finding it difficult to retain her easy casual tone.

"Mr. Heath's heading for another outbreak," she said at last. "He came past the house last night singing. He sounded quite tipsy."

She threw him a quick speculative glance. She'd meant, of course, to detract his attention by a piece of local gossip. She always held that men were greater gossipers than women. But he merely nodded and made no comment. She tried another tack.

"Arnold Kemsing's taken Mr. Ransome's studio for June. The novelist, you know. He's a painter, as well, and he wants to paint Stella's portrait. She went for her first sitting yesterday, and she's there again to-day."

"Really?" he said, and she saw with relief that he had ceased to think of the distance of Cornwall from the Eastern Counties.

Stella had always been the only one of the six children who seemed to belong to him. Pen was in love with him when Stella was born. She had been *their* baby, not, like the others, Pen's alone. It had delighted Pen that he should want to nurse and play with her. Often when Pen was tired he had bathed and put her to bed alone. Then—very very gradually—the maternal instinct, which had at first so touched and charmed him, had filled her whole being, engulfing every other interest and stultifying every other emotion.

"I was sorry to miss her birthday," he went on.

"Yes . . . she liked your bag," said Pen generously, and added, "It's so lovely having her at home."

"I should have thought she'd have wanted to get down to a job of some sort when she left school," he said casually.

Pen trembled with sudden unreasoning anger.

"Of *course* not!" she said, trying to speak calmly. "She's been looking forward for *years* to living at home with me and helping me."

She had deliberately shut out of her memory that vision of Stella—sulky, defiant, demanding to leave home and "do something"—and remembered only the docile, contented Stella of the school holidays, the radiant happy Stella of the past week.

"Oh, well . . ." he said, a little puzzled.

The car drew up at the gate of Sea Meads, and Rosemary, Roger, and Valerie flung themselves upon him. He hoisted Valerie up onto his shoulders.

"Now, children, leave Daddy alone," said Pen rather sharply. "He's had a long journey and he's tired. He wants to go up to his room and wash. You mustn't make nuisances of yourselves."

Rosemary and Roger withdrew, abashed by the edge of irritation in her voice, and she lifted Valerie down from Charles's shoulder.

"You aren't a baby any more, are you, Val? You're a big girl, remember."

She shoo'd them into the garden and took Charles up the winding wooden stairs to the attic bedroom.

"I thought you wouldn't mind being in here, dear," she said, and, though her tone was light and impersonal, she flushed slightly and avoided his eyes as she spoke. "I've got Val in my room, and none of these rooms are large enough for three. There's a lovely view of the sea from here, isn't there?"

"Isn't there!" he agreed with a trace of irony in his voice.

She turned quickly to the door.

"Well, I'll leave you to do your unpacking. We'll have tea when you're ready."

He stood at the window when she had gone, staring unseeingly out over the sea. He still loved her. Things would be so much simpler if he didn't. Making one excuse after another, she had refused to live with him since Valerie's birth. Though she probably didn't realise it, it was partly to avoid having to live with him that she had deliberately put two hundred miles between them by coming to Merlin Bay. Probably she honestly believed that it was for the sake of Rosemary's health. She had always been able to make herself believe whatever she wanted to believe. It wasn't that she disliked him. She would be quite kind to him if he would be willing to take his place in the household as one of the children—to be managed, humoured, and petted. She refused him any other relationship and he refused to accept that. He still felt humiliated by the memory of his last visit here. He had been made to feel that he was of far less importance in the household than Dandy. . . . He wouldn't have come down this summer if he hadn't meant to settle the thing one way or the other.

Right from the beginning she had stood between him and the children, jealous of their affection for him, of his claims on them. He hadn't realised what was happening at first, and when he did realise it was too late to do anything. He mustn't play with them when he came home from work because it over-excited them just before bedtime. Her rigid rules of diet and routine forbade him to give them "treats" of any kind. Quite unconsciously she had made a sort of bugbear of him to them. Daddy mustn't be disturbed, mustn't be worried. Daddy, according to her, was always "busy." They mustn't ask him questions or go to him for advice or comfort. When Val was born she would hardly let him touch her. He held her in the wrong way. He upset her stomach by jolting her, upset her nerves by playing with her. He must have no share in their children. They must belong to her entirely. And yet she *had* been in love with him when she married him. She had been in love with him till Stella came. It was Stella's coming that had seemed to arouse those instincts that had dominated her ever since. And, of course, she *was* a good mother. She gave up her whole life to the children. She did honestly care for them more than for anything else in the world. . . . He wondered how she would take what he was going to say to her, and—what her decision would be. . . .

He washed, put his clothes away in the little chest of drawers, and went downstairs. He felt like a visitor in this house—as Pen probably meant him to feel. He had had no hand in the arranging of it. Everything in it had been planned by Pen. Things had to be shown and explained to him as though it were not his home. All he was good for, he thought, with a tinge of bitterness, was to earn the money that kept it going.

"Mummy," Rosemary was calling, "Granny's just gone by in a side-car."

"Nonsense, dear," said Pen.

"She *has*," corroborated Roger, "and Mr. Forrester was driving it."

What *would* Mother do next, thought Pen irritably. Charles's coming had made her feel unaccountably irritable. It really *was* the last straw having him here on the top of everything else. She would be very careful, however, not to show him how she felt.

Miss Hinkley was in the hall, putting on her gloves, as he came down.

"Hello, Aunt Sarah," he said, smiling at her. "Nice to see you here."

She beamed at him. She had adored him since the days when she used to help his mother put him to bed on the nurse's afternoon out.

"I'm having a *lovely* holiday, Charles," she said.

"Good! Pen looking after you all right? Now where are you running off to just when I've come?"

"Well, dear," she said, with a laugh that was deprecating and a little excited, "I didn't mean to, because I've been so looking forward to seeing you, but Mrs. Bevan's just sent to ask me to go in to Agnes again. It's that silly story I told her." Modest pride quivered in her voice. "She wants it again and again and she won't hear it from anyone but me. We keep putting a bit more on to it every time. I told her yesterday that the chairs were made of chocolate and the floor of toffee and she got so excited that we had to stop. ... She's such a dear girl and really quite intelligent. ... A little backward, certainly, but so sweet and affectionate. ... Well, dear, see you this evening."

She drifted off through the open door, turning at the gate to wave to him with a hand encased in a much-darned black cotton glove. Gloves were to Miss Hinkley the essential badge of respectability. She would rather have starved than gone out without them, even in Merlin Bay.

He smiled after her.

"Poor old thing! She does love to think she's helping someone. It makes her feel important again."

"Well, she's hardly 'helping' exactly," said Pen, a little tartly. "Just telling that ridiculous story she's made up over and over again to Agnes Bevan. I should think that Mrs. Bevan's sorry she ever started it. I told you about the Bevans, didn't I?"

He nodded. Pen was a conscientious letter writer. She wrote bright chatty letters each week to him and Gordon and Susan. He had an idea that any of the three letters would have served equally well for any of the three.

He followed her into the little sitting-room, where tea for two was laid on the table.

"The children have taken their tea out into the garden," she said. "I thought you'd like to have it in peace the first day."

He glanced out of the window and saw Rosemary and Roger and Valerie sitting on the lawn with mugs of milk and plates of bread and jam and sponge-cake. He couldn't reasonably object, and yet he felt that it was all part of her policy of separating him from them, of making him a guest, a stranger. . . .

As soon as she had poured out his tea, Stella came in.

"Hello, Daddy!"

She kissed him and perched for a moment on the arm of his chair, her hand in his.

"Darling," said Pen, "there *are* other chairs, and Daddy wants to get on with his tea. It's really too hot, anyway, to have people sitting on top of one like that. . . . If you'll get another cup you can have some tea. I wasn't sure when you'd be in."

Stella rose.

"No, thanks, darling. I had tea with Mr. Kemsing after the sitting."

"How did the sitting go?"

"All right, I think. . . . I'm just going out to stretch my legs. It gives one such a cooped-up feeling, standing in the same position for hours and hours. . . . I'll go for a run along the beach. See you later."

She blew Charles a kiss and went out. They saw her running down the path to the sands.

Charles stirred his tea thoughtfully. The sight of Stella had startled him. She was—different in some way. The child he remembered as lately as last summer had vanished.

"Who is this fellow she's sitting to?" he said slowly.

"I told you, didn't I, darling?" said Pen patiently. "He's Arnold Kemsing, the novelist, but he's a painter too, though his paintings aren't as famous as his novels."

"Do you know anything about him—apart from his work?"

"He's a man of very good standing, naturally," said Pen with dignity, "or I shouldn't have allowed Stella to sit for him."

"But you know nothing of him apart from his work?" he persisted.

"Of *course* I do, Charles," she said, the note of irritation peeping out at last. "He came here to ask permission to paint Stella. He's a most *charming* man."

He remembered the subdued excitement of Stella's manner, the new eager radiance that seemed to shine out from her.

"Is she in love with him?" he asked bluntly.

The colour flooded her cheeks, and for a moment she was too angry to speak. Then she laughed unsteadily.

"My dear Charles, what a ridiculous idea! Stella's an absolute child. She's never been in love with anyone in her life and won't be for years. Why, she's so devoted to me that there's no room for anything else. I know that some girls of her age do go in for that sort of thing, but Stella isn't one, I'm glad to say."

He glanced at her, surprised and faintly touched by her blindness. They're her whole life, he thought. She can't bear to face the idea of their going away from her, because it would leave her nothing.

"After all," he said gently, "it's quite natural for a girl to fall in love with a charming man."

"He happens to be old enough to be her father," she said, in the tone of one who brings forward an unanswerable objection.

He shrugged and said nothing further.

She quickly resumed her armour of kind bright aloofness and began to detail plans for his holiday.

"We must have a picnic in Beesley Woods one day. The children get a little tired of the beach, of course, and enjoy going inland. And Mother wants us to have the hotel car for some drives while you're here, and we must go to Faulkland Cove. It's so charming. The Forresters have a cottage there, but it's quite unspoilt. I expect

Martin will be glad to have you here. He's looked a bit bored, poor boy, with only Mother and Florence and that friend of Florence's to go about with."

She's putting me in my place, thought Charles grimly. I've no right even to discuss the children with her. I'm merely her guest, to be entertained and kept happy and occupied. She was explaining the ways of the household to him.

"The children start using the bathroom soon after seven, because of getting off to school, so if you could finish in it by then, or use it later ... I expect you'll be having a morning dip, won't you? Breakfast's a bit of a muddle with the children, of course, so I could get you yours after I've seen them off."

Rosemary came in.

"Can I do my home-work, Mummy?" she said. "I do home-work now," she explained importantly to Charles. "Roger doesn't yet."

"What have you to do to-day?" asked Charles.

"I've got to write about the journey of a raindrop to the sea," she answered.

"Come along, dear," said Pen, rising. "I'll get you settled."

She took her to the dining-room and settled her at the table, with her exercise-book and pencil, her "people" sitting round in a bedraggled-looking semicircle. Rosemary always insisted on her "people" sharing her home-work.

Charles was carrying the tea things into the kitchen when Pen returned.

"I'd rather do that myself, dear," she said kindly. "You don't know where the things go or anything, and it makes more trouble for me in the end."

Roger and Valerie brought their tea things in from the garden and went out again to play. They had been a little tiresome all afternoon (Pen put it down to the excitement of Charles's coming), and now they began to quarrel. Roger kept teasing Valerie by following her about and stamping on her shadow, and at last Valerie began to cry.

"Don't be silly, Val," said Pen. "It doesn't hurt you."

"It hurts my shadow," wailed Val. "It hurts it badly."

"Leave her shadow alone, Roger," said Pen.

She finished clearing up in the kitchen, then got her mending bag and came back to Charles in the sitting-room. She was determined to do her duty by him, to be the attentive, pleasant, affectionate wife, interested in all his doings. After all, it was only for a month. . . .

He turned round sharply from the window as she entered.

He'd decided to have it out with her here and now. There was no sense in putting it off. He'd give her the month to think things over and come to a decision.

She sat down and took out a sock of Roger's.

"Now tell me all your news, darling," she said, with that maddening air of entertaining a child.

"Pen . . .," he began.

She examined a large hole in the heel carefully before she answered, then she said "Yes," absently, still exploring the cavity with her hand, her mind evidently still chiefly concerned by the problem of how best to tackle it.

"I want to talk to you."

She glanced at him with a questioning smile, but beneath the smile he saw something vigilant, on its guard, prepared to meet and resist attack.

"Yes, dear?" she said again, and added, "Did you ever see anything *like* the holes Roger makes in his socks?"

"Listen, Pen," he said. "We've got to have this out."

The door opened and Rosemary's head came round.

"How do you spell 'ditch'?" she asked.

"D-i-t-c-h," said Pen slowly.

"Thanks," said Rosemary, and disappeared.

"What were you saying, dear?" said Pen, as the door closed.

"I was saying that——' "

Valerie's voice, upraised tearfully, came through the open window.

"Mummy, he's stamping on my shadow again."

Pen looked out and saw Roger running after Valerie round the garden, laughing mischievously, stamping and jumping on her shadow.

"Leave her alone, Roger," she said.

"I'm not touching her," said Roger. "I'm only running on the grass. I can't help it if her shadow's there."

"They're a bit over-excited," she said to Charles reproachfully, as if he were the cause of the disturbance. "What were you saying, dear?"

"I was saying that you've got to make up your mind one way or the other. We've got either to have a home together or——"

The door opened and Rosemary's head appeared.

"How do you spell 'mountain'?" she asked. "I can do the 'moun' part, but is it 't-a-n-e' or 't-a-i-n'?"

"T-a-i-n," said Pen.

"Thanks," said Rosemary, and disappeared.

"Yes, dear?" said Pen to Charles again. "You were saying?"

She still sounded as if what he was saying couldn't possibly be of any importance.

"I was saying——"

"Mummy, he won't stop," wailed Valerie. "He's still doing it."

"Well, take your shadow up," taunted Roger. "If you leave it lying on the grass, of course people tread on it. Take it up and put it away."

"I can't."

Pen went to the window.

"Val, dear, it doesn't hurt you, and Roger——"

Charles lost his temper, pushing her aside and shouting, "If you don't stop that nonsense at once, both of you, I'll come out to you."

They stared at him aghast, then went to the back of the shed to play shop, their quarrel forgotten.

It was the first time he had ever interfered in Pen's treatment of the children, and the colour flooded her cheeks.

"Really, Charles——" she expostulated.

"Now we can get to business," said Charles shortly, but apparently they couldn't, for the door opened and Rosemary's head reappeared.

"How do you spell——"

Charles cut her short.

"Can't you use a dictionary?" he snapped.

She looked at him sideways under her lashes.

"Well..." she said. "Yes, I suppose I can."

"There's a dictionary on the dining-room bookshelf," said Pen.

"All right," said Rosemary, disappearing again.

She pouted a little to herself as she took the dictionary from its place on the shelf. It was dull looking up words in the dictionary. It was much more interesting going to ask Mummy and Daddy.

Pen had surrendered her pose of indifference. She even forgot to go on with Roger's sock.

"What is it you want, Charles?" she said.

"I'll tell you as shortly as I can," he said. "I'm tired of living a homeless life."

"Homeless?" she said, as if she didn't understand.

"Yes, homeless. This is no home for me. I can get here with difficulty at Easter, Christmas, and for the summer holiday, but I can't live here. I don't belong here even when I do come. You see to that."

She opened her eyes wide.

"What *do* you mean, Charles?"

He waved that point aside.

"Never mind that. The point is that I want a home and that this place can never be a home—to me, at any rate."

"Why not?" she countered.

She wore an innocent bewildered expression, but Charles knew her well enough to realise that her every sense was alert. She understood exactly what he meant and she intended to side-track him, to beat down his every argument, to cajole and coax him, to deceive him as thoroughly as she deceived herself.

"It's too far away from my work," he said shortly.

An expression of self-righteousness came over her face.

"I know, darling," she said unctuously. "I'm so sorry, but we had to come here for Rosemary's sake, you know."

"You said Rosemary was better."

"I know, but it's only because this place suits her. It would be fatal to go back to London."

"I'm not proposing to go back to London."

She looked at him, wary, on the defensive, gathering her forces for resistance. He met her gaze, trying not to let his eyes wander to her temples, blue-veined, fragile-seeming as eggshell, beneath the cloud of soft fine hair. The sight of those temples had often melted his anger in the old days. He hardened his heart against them.

"I've consulted several doctors about Rosemary," he went on. "I've been to a Harley Street specialist. They all agree that the East Coast air would be quite as good as the air here. I don't want to—bother you in any way. I only want to have a home somewhere where I can come to it at week-ends and occasionally during the week."

He had played his trump card. She was still looking at him, so white and frightened now that it gave her a curious resemblance to Rosemary—Rosemary, waking from one of those nightmares that filled the world with terror. She rallied her forces with an effort.

"Those doctors can know nothing whatever about Rosemary," she said. "It's absurd for them to give an opinion without seeing her."

"I told them exactly what the trouble was."

"Without seeing the child they could know nothing," she maintained. "She was in Dr. Siddon's hands, and we came here on his advice. I shall not listen to anyone else."

"Siddon agrees with them," he said relentlessly. "He says that the East Coast would be just as good as this place. He told you that this would benefit the child, but he says that he had an idea you were coming here in any case and he was reassuring you."

"I never told him that," she flashed.

"I don't say you did, but he got the idea."

"The fact remains that she's been enormously better since we came here, and so have they all, and that's the only fact that counts with me. It's bad for children to be continually moving about. They've settled down here and they're beginning to do well at school. Besides, think of the expense."

"I have thought of it. That's my business."

She kept her eyes on him steadily. She was still very pale.

"And if I decide not to go?"

"Then we must separate finally. I can't go on like this any longer."

"You mean—divorce?"

He shrugged.

"Perhaps ... eventually."

"Have you—met anyone?"

He longed to say "Yes" just to see whether she would care at all, but he couldn't lie to her. Besides—she must know that he could never love anyone else. He might marry again for a home and companionship, but—he could never really love anyone else.

"No," he said.

She began to put the socks and sewing materials back into her mending bag. Her hands trembled a little, but that and her pallor were the only signs of emotion.

"I want you to make up your mind before I go back," he said. "We needn't discuss it again unless you want to. I think I've made it quite clear. We move to somewhere within reach of my work, the East Coast for preference, or—it's the end. You do understand, don't you, Pen?"

"Yes."

Her voice was hard. He looked at her despairingly. She was like granite beneath that delusive appearance of fragility. Probably she would let him go out of her life without a single regret.

"You'll make me a regular allowance, of course, if we separate?" she stipulated.

"Of course," he agreed bitterly.

That, of course, was all he meant to her now, all he had meant for years—money to bring up the children who had pushed him out of her life. He was shocked by the sudden fierce resentment of his children that swept over him.

She closed her work-bag and glanced at the clock.

"Why, it's past Val's bedtime," she said brightly.

She got up and went to the window.

He followed her with his eyes. She was so slight and childish in build that he could almost have broken her with one hand, and yet she was indomitable. . . .

"Val, darling," she called. "Come along. Bedtime."

She went out of the room without looking at him again.

Chapter Eleven

"I HOPE that wasn't too fast for you," said Michael Forrester, as the motor cycle stopped in front of the small whitewashed cottage overlooking the cove.

"No, I've loved it," said Mrs. Paget. "I'd have liked you to go faster still."

He dismounted and opened the door of the side-car.

"All right," he laughed. "I'll take your breath away going back."

He helped her out and glanced at the cottage.

"I expect Ruth heard . . ."

As he spoke the door opened and a woman stood in the doorway smiling. She had dark curly hair, warm brown eyes, and cheeks tanned to the colour of a ripe peach. There was a radiant air of health and cheerfulness about her.

"My wife, Ruth . . . Mrs. Paget," he introduced them.

"Do come in," the woman smiled. "You go down a step, and the door's rather low. At least, it's all right for you, but when first we came here Michael brained himself a dozen times a day."

"I know . . ." said Mrs. Paget dreamily, following her into the small passage hall, where a bowl of roses stood on an oak chest.

Ruth threw open the door into the sitting-room.

"Another step down," she warned her.

Sunshine poured into the little room, with its cream distempered walls and the gay jute rugs. The gate-legged table on which tea was laid was of unstained wood, as were the chairs, bookshelves, and writing desk, which was piled with green-backed exercise-books. There were bowls of flowers everywhere, and the only picture on the walls was a reproduction of Marc's "Blue Horses."

Mrs. Paget looked round the room approvingly.

"It's nice," she said. "It isn't fussy."

"It's old-fashioned now," said Michael, going to adjust the curtains so that the sun shouldn't shine on her. "Fuss is coming back. Frills and ornaments and what-nots."

"I had a what-not for one of my wedding presents," said Mrs. Paget. "It was inlaid with something and had little knobs all the way down."

Ruth, who had slipped out of the room, returned with tea-pot and hot-water jug.

"Of course, we know your daughter and the children quite well," she said. "Roger's in Michael's form. Have you got that school group, Michael? He looks rather a pet in it."

Michael went to a drawer of the desk and took out a photograph.

"Here you are," he said. "Though I have a suspicion that you're not really the proud grandmother type."

"Well, no," admitted Mrs. Paget. "Perhaps I'm not. But I'm quite proud of them as long as I don't see too much of them." She studied the group. "Oh yes, there he is. Doesn't he look like Charles! It's odd how family likenesses that you can't see at all in real life peep out in photographs."

Michael studied the group.

"Not knowing who Charles is——," he said.

"His father. My son-in-law."

"I don't think we've ever seen him," said Ruth. "I had a vague idea he was abroad."

"Oh no. But his work keeps him near London. He's coming down to-day as a matter of fact to spend his holiday here." She glanced at her watch. "He'll have arrived now, I suppose. He'll be coming round to the hotel after tea to pay his duty visit. I like Charles, but I can never think of anything to say to him." She studied the group again. "Which is the headmaster? ... Oh yes, he looks the modern type."

"He is," said Michael.

"Hearty," said Ruth.

"Well-meaning," said Michael.

"Limited," added Ruth.

"Who's the dressy woman with the little mouth?"

"Mrs. Orton . . . his wife."

Mrs. Paget studied her with interest.

"She looks what, for want of a better word, one generally calls common. I don't mean just uneducated, though she may be that, too. Am I wronging her?"

Ruth laughed.

"We don't have to be loyal, do we, Michael?"

"Not within these four walls."

"Well, then, you're not wronging her."

Mrs. Paget nodded as if satisfied.

"I do love *people*, don't you? Just for being people. Let me guess a little more about her. When you're as old as I am you've learnt to take away a character on the turn of an eyelash. It's a great game. I had an aunt whose rule was never to say anything unless it was kind and true and necessary, and she died of acute melancholia before she was forty. I attribute my longevity solely to my love of malicious gossip. . . . Let's go on with it." She held the photograph again. "The eyes are shifty and the mouth is obstinate."

"You're terribly terrifyingly right. Michael, I must change my chair and sit with my back to the light. I couldn't bear Mrs. Paget to reveal me to myself."

"It's all right," smiled Mrs. Paget. "My moment is over. Besides it's too late. I've got you docketed for ever. But seriously—I don't know much about boys' schools from inside. Martin went to one, of course, but I was only a parent. Can a woman like that do much harm in one, or does the monastic atmosphere defeat her?"

"She can do enough," said Michael. "For one thing, her hearty husband is as wax in her hands."

"I knew she hadn't that mouth for nothing, of course," nodded Mrs. Paget.

"And anyone she doesn't like gets the sack sooner or later," put in Ruth. "Do have one of those little cakes. You needn't be nervous. They have a home-made look, but it's deceptive. They're quite wholesomely mass-produced in Penzance."

"Thanks," said Mrs. Paget. "I could never make cakes, either. I always began to think about something else, and that's fatal. . . . How does your husband manage to keep his post? Or does she like him?"

"She *loathes* him, doesn't she, Michael? But, you see, Michael has lived here all his life, and has what you might call a local pull. Also, he's a Cambridge blue, and that goes down awfully well with parents. Anyway, he wouldn't care two hoots if she did get him the sack. He could find another job easily enough, couldn't you, pet?"

Michael had lit his pipe and was leaning back in his chair, smiling at them.

"I suppose I could," he said, "though I'm fond of this place. I was raised here, you know."

Mrs. Paget looked at him, then looked quickly away. She had been rattling on about whatever came into her mind in an attempt to make the occasion seem natural and ordinary, but it wasn't any use. The very sight of him brought this strange fluttering pain to her side, and his voice swept her back into the past so bewilderingly that she had to keep her eyes on her hands—gnarled and yellow against the grey silk of her skirt—to assure herself that she was an old woman, not a young girl in a pink alpaca dress. . . .

She made another effort, taking up the school group again from the table.

"Who's the other woman—the one at the end of the back row?"

"That's Mrs. Heath. Her husband used to be headmaster. But I suppose you know all about them."

"Yes, I'm shockingly well up in the local news."

"She was a marvellous H.M.'s wife, wasn't she, Michael?"

He nodded.

"And Ma Orton hates her even more than she hates Michael. She's a perpetual reminder of what she—Ma Orton—ought to be and isn't. She's always trying to make her husband get rid of her, but he's just enough sense not to. She's a wonderful teacher and has the heaven-sent gift of managing parents, which Ma Orton conspicuously lacks. . . . Why *are* we telling you all the gossip?"

"Because you know I love it," said Mrs. Paget simply.

They had finished tea now, and Michael carried the things out into the kitchen.

"We haven't a maid," explained Ruth. "There aren't such things here. There are only 'women' who go to two and three houses a week. It makes it so much more interesting to know what your neighbours have for dinner and whether their tomatoes are really doing as well as they make out."

Michael came back, closing the door behind him.

"Mrs. Forrester was just saying——" began Mrs. Paget, but he interrupted her.

"Why Mrs. Forrester?" he said. "You called me 'Michael' the minute you set eyes on me. You can surely call her 'Ruth' after" (he glanced at the clock) "nearly an hour."

"Yes, do," said Ruth.

Mrs. Paget looked at him and the laughter died out of her eyes. She had known since she came to this house that she was nearing the heart of the mystery, that she was soon going to know what Michael wanted her to know. All the time she had been here, while she chattered and gossiped, that feeling of unreality had grown stronger and stronger. She could hardly believe that ordinary life was going on outside this charmed room, that she would go out to find Martin, Florence, Violet at the hotel, Pen and Charles at Sea Meads. She couldn't help feeling that life itself was suspended as she sat in the little room with Michael. Even Ruth was unreal, dream-like. Only she and Michael were real.

Her heart began to beat quickly as she said, "Did you say you'd lived here all your life?"

"Do tell her the story of your life, Michael," said Ruth. She had curled up in her chair and lit a cigarette.

"She'd never believe it," objected Michael.

"I know she wouldn't. But she'd love it."

"Do tell me," said Mrs. Paget, a little breathlessly.

Suddenly she was so strongly conscious of Michael, the real Michael, that she almost felt his hand close over hers on the arm of the chair.

"Do tell me," she said again.

Michael filled his pipe again and lit it in silence.

"I hardly know where to begin."

"Begin where you were born of poor but honest parents," said Mrs. Paget, with a lightness that rang untrue even to herself.

"But I wasn't, you see. That's the point. My mother was companion to an old lady, and my father was the old lady's nephew."

He stopped and Mrs. Paget said "Go on, please," so unsteadily that he glanced at her in quick surprise.

"Well . . . my mother had been married when she was nineteen to a blackguard who had spent what little money she had and then deserted her. She was passionately in love with my father, but I don't think he ever was with her. The affair went on for some time, and then the inevitable happened. He fell in love with a girl he met and got engaged to her. Just about that time my mother found that she was going to have a baby. She loved him so much that she decided to go through with it without telling him. She'd saved some money and she managed it quite well at first—gave up her post, went to hospital to have the child, then came out and set to work to keep him. But she couldn't get a job. She ran through her savings and was desperate. Then, by chance, she met a woman who was cook at her old employer's and who told her that my father had just got married and was spending his honeymoon at a little place in Cornwall called Merlin Bay. She decided to go down there, meet him secretly, and ask him for money. She was sure that if he knew about the child he'd help her. She left the child with her landlady and spent her last penny on the fare. She didn't want his wife to guess anything, so she didn't go to the cottage where he was staying, but hung about on the beach waiting for the chance of seeing him alone."

"I *said* she'd never believe it," put in Ruth. "She'll only think you've been reading Victorian melodramas. There's always the bride and the old mistress—the bride in pale blue, the old mistress in red."

"Go on, please," said Mrs. Paget again.

"Well, she was sitting on a rock at the foot of the cliffs," continued

Michael, "when he came along. He looked happy and carefree and was smiling to himself. I suppose he was thinking of his wife. He didn't see her till he was right onto her, then his face froze into a look of such horror and revulsion that she couldn't say anything. She even forgot what she'd come for. . . . They stared at each other without speaking for a few moments, then she turned and ran away. She never saw him again. . . . She hung about the beach, stupefied by misery, till suddenly a kind of recklessness came over her, and she decided to go to the cottage and brazen it out for the child's sake. She went to the cottage, but they'd gone. In little over an hour from her seeing him they'd cleared out, bag and baggage. She was desperate. She said that if she'd had the child with her she'd have thrown herself over the cliff with him. She hadn't any money to get back to London. . . . Then, as she was wandering about the bay, the Vicar of Anshall—the next village, you know—who was coming for a walk along the beach, found her and took her home to his wife. His wife was lame, and they were beginning to need a companion-help in the house. Also they were childless and had always longed for a child. So they sent for me from London and we were installed in the Vicarage. To cut a long story short, my mother died when I was five, and they adopted me and brought me up as their own son. They're both dead, too, now, God bless them." His face had grown serious. "They were the best parents a boy ever had."

"And did you never——" began Mrs. Paget.

"No, he never found out who his father was," said Ruth. "Isn't he unenterprising?"

Michael smiled.

"My mother would never tell anyone his name. I suppose that my adoptive father might have found out by enquiries in Merlin Bay, but he didn't want to know. His one dread was that someone might appear to contest his claim on me. When I was in my teens, I suddenly decided to investigate the matter on my own—I'd read a story in which the illegitimate boy's father turned out to be a duke—but I had no luck. Even in those days there were a lot of summer visitors to Merlin Bay, and no one remembered them.

Several of the women who used to let rooms had died meantime. I found out that a couple who might have been they had stayed at the cottage that's been turned into a shop now, but no one remembered their name. I gave it up finally. After all, it really doesn't matter."

"So, you see," said Ruth, "he's that backbone of old-time melodrama—the man whose mother hadn't got her 'lines' and who doesn't know who his father was."

Mrs. Paget was silent for a moment because she couldn't be quite sure of her voice. When she spoke, however, it was firm and steady.

"I can tell you who his father was," she said. "He was my husband."

Chapter Twelve

"I WANT your head like this . . ." said Arnold Kemsing.

He put one hand on her shoulder and with the other tilted her chin slightly.

His touch sent little waves of happiness through her, making her body seem so insubstantial that it was hardly there at all.

"But I *was* like that, wasn't I?" she said, laughing tremulously.

His touch lingered on her shoulder, its very lightness a caress. His face was close to hers, and it was by an almost superhuman effort that he resisted the temptation to kiss her.

"You're such a confounded little fidget," he said, returning to her easel. "You can't stay still for two seconds."

His voice was, like his touch, lightly caressing. (I wonder if I could ever be happier than I am now, she thought, even if . . . even when . . .)

Her eyes met the eyes of the woman in the photograph. He'd never mentioned her since that first meeting. That alone showed he didn't love her. And, if any other proof were needed, there was the fact that they were so obviously living apart—he was here and she in Scotland—and there was no talk of his joining her. She'll be glad to be rid of him . . . and I'll make him happy . . . I *will* make him happy. . . . Again panic seized her lest he should think of her as a child, not as the cultured woman of the world she wished to appear to him. She had tried so often to discuss his work with him, but somehow she had never succeeded. She made another effort.

"I did so love that description of the dawn in *Starlight*" she said. "It reminded me of Wordsworth."

"What particular part of Wordsworth?" he asked.

"Oh . . . just Wordsworth," she said vaguely.

He smiled wryly behind his easel. How adorable she was when she was just being herself, how impossible when she tried to be someone else!

"You're letting your chin drop again," he reminded her.

She tilted it obediently.

"And I love that part where Mavis goes to Peter when she hears that he's ill. His wife was a *beast*."

He put down his brush.

"That's enough for to-day," he said cheerfully. "You've been very good, on the whole. Now let's have tea."

Immediately she was a child again, running about with plates and cups and putting on the kettle, while he took off his smock and washed his hands at the kitchen sink. She loved getting tea for the two of them like this after the sitting. He watched her with narrowed eyes, wondering how long he'd be able to resist the temptation to make love to her. She had a mouth like Botticelli's Venus and he'd always wanted to kiss Botticelli's Venus.

"Now," she said happily, "come along. It's all ready."

"I saw you on the cliff the other day," he said, putting two lumps of sugar into his cup and stirring it slowly, "but you didn't see me. You were with a nice-looking young man, so I didn't like to intrude my middle-aged presence."

"Middle-aged!" she said indignantly. "What a dreadful word! It means dull and fat and stuffy and stodgy and—everything you aren't."

"Nonsense! It means just middle-aged, which I am. . . . Anyway, who was the nice-looking youth?"

She crinkled up her nose contemptuously.

"Oh, *him!*" she said. "It was Tim Bevan. He isn't anybody. I mean, he's just a boy. . . ."

"Is he younger than you?"

She blushed. She didn't know whether he was teasing her or not. She felt annoyed that he had seen her with Tim . . . just as if she were an ordinary girl who was satisfied with the friendship of an ordinary boy. Ever since she'd known him she'd been trying to make him understand how different she was from ordinary girls, and she still didn't seem to have succeeded.

"Actually," she said, with dignity, "he's a little older. In actual years, I mean. But I've always been much older than my age. I've always been interested in serious things."

She felt rather guilty as she said this, because she'd only been interested in serious things since she began to read his books.

"What serious things?" he said.

She still couldn't tell whether he was laughing at her or not. She hoped he wasn't. . . .

"Oh—just serious things," she said. "I mean, when Moina in *Devil's Guerdon* quoted that verse from Shelley's 'To Night' I looked it up and learnt it all by heart. . . . I couldn't say it now," she added quickly, "but I could then. I said it every night when I went to bed for almost a week. Your books have made an enormous difference in my life."

"Splendid!" he said, rising and throwing away his cigarette. "Now what about washing up? Or shall we leave it for Mrs. Muggins?"

She giggled.

"She's not called Mrs. Muggins."

"Isn't she? It suits her far better than whatever she is called, then. Shall we leave it to her?"

"Of course not. Anyway, she's called Mrs. Pearson. It won't take us long."

"Very well. I'll dry. I've brought the art of drying to a fine perfection, but I'm still a bad washer."

She looked forward all day to this half-hour of domestic intimacy with him after the sitting. It seemed to set the seal of certainty upon her dreams. They would come here every year after they were married. They would often talk of this summer. He would say, "Do you remember that first summer here when I painted your portrait? Did you *know*—even then?" And she would admit that she had known even then, known that they belonged to each other inseparably for ever. Of course, the divorce would be rather a nuisance. Mummy and Daddy would probably make a dreadful fuss about it. She must just be firm. After all, love couldn't be worth much if you hadn't to suffer for it. Someone in one of his books said something like that—she couldn't quite remember whether it was Mavis in *Starlight* or Moina in *Devil's Guerdon*.

She poured away the washing-up water, washed her hands under the tap, and dried them on the roller towel behind the door, carefully avoiding the dark patch where Mrs. Pearson had evidently dried hers that morning. Then she turned to him and said, "Well . . ." rather uncertainly.

She always hoped that he would suggest her staying a little longer, so that he could read a manuscript to her or discuss a plot, but he hadn't done so far.

"You've been a brick," he said. "Same time to-morrow? Or are you getting bored?"

"Oh *no*!" she gasped, horrified at the mere thought. "Of *course* not!"

He put his hands lightly on her shoulders, and again happiness flamed through her from his touch.

(I'm little short of heroic, he told himself complacently. It's the wistful droop at the corners that gets me. . . . I could stand the rest.)

"Well . . . good-bye," he said, removing his hands. "Take care of yourself."

She went back slowly over the cliffs to Sea Meads. He *was* in love with her. She'd felt it as he stood there with his hands on her shoulders. He'd been fighting for self-control . . . *fighting* for it . . . like Peter in *Starlight*, when he and Mavis met by accident in the wood. He was too chivalrous to tell her that he loved her. He would tell his wife, probably, when next they met and ask her if she would divorce him. He could easily divorce her, of course, because she had innumerable lovers, but he was too chivalrous to do that. She'd laugh at him and sneer at him, but she might be willing to divorce him, because she'd never really loved him—not even when she married him. Oh dear, she did hope that Mummy and Daddy wouldn't be *too* stuffy about it. If they were, she'd just have to wait till she was twenty-one. It would be an eternity, but then her love for him was deathless. Deathless. It was the word he had used himself about Mavis's love for Peter.

She slowed her pace as she drew near Sea Meads. She felt that her love must shine out of her for everyone to see, and she didn't want anyone to see yet—especially Mummy. The house, however, was empty. She went round to the back garden. Pen was sitting on a deck-chair stitching buttons onto a Liberty bodice of Rosemary's. The three children were on the sands with Charles.

After tea he'd said, "I'm going for a walk along the sands. You coming, Roger?"

And not only had Roger sprung up eagerly, but Rosemary and Valerie had flung themselves on him, crying, "Me, too, Daddy."

Just as they were setting off Charles had turned to her and said, "You coming, Pen?" but she'd answered brightly, "No, thanks. I've got masses of things to do."

Left alone, she felt disproportionately hurt and lonely and resentful. Charles really might have stayed to help her with the "masses of things," she thought, forgetting that, ever since he'd come there, she had firmly refused to allow him to help at all. They'd gone off so quickly that she hadn't had time to collect her forces, or, of course, she wouldn't have let him take Valerie. He'd only get the child over-tired and over-excited just before bedtime. And Rosemary . . . Rosemary wasn't strong enough for those "walks" of Charles. A man never noticed when a child's energy was flagging, when ordinary high spirits gave way to the nerviness of exhaustion. And Roger—surely there was something Roger ought to be doing. Though he hadn't officially started home-work, he often brought home some piece of work to finish or do over again. It didn't help matters to remember that yesterday, when Charles had gone into Penzance to do some shopping for her and she had suggested a walk to the children, they hadn't wanted to leave their games in the garden. To-day even Dandy had deserted her, scampering after them down the cliff path.

A wave of mingled irritation and self-pity engulfed her. Charles's visit was unsettling the children, as she'd known it would. She was trying to forget what he had said to her on the evening of his arrival. In any case it wasn't to be taken seriously. He'd probably forgotten it himself by now. He hadn't mentioned it again. He had been tired by the long journey, and it was just an outbreak of nerves. Men were only children, after all. Their fretfulness took the form of portentous domestic ultimatums, but they were no more to be taken seriously than children.

She looked up as Stella appeared. She'd tried to forget, too, what Charles had said about Stella's sitting to Arnold Kemsing. It had been absurd and even offensive, just as if she, Stella's mother, didn't know everything that went on in the child's mind, but it nevertheless remained at the back of her thoughts—a tiny pinprick of uneasiness. There was a sort of—glow about the child that hadn't been there a month ago. Suppose the man were trying to make love to her. Oh, but Stella would have told her. At once. At the first sign.

"Where is everyone?" said Stella, sinking onto the grass at her feet.

Pen smiled at her.

"Daddy's been a perfect angel and taken off the children to give me an hour's peace," she said.

Put like that, it sounded better. It even made her feel a little better. . . .

Stella pulled up a stalk of grass and began to nibble it.

"Sorry I wasn't here to give a hand," she said perfunctorily.

Pen looked at her.

"How many more sittings are you going to have with Mr. Kemsing, darling?" she asked carelessly.

A guarded look came into Stella's eyes, and her heart began to beat quickly.

"Oh, I don't know," she said. Her tone was as careless as Pen's. "He's not nearly finished yet."

"Darling," said Pen, coming to a sudden decision, "Daddy and I have been talking it over and we don't want you to go on with them. Surely he can finish it from memory now. . . . You see," she continued a little lamely, "it's such lovely weather that we think it would do you far more good to be in the fresh air—" She felt suddenly out of her depth. She didn't know the grown-up Stella.

(Oh, but there wasn't one, of course!) She only knew the child. She went on in her bright, brisk, reasoning-with-children voice, "It was very nice of him to want to paint you, but——"

Panic and a hot heady anger seized Stella. How *dared* they interfere? How *dared* they try to stop her? She'd *die* if she didn't go on seeing him. . . . Furious protests rose to her lips ("I won't. I won't. You *shan't* stop me. I'll go whatever you say. I don't belong to you. I belong to myself—to him"), but she choked them down. Mother was so quick to understand and find out, and once she knew she'd certainly stop her going. Artifice, almost as instinctive as her first anger, sprang to her aid. She stared at Pen with wide innocent eyes, a little smile of bewilderment on her lips.

"But, Mummy," she said, "why? I mean, it's such fun being painted by a real artist."

Pen looked at her and anger seized her in her turn—a sudden fierce anger against Charles. She felt that he had somehow soiled and degraded the child by even hinting that it was possible for the man to make love to her. As if Stella would have stayed there one *second* had that happened. She hadn't even a suspicion of that side of life. For all her eighteen years she was as much a child as Rosemary where that sort of thing was concerned. She'd never listen to Charles again or let him interfere in her treatment of the children. . . .

"Very well, dear," she said. "As long as" (No, she mustn't put ideas into the child's head) "as long as you don't get too tired or anything." Despite herself, a faint anxiety lingered. "Stella, darling, you do tell me everything, *everything*, don't you?"

Stella's gaze grew more candid and ingenuous than ever, though her heart was galloping.

"Of course, Mummy," she said.

"*That's* all right, then, darling," said Pen, dismissing the matter with a sigh of relief and a fresh hardening of her heart against Charles.

She took up a cricket shirt of Roger's with a hole under the arm.

"I think I can patch this so that it won't show. He's getting so fussy about patches nowadays."

Stella sat with her eyes on the ground pulling up bits of grass. She was bitterly ashamed of her victory, but she didn't regret it. She couldn't have *lived* if they'd stopped her going. Suddenly she felt afraid of betraying herself even now. She rose to her feet.

"I think I'll go for a little walk," she said unsteadily.

"Yes, do, darling," said Pen. "You must be feeling cramped sitting all that time. . . . You might catch up Daddy and the children if you run. They haven't been gone long."

But Stella didn't want to see Daddy just yet—not till she felt more sure of herself.

"Where's Miss Hinkley?" she said.

"At Green Gates," said Pen. "It's *too* absurd. Mrs. Bevan asked her to tea again. I suppose she's telling those silly stories to Agnes. It can't be good for her."

"I'll go round there," said Stella, "then I can walk back with her."

The reaction that so often followed her visits to Arnold Kemsing was setting in. She felt nervy and depressed. She wanted the reassurance of Tim's ingenuous admiration.

"Very well, dear," said Pen absently. She was thinking that in future she would be very firm with Charles and make him understand quite clearly that he must not interfere with the children. He was at home so little that he couldn't possibly know anything about them.

Stella went quickly along the cliff path. From below she heard Roger's voice, then Daddy's, then Valerie's. . . . Looking down at the beach, she saw Charles, his feet bare, his trousers rolled up above his knees, walking along in the surf with Valerie on his back. His pipe was in his mouth, and Valerie hung onto his neck, shouting, "Gee-up . . . gee-up." He started, reared, bucked, and ran forward, making little splashes in the surf. Valerie's laugh pealed out. Roger ran behind, imitating Charles and shouting, "I'm a pony . . . I'm a pony. . . ."

Rosemary was hunting in the sand for the tiny horn-shaped shells that could be found there. Beryl had gone away on a visit to her godmother (it was term time, of course, but the godmother was wealthy, and Beryl's mother thought the change would do her good), and the evening before she went, when they were playing together on the beach, she had picked up one of the shells from a handful of sand and said "Isn't it sweet?" and then the lovely idea had come to Rosemary of collecting as many as she could for a surprise for her while she was away. She had borrowed from Pen a box that had had toilet soap in and she wanted to fill it, if she could.

"I've got twenty now, Daddy," she called excitedly. "I found quite a lot all together. They were having a sort of meeting."

"Gee-up, gee-up, gee-up!" shouted Valerie.

Stella walked on slowly to Green Gates. There she found Mrs. Bevan and Miss Hinkley sitting on deck-chairs in the little garden, with Agnes, quiet and happy for the time being, at their feet, engaged in threading brightly coloured beads onto a string. Miss Hinkley sat very upright, as usual, still wearing her black cotton gloves. She had taken them off for tea but had put them on again immediately afterwards. They were talking about Agnes, agreeing that she was only very slightly backward and that she was improving a little every day.

Mrs. Bevan had never found anyone before to take this interest in Agnes. People generally became embarrassed when she mentioned her, as if there were something indecent about her, something not fit to be discussed in polite society. Even Tim went stiff and resentful when she tried to discuss Agnes with him, to point out how sweet and affectionate and well-meaning she was and how she was improving a little every day. She felt passionately, extravagantly grateful to Miss Hinkley for seeing what ought to be obvious to everyone.

"It makes me so angry," she was saying, "when people say she should be put into an institution. Even if I could bear to part with her, she'd be so unhappy and frightened. They seem to think that just because she's a little—different, she can't suffer like other people. She can suffer a good deal more. She's very highly strung."

"Of course," said Miss Hinkley, nodding her battered black straw hat in fervent agreement, "and really she's much less trouble to look after than a lot of children they call normal."

"So affectionate," said Mrs. Bevan, pleading for more.

"So sweet-natured," said Miss Hinkley. "So forgiving," put in Mrs. Bevan. "It doesn't matter how Tim snubs and ignores her, she never bears malice against him. And so generous. She's always trying to give things away."

"So kind," said Miss Hinkley. "She can't bear to see or hear of suffering. And when I think of other children I've known, and the way they've tortured insects. . . ."

"She's excitable, of course, but then lots of children are that."

"Of course," agreed Miss Hinkley, nodding the black straw hat till the rusty trimming fairly rattled.

She was enjoying this holiday more than she ever remembered enjoying a holiday before. To be wanted, to be needed, to be loved—for there was no doubt that Agnes loved her. She cried when she went away. She demanded her loudly and imperiously at all sorts of unreasonable hours. And Miss Hinkley loved Agnes in return with a love that she had seldom given to anyone in all her life before. She loved her so much that she honestly thought that she was improving a little every day.

To sit like this in the garden with Mrs. Bevan, watching her, loving her, talking to Mrs. Bevan about her, gave her the purest thrill of happiness she had known for years. It melted away the hard shell of loneliness, which had enclosed her heart so long that she now hardly realised it was there.

Stella appeared at the garden gate and stood motionless, her eyes fixed on the scene in aloof distaste. How dreadful Agnes looked, sitting there, flushed and moist, jabbing excitedly at the beads! She half decided to pretend that she was just passing the house on her way somewhere else. She didn't really know why she'd come. It would have been better to go for a walk by herself, carrying her precious dream with her, hearing his voice, seeing his face, watching the half smile that hovered about his mouth ... instead of coming to these horrible ordinary people—Agnes, Miss

Hinkley, even Mrs. Bevan and Tim—who would obtrude themselves between her and her memories.

"Hello, dear," said Mrs. Bevan, looking up. "Come in."

She went in uncertainly and closed the gate behind her. Agnes greeted her with an excited shout.

"Watch me," she said. "I'm threading beads. I'm threading beads."

She spoke, as usual, so unintelligibly that Stella did not catch the words.

"What does she say?" she asked Mrs. Bevan.

"She says she's threading beads," said Mrs. Bevan a little coldly. It was so absurd of people to pretend they couldn't understand what Agnes said. She spoke quite distinctly. . . .

Just then Agnes got into a muddle with her string and turned crimson with anger.

"It won't go in. . . . It won't go in," she bawled and, flinging the string of beads onto the ground, began to howl at the top of her voice.

In a moment Mrs. Bevan and Miss Hinkley were on their knees on either side of her, soothing, coaxing, consoling.

"It's all right, darling . . ."

"This way . . ."

"See, it's gone in all right now."

"You're so clever, darling. Try again. . . . See, it's quite easy . . ."

"Watch Mummy . . ."

Stella stood looking at them dispassionately, thinking how awful they were. . . .

Agnes's howls died away, but she had wearied of the beads.

"Tell me the story," she gulped to Miss Hinkley.

"I'll tell you another story this time, a lovely story," said Miss Hinkley persuasively, "called 'King of the Golden River.'"

Agnes's face darkened.

"No, I want the merman story," she yelled. "The merman story. . . . The merman story."

"Very well, dear," said Miss Hinkley resignedly. (She really was a little tired of that story.) "Once upon a time . . ."

Agnes settled down to listen, a beaming smile upon her tear-stained face.

Mrs. Bevan looked up at Stella.

"Tim's in his room, dear," she said. "Go and bring him out. He's been working long enough."

She hated to see Stella standing there looking at Agnes as if she were some sort of monstrosity—her darling Agnes, who was listening so intelligently to Miss Hinkley's beautiful story.

Stella went indoors, up the winding wooden staircase, and knocked at the door of Tim's room.

"Come in."

He was sitting at his desk, studying an accountancy manual. He sprang up eagerly as she entered.

"Stella! I say, how topping of you!"

"I came for a walk and to take Miss Hinkley home. Your mother said you'd worked long enough."

"Did I hear Agnes kicking up a shindy?" he said.

Stella perched on the end of his desk and nodded.

"Yes—something about her beads—she's all right now. Miss Hinkley's telling her that dreadful tale again."

She looked curiously round the room. She'd never been in it before. It was plainly furnished—desk, bookshelves, upright wooden chair, narrow camp-bed, the walls bare except for a reproduction of Van Gogh's "Drawbridge at Aries" over the mantelpiece. There was about it a suggestion of a retreat. It was his fortress, inviolable, impregnable, into which he could retire, shutting out the demands of his world—Agnes's loud insistence, his mother's unspoken reproaches. It struck her suddenly and surprisingly how little, after all, she knew him. They had seldom discussed anything but superficialities—their own doings and the doings of their families and neighbours. She took up a small paper-backed book that lay on his desk and looked at it curiously. *"The World's Masters: Picasso,"* she read the title. "He was an artist, wasn't he?" She opened it idly. "What on earth's this?"

"The title's underneath," he said. " 'Harlequins.' "

He was shy of speaking of the things that interested him deeply.

He had always longed for his mother to share his interests, and she would have done so, he knew, had not Agnes been there, for they had the same tastes and their minds worked on the same lines, but invariably when they were drawing near to each other Agnes's loud demands would interpose themselves and draw her away from him again. In his secret bitterness of heart he had kept empty the place that should have been hers. If she wouldn't fill it, no one should. But now that Stella was there, looking with childish ingenuous eyes at his treasures, he felt a sudden longing for her sympathy.

"It isn't like anything at all," she was saying.

Shyly, stumblingly, he began to try to explain.

"It isn't meant to be," he said, "not in that way. It isn't—just a copy of something. It's—well, it's rather what the artist felt when he'd seen it. In the preface it calls it 'form in the abstract.' " He stopped and added rather lamely, "People don't really understand it even yet."

She thought of the portrait that Arnold Kemsing was painting and felt suddenly indignant, as if Tim had deliberately belittled it.

"If it's a painting *of* something it ought to be like it," she said.

"That's an old-fashioned idea," he retorted.

She was suddenly furious with him.

"Well, anyway—"she began hotly, when a shrill cry from Agnes in the garden interrupted her, and Tim went to the window and stood in the shadow of a curtain.

"Must you *watch* them?" she said irritably.

She had thought of Tim as her slave, her property, and the discovery that he held the key to worlds that were closed to her was oddly disturbing.

"Yes, I must," he said shortly. "If she gets in a temper I shall have to go down or she'll start knocking Mother about. She's bruised all down one side already. . . . I'm the only one who can hold her. Not that I get much thanks for it," he added bitterly.

Stella stood at his desk, idly turning over his books. Depression had descended on her again. Her amulet had ceased to work. She thought of Arnold Kemsing, and the familiar thrill of happiness failed to visit her. He seemed far away and unreal, like someone she had heard of but had never met.

She took another book from the bookshelf and, opening it at random, read aloud:

> "Foster the light, nor veil the man-shaped moon,
> Nor weather winds that blow not down the bone,
> But strip the twelve-winded marrow from his circle."

The vague dejection that oppressed her seemed to focus itself on the words.

"It's *stupid,*" she cried impatiently. "It doesn't mean anything at all."

He turned from the window and took the book from her hand. His mother and Miss Hinkley had soothed Agnes. She was sitting on the grass quite happily again between them.

"It's not stupid," he said shortly, putting the book back among the others.

His tone and action seemed to shut her out, as if he had weighed her in the balance and found her wanting. She was angry and unhappy and afraid. . . . She could hardly remember what he looked like, though it was less than an hour since she had seen him last. Unreasonably, she felt as if Tim were responsible.

"I suppose you mean it's I who am stupid?" she flamed, then, anxious to justify herself, added, "After all, the object of words is to *mean* something, isn't it? Those don't mean anything at all."

"The object of words is to make you *think*" said Tim, "to stimulate your mind, if you've got one." His eyes were coldly hostile. He was, for no reason at all, suddenly as angry as Stella. "I suppose the sort of poetry *you* prefer is the sort that sends you to sleep. Like—

> "Birds in the high Hall-garden
> When twilight is falling,
> Maud, Maud, Maud, Maud,
> They were crying and calling."

"I've never even heard of it," she said with dignity, "and, anyway," defiantly, "I *do* think it's beautiful. And you needn't sneer at me as if I'd never read anything. I *have*. I've read *all* Arnold Kemsing's books."

He sneered in earnest now.

"That tripe!" he said.

Her cheeks flamed and for a moment she was too angry to speak. Then, just as she was gathering her forces to reply, Agnes interrupted them again, pounding up the stairs so heavily that the little house seemed to shake from top to bottom. She burst tumultuously into the room.

"When's the new moon, Tim?" she panted. "When's the new moon?"

Tim turned tight-lipped to the calendar.

"The 27th," he said, and added quite gently, "You mustn't come into this room, Agnes. I've told you so before. I'm always busy when I'm in here."

"But I wanted to know. . . . Show it me on mine, Tim, in my room. Show it me. . . ."

Mrs. Bevan appeared on the landing. Her face was white with exhaustion.

"I'm sorry, Tim," she said wearily. "I tried to stop her coming. She wouldn't believe anyone but you about the new moon."

"Come, Tim," said Agnes urgently.

He followed her into her room, his face set and rigid. He hated going into her room. It was so full of her hot turgid vitality that it affected him with physical nausea.

"Show it me," she shouted.

He took a pencil from his pocket and carefully pointed to the 27th on the calendar.

"There it is."

"I'll go now . . ." murmured Stella, slipping downstairs.

She had quarrelled with Tim, and she was utterly miserable and wanted to cry. Tim didn't mean anything to her, but somehow it was hateful to have quarrelled with him. . . . About nothing, too. Nothing at all.

"Can I be in your room, please, Tim?" Agnes was saying, her large dull eyes fixed on him appealingly, her full lips moist and shining. "I want to be in your room with you."

"No," said Tim firmly. "I'm busy."

"It's her bedtime in about ten minutes, Tim," pleaded his mother. "She won't be a nuisance."

"I'll come down with her, if you like," said Tim, "but I don't want her in here."

Even now, though she had only been in the room for a few minutes, he would feel her presence there for the rest of the evening—stifling, nauseating.

"Very well, dear," sighed Mrs. Bevan. "Come along, Agnes. Don't bother to come down, Tim."

Tim shut the door, sat down at his desk, and opened his accountancy manual again.

At the garden gate Agnes was saying goodbye to Stella and Miss Hinkley, shouting louder and louder as the distance between them lengthened.

He dropped his head onto his hands with a shudder. . . .

Chapter Thirteen

"No news, I suppose?" said Martin.

Jessica shook her head.

"None. . . . I shan't have any till he comes back. I never do."

She looked worn and anxious—her cheeks pale, dark circles under her eyes. He had seen in the sitting-room of Cliff Cottage a photograph of her and Brian taken just after their marriage, and it was almost inconceivable that the few years should have wrought such a change. He hated the man who was responsible for it and who had himself remained as gay and careless and youthful-looking as ever.

To Martin she was lovelier now than she could ever have been in those days. He loved the honesty of her tired grey eyes, the sudden rare sweetness of the little lop-sided smile, the suggestion of indomitable courage that belied the slightness and frailty of her physique. They were walking through Beesley Woods, snatching a few precious moments together. It was Sports Day at Cliff End School, and Jessica would have to be on duty there within an hour or so.

He noticed the frequent glances she gave her watch and said impatiently, "Can't you cut the thing?"

She shook her head.

"I daren't. It would give Mrs. Orton a handle against me, and she'd be only too glad to use it."

"Let's sit down," said Martin, pulling some brambles aside from a fallen log. She sat by him, elbows on knees, chin in hands, and gazed unseeingly into the distance. There was a long silence, then he said, "Do you worry about him—terribly?"

She turned to him with a faint smile and put her hands down onto the log on either side of her.

"I can't help it. I keep wondering where he is and what he's doing. It gets worse each time. Anything might happen to him. . . ."

"What will happen, I suppose," said Martin grimly, "is that he'll come home a wreck and you'll have to nurse him back to decency."

"Oh, that!" she said, as if that were the least of her fears. "I've so often done that."

He caught her hand.

"Jessica, why do you stand it? It isn't as if you loved him. . . ."

"But I do, Martin," she said. "Oh, not as I love you—I've never loved him like that—but I love him as I'd have loved my child if it had lived. He *is* a child. That's why he was such a success as a schoolmaster. He understood the boys. He entered into all their interests. They adored him and he loved the life. He misses it terribly. Even now he keeps talking about starting again and getting another post, though he must know in his heart it's impossible."

"It's so damnable for you."

"Lots of women have worse to put up with. . . . I want you to understand about him, Martin. He's kind and generous, like a child, and irresponsible like a child. Even—this doesn't really worry him. Each time he says he's learnt his lesson and it will never happen again, and each time he absolutely believes it. He doesn't even feel his position at the school. He'll go there to watch the matches quite happily."

"It's intolerable. . . . He can't love you."

"He needs me, Martin."

"Not as I do."

"More than you do. If it weren't for me he'd go all to pieces. He depends on me so utterly. . . . Oh, Martin, let's not think about him."

"How can we help it?"

She looked at him. It was difficult to believe that she had known him for so short a time. Her love for him seemed now so essential a part of her that she couldn't understand how she had ever lived without it. It sprang from the roots of her being and was the background to everything she thought and said and did. Despite the anxiety that tormented her, her spirit drew a deep enduring peace from his. It had happened so suddenly. Certainly it hadn't happened that first evening when he came with Roger's exercise-book. She had been too frightened and uneasy about Brian to have room for anything else in her heart. Then a few days later—the day she had got up in the morning and found Brian's note, "Going away for a week or so. Don't worry"—he had met her in the village and walked home with her, and she had thought how kind he was and had felt less unhappy and afraid after he left her. And the day after that he had come to ask her if she would like him to go to London to look for Brian (he seemed quite confident of being able to find him), but she had told him how useless it would be.

"Even if you found him—and I don't think you could—you wouldn't be able to do anything with him."

"Come out for a walk," he had said at last. "It'll do you good."

They had walked through the woods to a little village beyond Beesley, where, guessing that suspense and anxiety had taken away her appetite, so that she had not eaten a proper meal since Brian went, he had gone into a farmhouse and ordered a "high tea" of eggs and bacon.

Sitting in the farm kitchen, he had talked to her as if he were trying to charm away a child's shyness (his friends would have been amazed to hear him), and gradually the tension at her heart had eased. She had even laughed at his description of the pig-faced monkey whom his coolies had trained to pick coconuts for them. ... To her surprise she found herself making a large meal and enjoying it. And that night, lying awake, she realised, with mingled dismay and exultation, that she loved him, as she had never loved Brian even in those far-off days when she had imagined herself to be in love with him. And somehow it had seemed as if she had always known that it would happen. So inevitable was it that, looking back, she didn't remember when she had admitted her love in words. Something deeper, stronger than words united them.

He put his hand over hers on the fallen log.

"Jessica," he said suddenly, "come away with me. I could get a job in England. Or, if I couldn't, Malaya isn't so bad. White women do live there. . . ."

Her eyes dwelt with brooding tenderness on his face—the sallow furrowed cheeks, the brown eyes, honest, unhappy, devoted.

"Oh, my dear . . ." she said, with a little catch in her voice.

"He wouldn't feel it as much as you think he would," Martin persisted. "I see him probably more clearly than you do. I know his type. Nothing goes deep with him. He'd make a scene. He'd probably cry and threaten to commit suicide, but he'd be perfectly happy again in a month's time."

"Oh, Martin, it's no *use*. I've thought and thought. . . . He can't do without me. I'd feel like a mother who's deserted her child. I'd never have a moment's peace of mind, wondering where he was and what he was doing. . . . I don't love him, but he—belongs to me. He's part of me. . . ."

"If it's money . . ." he said slowly. "If I got a good job in England you might give him an allowance—just to keep him."

She looked at him pityingly.

"Martin, do you think you *could* get a job after all these years out of England?"

"I don't know," he said uncertainly, and then, "Hasn't he any money but what he earns? Didn't he get something for the school when he sold it?"

She shook her head.

"He didn't sell it. It's run by a board of governors. They don't interfere much. They didn't sack Brian till things had got pretty bad. . . ." Her eyes grew dreamy. "I remember how pleased we were when he got the job. We were staying in London and we'd gone to the Crystal Palace the day we heard. We'd been reading *Kips* and we wanted to see the Labyrinthodon, who was like Coote, you know."

"I don't think I've read it," he said absently. "I've not read much."

He felt that he was up against the ruthless indefinable power of those years she had spent with her husband before he met her—each day, each hour, each casual memory forging chains that were more binding than love itself. He remembered the man's pleasant weak mouth and wondered why it was that weakness was often so much stronger than strength.

She looked at her watch and rose.

"We must go back now . . ." she said.

"Just kiss me once here," he pleaded, and she turned to him readily with lips upraised.

Then they walked on, both a little shaken, hand in hand.

"Do you know," she said, "when I'm away from you I can feel as worried and unhappy and anxious as possible, but when I'm with you it all clears away, and I can't feel really worried about anything—even Brian. When I read in novels that a person's heart sang I used to think it such a ridiculous expression, but now I don't. I know what it means. My heart sings all the time I'm with you. . . ."

They had reached the end of the wood, and he helped her over the stile into the road. The 'bus had stopped in the distance, and they could see Pen and Rosemary getting onto it. Charles followed, swinging Valerie in front of him to the top step.

"They're going already," said Jessica. "I must hurry."

They walked down the road towards the 'bus-stop.

"Will they make a fuss if you're late?" he said anxiously.

He had met and disliked the Ortons and hated to think of her as their employee.

"I shan't be late. I don't begin to function officially till teatime, but if I'm not there from the beginning it will be a black mark against me. You know the sort of thing. Lack of public spirit. Bad example. Don't you remember?"

He smiled—his slow uncertain smile.

"I suppose I do."

"Anyway, I do want to see it all, or rather I would if you weren't here. . . . Don't think of my teaching as a sort of martyrdom. I do love teaching and I love the boys. It gives my maternal instinct an outlet, I suppose. And—it's good for me to get away from Brian for part of the day. Good for Brian, too. I do enjoy my work, Martin."

He set his lips.

"I want to take you right away from it all," he said stubbornly.

The determined courageous brightness faded from her face, and a look of longing that was almost despair took its place.

"If only we could . . ." she breathed.

The hotel car passed them. Florence and Violet sat alone in it behind the chauffeur. Florence's hat was perched at a wilder angle than usual, and her eyes were red-rimmed as if she had been crying. Violet was pale, her mouth set in a tense angry line. When she saw Martin and Jessica she looked away again quickly, and a dull hot flush crept up from her neck, suffusing her face in patches.

"Isn't your mother coming?" said Jessica.

Martin smiled, though the sight of Violet had given him a sudden qualm of uneasiness, he didn't know why.

"Yes. Forrester's taking her in his side-car. She's struck up a tremendous friendship with the Forresters, you know."

"Isn't she a sport?" said Jessica slowly. "I wonder how we shall look back on this when we're both as old as she is. Will it be a sort of dream—something that you can't believe ever happened—or will it be the reallest thing in our lives?"

"It will be real, all right," he said grimly. "Or rather it will be the beginning of the only real thing in our lives. We shall be looking back on it together, you know."

She sighed and slipped her hand into his. His tightened over it.

"Make no mistake about that," he added.

He spoke firmly, striving to master the feeling of hopelessness that had suddenly assailed him.

Mr. and Mrs. Orton stood just outside the pavilion of the sports-ground, holding a small court of parents. Mr. Orton was a tall, muscular, handsome young man, with hail-fellow-well-met manners and a disarming *naïveté* of outlook. He was immensely popular with the boys, and generally had half a dozen or so hanging onto each arm. He had in him something of the inherent childishness that had made Brian Heath, too, a successful schoolmaster, but he was mentally much more limited. A clever boy could easily "stump" him, and there was a touch of contempt in his older pupils' affection for him, while something faintly propitiatory underlay the heartiness of his manner to them. His wife, who completely dominated him, had been the daughter of a Cambridge tobacconist, and had become engaged to him while he was still at college. She was pretty in a sharp, somewhat shrewish fashion, with small pinched mouth, hard blue eyes, a dazzling complexion, and fair frizzy hair. She had always disliked Jessica. It was galling that parents should defer to her and ask her advice about their children, should treat her, indeed, as if she were, in a way, the headmistress of the school. In fairness, Mrs. Orton had to admit that Jessica did nothing to encourage their attitude, but this only made matters worse, depriving her of what would have been a legitimate grievance. At first she had thought that she had only to bide her time, to wait till the boys who had actually known her as the headmaster's wife had left the school, but in this she had been disappointed. A new generation had sprung up, and their parents, too, consulted Mrs. Heath, relied on her judgment, seemed to place their children particularly under her care. Mrs. Orton was a clever woman. She never openly dominated her husband, but she had her own methods of getting her way. On this point, however, he was unexpectedly firm, refusing even to consider dismissing Mrs. Heath. He was in love with his wife and had never regretted marrying her, but he was not quite so stupid as not to realise that she did little to enhance the prestige of the school. Her uneducated accent, her intermittent and highly unconvincing affectations of gentility, her general lack of culture, would have alienated the parents had not Mrs. Heath been there as well—so obviously a lady and a good sort, so capable and pleasant, so sincerely interested in her charges. "I'll introduce you to Mrs. Heath," he would say to vacillating parents. "She'll probably have charge of your boy if he comes here," and after a talk with Jessica the parents would generally enter their boys for the school. She was useful, too, in soothing unreasonable parents, in adjusting those hundred and one little difficulties that arise from time to time in school life. His wife was capable enough, but she spoke a different language from these people, and he tried as far as possible to keep her in the background.

"We'd never find anyone else to do all she does," he would say, when his wife urged him to dismiss her. "She's a good teacher, and she has a way with parents. She's too useful, my dear, for us to get rid of."

Mrs. Orton always treated Jessica with consideration, even apparent affection, in front of parents, compensating for this amply on other occasions. This afternoon several of the parents had already asked for her, and Mrs. Orton had taken mental note of the fact that she was late, storing it up as a useful weapon when opportunity arose.

As soon as they reached the sports-field, Valerie and Rosemary ran off to find Roger, and Pen and Charles joined the group round the headmaster. Charles felt ill-at-ease and self-conscious. Most fathers present, he imagined, had themselves inspected the school, interviewed the headmaster, and made the necessary arrangements before sending their boys to it. In his case Pen had done it all, and he was just brought to the sports along with the other children. He wished to heaven that Pen were a little less competent. He wondered what the headmaster and staff thought of it. Probably looked on him as either a "henpecked husband" or a philanderer who parks his wife and family in some out-of-the-way corner in order to leave himself a clear field. The former, of course, was nearer the truth, though it wasn't *quite* the truth, he told himself grimly.

Mr. Orton stood listening to a small woman with an enormous bosom and osprey-trimmed hat, who was pouring out a lengthy grievance about her son's cap. It had been lost for four days, and then, the very day she'd bought him a new one, his old one had reappeared on the peg.

"Have a talk to Mrs. Heath about it," he said, adding vaguely, "That sort of thing's her province."

He turned to greet Pen and Charles.

"Good to see you down here, Mr. Marlowe. ... Your boy's

shaping well, very well indeed. Where are the little girls? Oh, I see them. Shooting up, aren't they? Both go to school now, I suppose."

"Val's only five," said Pen, "but she went for the first time this morning."

Pen had been almost in tears when she saw her off, and had with difficulty prevented herself from taking a 'bus to Maple House School halfway through the morning to make sure that she was all right.

"Poor little thing!" she said to Charles. "It'll be the first morning in all her life she's spent away from me. I sent a note to say that if she's really *terribly* home-sick they must let Rosemary bring her home."

She suddenly became very solicitous for Charles's comfort and welfare, cross-examining him about the state of his underwear, and suggesting that he came down to sit on the beach with her, but that wasn't what he wanted—to fill the gap in the day's routine left by Valerie's going to school. He had refused somewhat curtly and had gone for a long walk alone. To Pen the morning had dragged interminably. It was the first time since Stella's birth that she hadn't had a baby to look after. She felt like an automaton wound up but prevented by some obstacle from functioning. It wasn't very kind of Charles, she thought aggrievedly, to have left her alone, for Stella was having a sitting with Mr. Kemsing. Perhaps it would have been better to have put off Val's going to school for another year. If the child found it very tiring, of course, she would do. . . .

And at one o'clock Valerie had returned, glowing with excitement and happiness, full of the adventures of the morning, and demanding to go to school again in the afternoon instead of to Roger's sports. She was irritated when Pen tried to hug her.

"Don't, Mummy. *Don't!* I'm a *big* girl. I go to school."

Pen was relieved that she had been happy at school, and at the same time vaguely hurt and disappointed.

"You must send them both in for the visitors' race," Mr. Orton was saying. "We're having it after tea this year so as to rope in the late-comers."

Jessica came up and shook hands with them.

"I'm not late, am I?" she said to Mr. Orton, and added a little breathlessly, "Brian's so sorry not to be here. He had to go to London on business. . . ."

Mrs. Orton turned from speaking to a tall grim-faced man with a black moustache and bristling eyebrows. She was finding him rather heavy going.

"Oh, there you are, dear," she said affectionately to Jessica. "I want you to meet Mr. Cossack. He's Mrs. Burton's brother-in-law, and he's thinking of sending his little boy next term. Perhaps you can tell him anything he wants to know."

She flashed her hard tight smile onto Pen and added, with the nauseating effusiveness she kept specially for parents, "I *do* hope your mother's coming. *So* charming."

"I saw her with Mrs. Forrester a moment ago," said her husband.

Pen and Charles wandered over to the seats under the trees at the side of the field.

"There's Martin, with Val and Rosemary," said Pen. "Oh, and there's Mother." She waved to Mrs. Paget, who was sitting some distance away in a deck-chair next to Mrs. Forrester. "Do you see Stella or Miss Hinkley?"

Stella and Miss Hinkley had gone to call at Green Gates. Mrs. Bevan had said that they might take Agnes to the sports if she was in a good mood. If she was in a bad one Miss Hinkley would probably stay with her and Stella would come to the sports alone.

Charles glanced round.

"No. There's the Hundred Yards just getting ready."

Pen fixed her eyes anxiously on Roger, who stood, tense and quivering, among the others at the starting-place. He looked so small and earnest. . . . Her heart yearned over him.

"I hope he'll remember what I told him about starting," said Charles.

Mrs. Paget was watching Michael herd the Hundred Yards' competitors into their places.

"Everything about him is *my* Michael," she said. "The way he smiles and laughs, the way he moves, his voice—everything."

Ruth turned her brown eyes from her husband to the old woman beside her.

"It's made Michael very happy," she said.

"It's made me very happy, too," said Mrs. Paget.

"He seems to think that it makes you his mother, somehow."

"I know. I feel like that, too. And, again, sometimes, when I've been with him, he's so like Michael—*my* Michael—that it gives me quite a shock to look in the glass and see that I'm really an old woman."

Ruth laid her hand in a fugitive caressing gesture on the grey-silk knee.

"You must come down here again. Often."

Mrs. Paget shook her head.

"I don't think so, my dear. Michael wanted me to know about this. He wanted me to meet you—both of you. I think that means that the time's very near when I shall join him. I'm an old woman. It may be fancy, but somehow I don't think it is."

"I hope it is," said Ruth.

"Why, my dear? I sometimes feel very tired."

"Anyway, we shall never forget you—Michael and I."

Mrs. Paget's eyes went to Martin sitting on the grass with Rosemary on one side and Valerie on the other ... to Florence sitting on a deck-chair next to Violet ... to Pen and Charles on one of the wooden forms beneath the trees. It seemed strange to see Pen accompanied by the stocky shaggy figure of Charles. One was so used to seeing her alone or with the children.

"It used to make me rather sad," she said, "that none of them were like Michael. ... They never meant anything to me compared with him. Perhaps that's why Pen's gone to the other extreme."

"She's a wonderful mother," said Ruth.

"Yes, that's her trouble," said Mrs. Paget.

Stella and Tim sauntered across the grass to them.

"Hello!" said Stella. "We've just arrived. Have we missed much?"

There was a burst of clapping.

"Only two races," said Ruth. "They're over so quickly. All this practice and preparation and heart-burning for a few seconds. It does seem rather silly, doesn't it?"

"I suppose Roger didn't win the Hundred Yards?"

"He came in second."

"He's been practising awfully hard."

"Hasn't Miss Hinkley come?" asked Mrs. Paget.

"No, she's staying with Agnes."

"Agnes ate too much lunch," put in Tim stonily. "She's being sick."

"Poor child!" said Mrs. Paget perfunctorily.

"Where is everyone?" said Stella, looking round. "Oh, there's Uncle Martin with the children."

She waved to him across the field and walked on with Tim.

"I nearly had a puppet-show last night, Uncle Martin," Rosemary was saying.

"Why not quite?" said Martin.

He was sitting cross-legged on the grass between them. As he talked and laughed with them his eyes never once left Jessica. She was still hemmed in by a crowd of parents, but he was ready to spring to his feet and join her the moment she was free.

"Mummy gave me some flour and water to make them, and I made some lovely dough, and then I made the puppets with it, and I put them to dry in front of the fire, and when I wasn't looking Dandy came along and ate them, and it was bedtime so I couldn't make any more."

"I went to school," put in Valerie proudly.

"He ate a witch and a princess and prince and a fairy."

"I crayoned a frog."

"Wouldn't you have thought they'd have given him tummy-ache?"

"And I made a house with bricks."

"She only does baby things, Uncle Martin."

"I *don't*, I *don't* do baby things. I made a flower out of pasterine."

"She means plasticine, Uncle Martin."

"I *said* it."

"She was very good," said Rosemary in her most elder-sister manner.

178

"I was very good," said Valerie, appeased. "I'm a *good* girl."

"Splendid!" said Martin, stubbing his cigarette-end on the grass.

"Oh, *please*, Uncle Martin," said Rosemary, leaping upon it. "May I have it?" She unfolded the paper, took out the morsel of tobacco and slipped it into the leather purse she wore over her shoulder. "I'm collecting tobacco for Bear. He's got a tobacco shop and all the others buy their tobacco from him."

"It's dirty, Rosemary," said Valerie, watching in righteous disapproval.

"No, it's not," said Rosemary. "The black part's only clean burn and the suck part's not wet at all." She turned with sudden anxiety to Martin. "Do you think there'll be time to go onto the beach before bedtime, Uncle Martin? I want to get some more shells for Beryl. I've got a hundred and ten. I want to have two hundred for her when she comes back. She's coming back next week."

Jessica had left the group of parents and was making her way alone down a path that led to the back of the school. Martin leapt to his feet to follow her.

Violet, engrossed apparently in conversation with Florence, had been aware in every nerve of Martin's gaze fixed on Jessica. The last week had been like a nightmare to her. Her love for Martin, which seemed to have sprung to life on the day of Stella's birthday picnic, had grown and deepened till it now possessed her wholly. It was a torment, putting her to agonies undreamed of before. At first she had clung blindly, obstinately, to the belief that he loved her, that he was merely waiting a suitable opportunity to propose to her. She seized on the veriest straws as proof of his imagined love. Even his telling her, on one occasion, that her wrist-watch strap was unfastened made her heart leap in sudden certainty of his interest and devotion.

She had attributed his frequent absences from the hotel to attacks of shyness at the thought of the proposal of marriage he had definitely decided to make to her. Even when she knew that he was going so frequently to Cliff Cottage she had at first thought it merely the disinterested desire of a naturally kind-hearted man to help someone who was in trouble.

"Poor Martin!" she had said gaily to Florence. "Such a plain woman, too!" and had glanced complacently at her own reflection in the glass.

It was, in fact, Jessica's worn, harassed, middle-aged appearance, and her obvious lack of any attempt to embellish her looks that had blinded Violet to the truth for so long.

"Oh no. . . . I understand Martin. As a matter of fact, I was sorry for the poor little creature and asked him to go and see if he could do anything for her in the way of getting in touch with her husband or anything. He's only doing it to please me—and terribly bored, poor darling!"

She had almost managed to persuade herself that this was true. Then one evening she had passed them on the beach, standing together at the foot of the ramshackle flight of wooden steps that led up the cliff to Cliff Cottage. They were looking at each other and did not see her pass, and after that she knew that they were in love. Oddly enough it increased, if possible, the tormenting ache of her desire for Martin, but to her love for him was now added a hatred of Jessica as consuming and passionate as her love. She lay awake all night, hating her, willing horrible catastrophes to happen to her, imagining the sweet worn face battered to a pulp, half gloating over her vision, half sickened by it. At meals a vision of the crooked smile would swim suddenly before her eyes, turning her faint, so that she could eat nothing. In the end her hatred seemed to take on a personality of its own, dominating every part of her.

There was virtuous indignation, too, in her hatred, for she quite honestly saw Jessica as an abandoned hussy trying to seduce an innocent young man, and herself as the pure high-minded woman who was trying to save him.

She managed none the less to reply quite pleasantly to Florence's futile chatter. She didn't want to start the old fool crying again. Florence had come into her bedroom before they set out, to ask her advice as to which hat she should wear, and Violet, who had just slipped out of the hotel after Martin to ascertain whether he was going to Cliff Cottage or not, had rounded on her. It had been a heavenly relief to vent her anger and humiliation on the ridiculous old frump, to lash at her, to ridicule her, to tell her what an utter fool she was. . . . And Florence had sat down abruptly on the bed and begun to cry.

Looking at her, it had been all Violet could do not to slap the silly crumpled face again and again and again . . . but she had controlled herself, realising even in her blind rage that she mustn't estrange her too irrevocably. She might even be able to help her with Martin yet, for Violet hadn't given up hope that he would recover from his infatuation. In any case, Florence was useful. . . .

"I'm sorry, dear," she said at last, sitting down and putting her hand to her head. "I've got such a dreadful headache that I simply don't know what I'm saying."

Florence was immediately all concern, fussing about her, still sobbing under her breath, her cheeks still red and tear-stained, blundering about the room, searching for aspirins, suggesting that Violet should lie down instead of coming to the sports.

"No, dear," Violet had said bravely. "I mustn't give way any more. . . . You forgive me, dear, don't you? It isn't *me*, you know. It's my nerves. I'm so highly strung."

"Oh *Vi*, of *course*," Florence had said in a voice that trembled with tears and devotion. "I *do* understand."

"I feel that you're my real friend," Violet had continued, "and that I needn't count my words beforehand as if you were only an acquaintance."

So that in the end Florence had felt Violet's outburst to be rather a compliment than otherwise.

And now they sat together under the chestnut tree, Florence happy in their reconciliation (those bitter moments when she had really thought that Violet hated her . . .) and Violet watching Martin and Jessica with compressed lips.

"Roger ran very well, don't you think?" said Florence.

"Yes, very," said Violet, who didn't even know that Roger had been running.

"Look. They're going to have the High Jump."

"Yes," said Violet, watching Jessica and Martin go round together to the back of the school building.

Stella and Tim strolled up to them.

"Hello," said Stella. "Your hat's crooked, Aunt Florence. Let me put it straight."

She straightened it and Florence made room for them on the seat.

"Do sit here," she said. "There's plenty of room."

She wanted to defeat the black loneliness that always lurked at the back of her mind and that Violet's outburst had intensified. She wanted to feel popular and beloved ("They're all so fond of me, my nephews and nieces," she had said last night to one of the residents at the hotel. "It's 'Auntie this' and 'Auntie that' all the time I'm with them").

But Stella only smiled vaguely and walked on with Tim towards the spinney of trees that bordered the playing-field. Florence looked after them with her foolish little smile, and threw Stella's straightening of her hat as a kind of sop to the demon of depression that lay in wait for her, trying to see her as an affectionate devoted little niece. . . . Her eyes roved round the field.

"Where's Martin?" she said.

Violet rose to her feet with a sudden jerky movement.

"Let's move about a bit," she said. "I'm getting stiff with sitting so long."

They walked down the field—past Pen and Charles, who were so intent on watching Roger in the Three-legged Race that they didn't notice them ("Hard lines!" said Charles as Roger fell out. "He's getting terribly hot," said Pen anxiously), and on to where Mrs. Paget sat with Ruth Forrester.

"We're just taking a walk round," explained Florence.

Mrs. Paget looked from Florence's flushed face, with its faint deprecating smile, to the tense lines of Violet's mouth, and felt a little stab of compunction. That sudden certainty of her own approaching death had given her also a startlingly clear vision of Florence—bewildered, adrift without her. She'll be Violet's drudge, she thought. She'll let Violet bully her as much as she wants to and Violet will hate her for it. They'll be two miserable old women and they'll never get free from each other.

She rose from her chair.

"I'd like to take a little walk, dear," she said, "if you'll give me your arm. The grass is rather rough."

She put her hand on Florence's arm and leant her weight on it, trying to seem as old and infirm as possible. Florence's depression fell from her suddenly. She felt again necessary, useful, beloved. (After all, she thought, what *would* Mother do without me? I mustn't regret having sacrificed myself to her all these years. . . .)

They walked slowly down towards the other end of the field. Violet slipped into the chair next to Ruth Forrester.

"What a darling Mrs. Paget is!" said Ruth, watching the old lady as she walked with exaggeratedly feeble steps by Florence's side.

Violet didn't answer.

Her eyes were fixed on the corner of the house round which Martin and Jessica had disappeared. The skin across her forehead felt tight as though a hot band had been placed round it, and a pulse in her throat pounded with deep rhythmic throbbing.

Martin and Jessica walked round the school building towards the gymnasium at the back, where tea was to be served. Mrs. Orton was coming out of the side door.

"Will you kindly see that there are enough seats this time, Mrs. Heath?" she said. "The seating at tea was disgracefully mismanaged last year." And passed on without looking at Martin. It always gave her great satisfaction to put Jessica in her place after she had been obliged to make much of her in front of the parents. Martin wasn't a parent and didn't count.

They looked after her. There was an angry flush on Martin's face.

"Does she always speak to you like that?" he said.

"Oh no," answered Jessica. "That's quite mild. She can be much worse than that."

"How on earth can you put up with it?"

She smiled—her little lop-sided smile.

"Oh, Martin, what does that sort of thing matter? It doesn't worry me at all. . . . And it's so childish. She knows quite well that most of the seats are in use on the field and that anyway I can't make ten seats out of five. As a matter of fact I dislike her so much that I'd hate her to be nice to me."

They entered the big bare hall. Trestle tables were ranged along the walls, laden with cups and saucers, jugs of milk, and plates of sandwiches and cakes.

"What is there for you to do?" said Martin.

"I have to give the signal to the kitchen to bring in the urns when I hear the first sound of the cheering for the Sack Race. And, of course, make bricks without straw in the matter of seats. Last year Mr. Orton forgot to tell the boys to bring the forms in from the field, and he's pretty sure to forget again."

He caught hold of her hand.

"Let me take you away from it all."

"Oh, Martin, not now. I mean, I've got to listen for the Sack Race cheering now. They've just started the Obstacle and it's the next but one. It's such an inopportune moment to make love to me."

She smiled at him, but there was desperate unhappiness behind her smile.

"I can't stand this any longer," he said. "You *must* let me take you out of it."

"We've been over all that. . . . Darling, don't let's go over it all again."

"It's killing you," he said. "You look like a ghost. Jessica, won't you think over again what I said last night? I'd be so careful."

She made a fierce little gesture of dissent.

"No, no," she said. "Not that. Not that furtive creeping-in-and-out sort of an affair. I've seen them. I've *hated* them. It wouldn't make us any happier. Believe me, Martin, it wouldn't. . . . Besides, though I don't love Brian, I'm his wife. It may sound old-fashioned but it does mean something."

"You're *not* his wife," he said hotly. "You're his drudge, his slave.

... You've won your freedom a dozen times over. ... You can't love me or——"

"Oh, Martin, I do. I do."

There came a burst of cheering from the field. She tore her hands from his.

"Oh dear! No, it can't be the Sack Race yet. Martin, do just move those benches about a little and make them look more than they are."

Pen sat, tense and rigid, watching the Obstacle Race. Roger fell out of a bottomless barrel, suspended from the branch of a tree, rolled over several times, picked himself up, did a sum, scrambled under a bench, threaded a needle, walked along a rope placed on the ground, cleared two hurdles of pea-sticks and arrived, purple and breathless, at the winning-post.

A roar of cheering went up.

"He's won," gasped Pen.

"Good fellow!" said Charles in a casual tone that slightly annoyed Pen. (As if it wasn't the most wonderful thing in the world that Roger should win a race!)

Roger made his way over to Pen and Charles, red-faced and panting, beaming ecstatically, surrounded by a group of friends who were thumping him unmercifully on the back. Rosemary and Valerie ran up to join the crowd.

"*Good* old Roger!" cried Valerie, joining excitedly in the chorus.

Mr. Forrester began to arrange the competitors for the Sack Race.

Roger's friends continued to thump him on the back.

"Well done, old chap!"

"You came an awful cropper out of that barrel."

"Did you hurt yourself, Roger?" said Pen anxiously.

" 'Course I didn't," said Roger.

Stella and Tim sat on the grass at the edge of the spinney.

"It was jolly good of Roger to win that," said Tim. "He was about the smallest in for it."

"Yes, wasn't it!" said Stella, but she wasn't really interested in Roger's having run the race.

"They're getting ready for the Sack Race now. A boy at my prep. school once broke his leg in a sack race. Can't think how he managed it; can you?"

Stella didn't answer. He'd kissed her this afternoon. She'd got up from her seat after the sitting, and he'd suddenly bent his head and kissed her lips. A sword-like happiness had shot through her, and all her secret doubts had vanished away. He loved her—he loved her as much as she loved him. It was all right. ... Their future lay together now, whatever happened. He had released her quickly and turned to busy himself with his palette and brushes. He was so chivalrous that he probably blamed himself for having let his feelings escape the strong guard of his reserve. But just as she was going, he had said quite casually, "My wife's coming down on Tuesday."

That meant that the crisis was approaching. He must have sent for his wife in order to discuss the situation with her and ask her to free him. ... She wondered what Tim would say when he knew, what everyone would say when they knew ... wondered if Arnold (somehow, though she loved him, it wasn't easy to call him Arnold even to herself) would ever write a book about it. Only, of course, she had to admit that it would be rather too much like *Starlight.* ...

Tim was drawing a little book from his pocket. His quarrel with Stella the other evening had made him very unhappy. He felt that he had been churlish and irritable, and he wanted to make up for it.

"I wonder if you'd care to have this," he said tentatively. "It's Blake's *Illustrations of the Book of Job.*"

"Oh, but it's yours, isn't it?" said Stella.

"Yes, but I can easily get another. They're only two shillings at the Tate. They're rather nice."

"It's sweet of you, Tim."

She, too, had hated quarrelling with him. ... She took the little book and turned over the pages.

"Job and God look just alike, don't they? ... What lovely little creatures round the borders. ... Satan's rather sweet, isn't he? ...

This one's lovely. . . . 'When the morning stars sang together and all the sons of God shouted for joy.' Whatever's this?"

"Behemoth."

"Isn't he a pet! . . . Oh, bother! That's the end of the Sack Race. They're going in to tea."

"Never mind. We needn't go yet. There's always such a scrum at the beginning."

"Look, there's Mr. Forrester taking Granny in. . . . Tim, I *do* love it. . . . Honestly, I do. . . . Isn't his beard lovely? Job's, I mean. . . . Here he is with everything all right at the end and all his sheep again. . . . It's a darling book, Tim." She glanced up. "Oh, do look!" she said in amused surprise. "Look at Uncle Martin red and het-up telling boys to bring in the benches. It's hardly his business, is it? And he isn't officious as a rule."

But Tim wasn't interested in Martin.

"I suppose it was silly of me to bring it here because you've nowhere to put it, but I just wanted you to have it."

"I'll keep it in your pocket till I get home. . . . Let me look at him again with his hair standing up when he's having nightmare. . . . But he *would* on that bed, poor darling! It looks terribly uncomfortable."

He watched her as she turned the pages, her dark lashes upturned on her softly flushed cheeks.

I do love Tim, she was thinking, but just as I'd have loved an elder brother if I'd had one. . . . The Jobs didn't seem to have had a house at all. They seemed to spend all their time sitting about on stone seats out of doors. . . . It's not a bit what I feel for—*him*. . . . What I feel for him is real love, the sort you read about in books, the sort that never dies. . . . I suppose that's the eldest brother trying to save the baby. . . . It was sweet of him to give it me. . . . I'm fond of Tim in the way that I'd hate him not to be there, but I don't really *love* him. . . .

Parents were having tea in the gymnasium and swarming all over the school. Roger drew Charles into a bathroom, and, turning up one leg of his running shorts, showed a rather grubby handkerchief, faintly bloodstained, tied round his thin leg between knee and hip.

"I caught it on a nail," he said, "when I was getting out of the barrel in the Obstacle Race. I didn't want Mummy to know. She'd only fuss. Is it all right, d'you think?"

He untied the handkerchief, displaying a long jagged scratch.

"Perkins said I'd be sure to get blood poisoning," he went on anxiously. "I won't, will I? He says people always die of it."

"No, you'll be all right," Charles assured him. "But I think we'll wash it and put something a bit cleaner than that on it. What about a bandage?"

"The first-aid cupboard's just outside, and Matron left it open, case anyone wanted anything."

Charles got some iodine and a bandage, then washed and bound up the small wound.

"Thanks awfully," said Roger. "That feels lovely. And I couldn't get it now, could I?"

"Not possibly," Charles assured him again.

"And you won't tell Mummy, will you? She'd *fuss* so."

Chapter Fourteen

ROSEMARY had been excited all day at the thought of Beryl's return. She had got her sums wrong in school because she would think of nothing else. (She's in the train now. . . . She's got to the station now. . . . She's at home now. . . . They said she'd be home for tea. . . .)

She had wanted to go straight to Beryl's house after school, but Mummy had said she must go home for tea first, so she'd gobbled up her tea as quickly as she could and was now hurrying up the sandy path to the rather ostentatious villa where the Egertons lived, the precious box of shells held tightly under her arm.

Last night she had been on the beach till bedtime collecting them and had just got the two hundred when Stella came down to fetch her. She had been so excited when she went to bed that at first she had not been able to sleep, and when she did sleep had had a specially bad dream from which she had awakened clammy and gasping with terror. She had lain there for some time rigid and motionless, her heart beating like hammer strokes, not quite sure whether she was awake or not. . . . She gave her head a little shake as if to shake the memory out of it and turned her thoughts to Beryl again. She'd made up a new game—about good witches and bad witches—for her and Beryl to play. She'd been tempted to play it with Val last night but had managed not to. She'd made it up for Beryl and didn't want to play it with anyone else before she played it with Beryl. . . . Like the shells, it was meant to show Beryl how much she loved her and how glad she was to have her home again.

The house was in sight now. . . . She ran along the path up to the gate, her small pale face alight with eagerness, fumbled at the latch for a moment before she could open it, then flitted up to the front door and, standing on tiptoe, put her finger on the bell. It seemed hours before the door opened and Beryl appeared—rosier and rounder and plumper than ever, the ringlets sleeker, the legs that emerged from the short blue frock stouter. Carry stood just behind her. Rosemary started forward, then stopped. Beryl was looking at her, unsmiling.

"You can go back home, Rosemary Marlowe," said Beryl clearly. "We don't want you."

The silence that followed was broken by Carry's snigger.

Rosemary stared at Beryl and the smile faded tremulously from her lips. It was just like a bad dream. She couldn't believe that it was really happening.

"But, Beryl," she stammered. "I thought . . . I've brought . . ."

She took the lid off the box of shells, and Beryl gave a high-pitched affected laugh, tossing back her ringlets.

"I hope you've not brought that rubbish for *me*" she said. "*I'm* not a baby, thanks, and I don't want to play with a baby. You can go back home and I don't want to have anything more to do with you ever."

Carry sniggered again.

"But . . . Beryl . . ." began Rosemary again in a little breathless voice.

"Playing with *dolls*!" went on Beryl with an exaggerated sneer on her small pink-and-white face. "Dolls and shells! I'm sick of you and don't want you ever to come here again. So there!"

With that she slammed the door to. Rosemary stood staring at the closed door for a few moments, her box of shells under her arm, then turned and walked slowly down to the gate. Beryl and Carry had appeared at the open window.

"Baby! Who plays with dolls?" they jeered.

Rosemary shut the gate carefully and set off down the lane homewards. Her knees felt unsteady so that she had to walk carefully, but she wasn't crying. She was glad she wasn't crying. At the bend in the lane she met Aunt Florence's friend. She stood there frozen, terrified that she would speak to her, because she knew that if she did she'd have to cry ... but she didn't seem to see her. She was walking very quickly and talking to herself in a funny quick angry voice.

Rosemary opened the gate of Sea Meads and went in by the side door.

"Is that you, Rosemary?" called Pen from the sitting-room.

"Yes," said Rosemary.

"Has Beryl not come back yet?"

"No."

She was horrified to hear herself tell the lie, but she didn't want Mummy to know what had happened. It wasn't that Mummy wouldn't understand. It was that she'd understand too well. She understood so well that she came right inside you, and Rosemary didn't want anyone to come right inside her. Somehow, that made things worse, not better. ... She went into the dining-room and opened the cupboard under the window-seat where she kept her toys. She knelt for a moment motionless, clutching the box of shells to her protectively. It was as if the shells had shared her hurt—scorned and rejected by Beryl—and she was trying to comfort them. She put them onto a shelf, then closed the cupboard and got up.

"Rosemary!" called Pen.

Rosemary slipped out by the side door again. She couldn't let Mummy see her yet. Mummy would know at once that something was the matter. She went down the path to the beach. Daddy was there with Val and Roger. She sat down in the shade of the sandhills and watched them. Though she was watching them, she didn't really see them. She only saw Beryl's face twisted into its scornful sneer in the frame of the shining ringlets ... Carry grinning maliciously in the background. Charles waved to her and she waved back automatically. Then Roger and Val, seeing two little girls who came down to the Bay every summer and had only arrived that morning, ran off eagerly to join them and Charles came over to Rosemary. His grey flannel trousers were rolled up above the knee and his feet were bare. He sat down by her and lit his pipe. Then he said quietly, "Anything wrong, old lady?"

She gave a little gulp and collapsed against him, sobbing. The story came out between her sobs. He couldn't make much of it. Some other kid had hurt her feelings. . . . It didn't really matter what had happened. The point was that she was upset. He put his pipe down on the sand and took her into his arms (Gosh! she was like a feather. There was nothing of her), and she sobbed on his shoulder in a luxurious abandonment of grief. A rush of tenderness for her filled his heart.

"There, there, old lady," he murmured. "Cheer up! . . . It's all right. . . . Never mind. . . . All in the day's work. . . . Nothing to worry about. . . ."

She knew that he didn't really understand what had happened and she was glad. She wanted his comfort but she didn't want anyone to understand what had happened—to look at it, handle it, ask questions about it.

"Don't tell Mummy," she said as she clung to him.

"All right, old lady. I won't."

Her sobs gradually died down.

"Shall we go and see what the others are doing?" suggested Charles after a bit.

She nodded assent and, still holding his hand, went with him to the further end of the bay, where Valerie and Roger were playing with the two little girls. The two little girls were twins and looked exactly alike, with snub noses, blue eyes, red pigtails, grey shorts, and white blouses. They had built an elaborate sand-castle with a wall and a moat, and the tide was slowly crumbling it. Helped by Valerie and Roger, they worked frantically to repair the breaches, rushing about with their spades, filling up holes with fresh sand. "Here, here! Put some here! It's getting in here! Quick! Quick!"

Then, yielding suddenly to the inevitable, they were seized by a lust for destruction as vehement as their defence had been and began battering down what was left, taking handfuls of sand from the castle and flinging it into the encroaching sea.

"Take it, then! Take it!" they shouted.

One of them raised a handful to her lips before she flung it out.

"Good-bye, darling castle. Good-bye!"

Rosemary watched them, smiling through her tears.

Violet Coniston walked with quick purposeful steps towards Cliff End School. She didn't see Rosemary coming back from the Egertons' villa. She saw nothing as she passed along the road. . . . She saw only Martin's face as it had looked last night. . . . The letter from her uncle had come while they were having dinner, and at first, with what some secret part of her knew to be wilful self-deception, she had seen it as the end of her troubles. A business friend of her uncle's was willing to interview Martin with the object of taking him into his firm. It was a good post with prospects. An honest, reliable, capable man was needed, and Martin's experience in Malaya, her uncle wrote, would be as useful as any other. She had folded up the letter with trembling hands and slipped it into her bag. That would settle everything, she assured herself. Martin would accept the post. He wanted to stay in England. He would soon forget the horrible woman who had ensnared him. She would *make* him forget. They would be happy together once they left this hateful place. . . . She waited till he got up from the table, then, stifling her secret doubts, followed him into the garden.

"Martin."

He wheeled round in surprise.

"Yes."

Even then he was hardly aware of her. She was merely an obstacle in his path, and his tone brushed her out of it impatiently. He was on his way to call for Jessica. They were going to walk over the cliff to Bramber Cove.

"Martin," she said in the tone of forced brightness that always jarred on him, "I've heard from my uncle. He's spoken to a friend of his, and the friend's willing to give you an interview about a post in his firm. Here's the letter."

She took it from her bag with trembling fingers and handed it to him.

He read it with a wild leap of the heart. So blinded was he that just at first he didn't realise its implication. He saw it only as a means of securing Jessica. He could stay in England and marry her. Brian would divorce her or she could divorce Brian. At long last he would make up to her for all her suffering. He raised his eyes to Violet's face. It was very white and a little nerve twitched with rhythmic jerky movements at the corner of her mouth.

"It's in Nottingham," she said. "We could live outside, of course. There's some quite nice country round."

Then he understood. He could have the job only on condition that he married her. His face seemed to go dead. In the silence he could hear her breathing quickly in short painful gasps.

His eyes slid from hers as he answered, "No . . . I'm sorry. . . ."

It didn't seem necessary to say more than that. He was turning away but she caught at him with a little sob.

"Martin . . . Martin . . . listen. Leave that hateful woman. I love you. I——"

He forced himself to look at her. A hot ugly flush had suffused her face and neck. Even her eyes were bloodshot. He could feel her breath on his cheek as she tried to draw his head down.

Gently he disengaged her hands and walked out of the gate without looking back.

She lay awake all night seeing that look of startled revulsion on his face. She thought that she would see it till the end of her life. Sometimes the picture faded and the picture of Jessica Heath's face came in its place, with the tired hazel eyes and little lop-sided smile. She knew and hated every line of it . . . even the powdering of freckles at the base of the nose and the faint lines that ran up from the side of the eyebrows to the temples.

So obsessed was she by these visions that when she saw Edith's letter waiting for her on the breakfast table the next morning her first impulse was to throw it into the waste-paper basket without even opening it. It aggravated her sense of injury that she should hear from Edith to-day—dull, plain Edith, who nevertheless had secured a husband and was the mother of three small boys. Edith had taught under her at the Kensington school and had admired her unquestioningly from their first meeting. Though Violet had been bitterly jealous of the marriage, some instinct had prompted her to keep up the friendship and retain Edith's ingenuous devotion.

After all, she hadn't so many admirers that she could afford to let any go. .... And now Edith wrote, asking—She turned over the pages impatiently. As if she could be bothered with that sort of thing now! Her hands were on the paper to tear it up when suddenly she stopped and sat there staring in front of her. .... Here, if she made proper use of it, was a weapon against her enemy. She folded it up and laid it by her plate, still staring in front of her, ignoring Florence's nervous attempts at conversation, not even making a pretence of eating.

Mrs. Paget, watching her, thought: It's time we went away. Something dreadful will happen if we don't. But she didn't want to go till the month was up. Every moment of her friendship with Michael was precious to her. She would never see him again after this month. She had been living in a waking dream in which only Michael was real, and even Michael was less himself than a bridge that took her back into the past—but that look on Violet's face shattered the dream ruthlessly. She remembered the eager laughing happiness that had been there when they came to Merlin Bay and pity shook her against her will. How selfish I've been, she thought. I wonder if I could have helped. But I'd probably only have made things worse if I'd tried. Just as Florence does. ...

Florence was still chattering nervously, in a futile effort to defy the fear of Violet that filled her heart like a black cloud. It was dreadful to be *afraid* of someone you loved as much as she loved Violet, but when Violet turned to her with those narrowed eyes and tight lips it set her heart racing with sheer terror. And she had to go on talking, talking, talking all the time, so frightened lest anything she said might be the wrong thing that she had to say something else quickly to cover it up. (How *could* Mother sit there, looking so happy and peaceful and obviously thinking of something else, not caring how desperately unhappy Violet was?)

"You've eaten hardly *anything* lately, darling," she said and, though she sat perfectly still, everything about her seemed to flutter timidly as she spoke. "I'm afraid the holiday hasn't done you much good. ... You really had a much better appetite when first you came. ... You'd got more of a colour, too. ... I really think I'll get a bottle of tonic for you. . . . There's a Boots in Penzance. . . . Martin would run in and get it. . . . I'll ask him when I see him. . . . He never seems to be here, does he? . . . Really, I think he——"

Violet rose with a quick jerky movement and went out of the room without speaking. Florence fluttered about in her seat for a few moments, obviously uncertain whether to follow or not, and finally settled down to another cup of tea.

"I don't think she's a bit well," she said tearfully. "I don't know what to do."

"Leave her alone," said Mrs. Paget. "She'll get over it."

"I—I do *help*," said Florence. "I'm sure I do. I mean, I don't know what she'd do without me. She's reserved, but she *does* depend on me. Our friendship means quite as much to her as it does to me. . . ."

She drained her tea-cup, dabbed at her eyes with a pocket-handkerchief and said chokingly, "I think I'll start another dish-cloth."

Violet joined them on the beach later, carrying a book. She spoke to them quite pleasantly, and the hard angry light that frightened Florence had gone from her eyes. Once or twice, engrossed apparently in her reading, she even smiled to herself. . . .

After lunch she went to her bedroom to rest and came out about tea-time, wearing her hat and coat.

"I'm going for a walk," she said to Florence, who was fluttering about outside waiting for her. "No, don't come with me. I'd rather be alone."

When she was ushered into the spacious sunny drawing-room of Cliff End School, she found Mr. and Mrs. Orton, Michael Forrester, and a man with a short black beard having tea there.

"How nice of you to call!" gushed Mrs. Orton, rising from the tea-table to greet her. "Do sit down and have some tea."

There had been from the first an indefinable bond of sympathy between Mrs. Orton and Violet. "Not so stuck-up as the rest of them," Mrs. Orton put it to herself, but she knew that it went deeper than that. "You know my husband and Mr. Forrester, don't you? This is Mr. Hardman, a friend of Mr. Forrester's, who's been lecturing to the boys on his travels in Albania. *Most* interesting."

"Well, I don't know," said the lecturer modestly. "One can't really give anyone much of an idea of a place in an hour. I only had a quarter of the photographs made into slides. . . ."

"Quite enough," said Mr. Orton heartily. "I mean, it was all most interesting. Gave the little beggars a fresh outlook on life."

He stood there by the window, large, smiling, handsome, the perfection of physical well-being.

"Well, if you're sure they enjoyed it . . ." said the lecturer.

" 'Course they did!" said Mr. Orton. "They'd enjoy anything that would get them out of afternoon school." The lecturer looked at him a little reproachfully. "Honestly, it made me think I'd like to go out there myself." The lecturer brightened. "Now tell me . . ."

"I won't have any tea, thank you," Violet was saying to Mrs. Orton. There was a tight dry feeling in her throat. She couldn't have swallowed anything. She looked about her. "What a charming room this is!"

She had queened it here once, of course, as the headmaster's wife. When she entered it now she had to knock at the door and stand humbly, awaiting orders. And—her heart surged with angry triumph—even that would be taken away if she managed this interview properly. Oh, and it was little enough. She deserved worse than the worst that could possibly happen to her.

"It's been such a pleasure to meet you all," she went on, "and to see such an admirably run school. I've had experience, you know." She gave a little laugh that was meant to be light and casual, but that sounded high-pitched and hysterical. "And I'm only too well aware how rare a thing a really well-run school is."

"That is kind of you, Miss Coniston," said Mrs. Orton. She was watching her visitor closely, convinced now that there was a purpose behind the visit. Well, she must just wait for her cues. She enjoyed these little games of intrigue. She always preferred herself to do a thing by roundabout than by straightforward means. It had been Jessica's refusal to understand this game, her barely concealed contempt of it, that had first roused Mrs. Orton's dislike.

"It's been so nice to have you all down here," she said. (One always began by a delicate exchange of compliments.) "We always like to know our boys' families, and it's so good for them to entertain their friends and relations at school."

"The sports were delightful," said Violet, and still managed to smile, though at the thought of the sports, of Martin sitting there, never moving his eyes from the woman's face, the blood surged and throbbed through her body.

The lecturer was taking his leave now. Violet lay back in her chair and looked about the room. It was a charming room, charmingly furnished, with grey walls, a mauve carpet, and chair-covers and curtains of grey and mauve printed linen. Somehow it didn't go with Mrs. Orton's air of rather flashy smartness. Had *she* furnished it like this? At the thought her fingers stiffened on the arm of the chair. . . .

Mr. Orton and Michael Forrester came back into the room.

"The cheque was all right, wasn't it?" said Mr. Orton.

"Oh yes," said Michael.

"I'd forgotten what he asked for, but that's what they usually have. I thought he was rather above the average myself; didn't you?"

"I like him personally," said Michael, "but I hate this modern commercialising of adventure. Love of adventure for its own sake doesn't exist any longer. It's just a commercial proposition, like any other. People go out to unknown or dangerous places merely in order to come home and lecture on them at so much a lecture. If Odysseus lived now, I suppose, he'd have a publicity agent and give lectures on his experiences in the Trojan war. It's a prostitution of something beautiful."

"Now, Mr. Forrester," said Mrs. Orton in arch reproach, "don't use naughty words."

Michael threw her an enigmatic smile and said, "Well, I'll go and clear those kids out of the cloakroom."

"Yes," said Mr. Orton heartily. "I can't waste any more time, either. Good-bye, Miss Coniston. Delighted to see you here any time."

He had judged from his wife's manner that for some reason or other the visitor was to be propitiated.

As the door closed on the two men, Mrs. Orton turned to Violet, waiting her lead. Were the preliminaries over and could they now get to business, whatever the business was?

"I think Mrs. Marlowe's so lucky to have the school near at hand for her boys," Violet was saying. "I know so many mothers who're worried to death by having no suitable school near for their children."

Mrs. Orton pricked up her ears.

"Of course, that must be *very* worrying," she said.

"A child's first years at school are so important," said Violet. "I'm always telling parents that. They're apt to think that the first school doesn't matter. I tell them that it matters far more than any later school."

"You're so *right*, Miss Coniston," said Mrs. Orton with a sigh. "I wish more people realised it."

"You take boarders as well as day boys, don't you?" went on Violet casually.

"Oh yes," said Mrs. Orton, copying the visitor's casual tone, but alert in every nerve. (She was certain that they were getting towards the point at last.) "We have about forty boarders. That's the side we're most interested in, of course."

Violet opened her bag and took out Edith's letter.

"I don't know how it is," she said with her light little laugh, "that all my friends think that I am an authority on every type of school just because I teach in one. Here's an old friend of mine writing to ask me to suggest a prep. school for her small boy. She takes for granted that I know all there is to be known about prep. schools."

Mrs. Orton's eyes were bright and wary.

"Perhaps I could give you a prospectus?" she suggested.

Violet waved the suggestion aside.

"There's no need for that," she said. "I know that Edith would take my word without any prospectus. She has two younger boys as well," she added, "who would naturally follow on to any school to which she sent the eldest. She has a large circle of friends and relations, too, all with young children. Have you noticed," she added casually, "how sheep-like parents are? When one member of a group sends a child to a school nearly all the others follow suit. If the child's happy, that is. That means so much more than any amount of prospectuses."

Mrs. Orton felt a little baffled. She still couldn't see where it was all leading to.

"Our children are certainly happy," she said. "Frank adores them and they adore him."

"Oh, I can see that," said Violet.

"And the place is run on most up-to-date lines. A carefully balanced diet and all that."

"I'm sure it is."

There was a silence during which Mrs. Orton once more awaited her cue. It came at last.

"Is Mrs. Heath a permanent member of your staff?" said Violet.

"Well . . .," Mrs. Orton temporised, waiting further guidance. "We took her on when her husband lost his job as headmaster."

"Out of kindness, I suppose?"

"Oh, of course."

Violet laughed harshly.

"But is it *real* kindness, do you think? Forgive me if I'm being impertinent. It's only that—I'm very conscientious, and I know that I'm taking a great responsibility in recommending a school to my friend."

"Of *course*, Miss Coniston," agreed Mrs. Orton fervently. "I admire you for it. And anything I can do to help . . ."

"May I be quite frank?" said Violet.

"Do, please," said Mrs. Orton, relieved that they'd got to it at last.

"If Mrs. Heath were not a member of your staff I should have no hesitation at all in recommending the school to my friend."

"You mean, her husband's——?"

"No, I mean the woman herself," said Violet. The hard angry

light blazed in her eyes again. Her lips were tightly compressed. "I mean that she's a loose woman."

"Miss Coniston!" said Mrs. Orton, acting instinctively her part of shocked horror. "*Surely* not!"

"Yes," said Violet. "I *know* it. I have proof. Don't ask me for it, please, because there are some things so horrible that—If my word isn't enough——"

"Of course it is, Miss Coniston," said Mrs. Orton. Triumph gleamed in her eyes, too. Frank couldn't hold out against this. "I'll speak to my husband to-night."

"She isn't fit to have dealings with children," went on Violet. "She can't be anything but an evil influence."

"I never dreamed . . .," said Mrs. Orton.

Violet lowered her voice.

"She made immoral advances to my friend's brother," she said. "He told his sister and she told me. She's nothing better than a woman of the streets." She had recovered herself now and smiled sadly. "It's very distressing for me to have to tell you this."

"I'm so grateful to you," said Mrs. Orton. "And, in a way, I'm not surprised. I've never liked the woman. I've always had a kind of feeling about her."

"I have a theory," said Violet, "that sensitive people can always feel evil in the atmosphere. . . . I felt it myself at once." She rose. "Well, I mustn't keep you, but I can take for granted, can't I, that if my friend's little boy comes here he won't be exposed to that particular influence?"

Mrs. Orton took her hand.

"You can indeed, Miss Coniston, and I'm more than grateful to you for having opened my eyes.

She stood at the window and watched Violet's figure disappear down the drive, a faintly derisive smile on her lips. She had a pretty shrewd suspicion as to how matters really stood (the woman had given herself away with almost every word), but she was determined that her husband should have no suspicion of it.

Chapter Fifteen

THE news that Brian Heath had returned to Cliff Cottage flew round Merlin Bay with the mysterious rapidity with which such news always travels.

But it was eclipsed by another piece of news that followed close on its heels.

Agnes had not been in bed that morning when Mrs. Bevan went to call her, and a frantic search of house and garden and village had followed. It was a fisherman who at last found her body, washed up by the incoming tide. At first the tragedy seemed inexplicable, for Mrs. Bevan had herself, as usual, tucked her up in bed the night before, then she remembered that when Agnes was a little girl she used to walk in her sleep, though it was so long since she had done it that they had now stopped taking precautions against it. That, of course, must be the explanation. Moreover, there had been a new moon last night, and Mrs. Bevan had often thought that that affected her in some way, that she seemed more difficult and excitable in the moon's first quarter. She must have gone downstairs in her sleep, opened the front door, unlatched the little green gate, walked right on to the edge of the cliff, and, still in her sleep, fallen over into the sea. After her first wild anguish Mrs. Bevan displayed a wonderful self-control. Miss Hinkley alone was allowed within the defences of her grief.

"You loved her," she said brokenly, "and she loved you. She loved everyone, my sweet darling, but only you and I really loved her. . . ."

"I shall never forget her, never," said Miss Hinkley. "So sweet, so affectionate, so intelligent . . ."

"You were so kind to her," said Mrs. Bevan.

And that, said Miss Hinkley, was her only comfort—that she had been able to give the darling child some little happiness during the last week of her short life.

Mrs. Bevan sent Tim to wire for his father and to make arrangements for the funeral, allowing no one but herself and Miss Hinkley to wash and arrange the beloved body, on which the waves had left no scar or blemish. In death Agnes's face wore a look of happy surprise, the grossness refined to something almost spiritual.

Martin heard the news as he was hurrying to Cliff Cottage. On him alone in Merlin Bay it made less impression than the news of Brian Heath's return. He found Jessica in the little kitchen, wearing the overall in which he had first seen her.

"Jessica, has——?"

She nodded.

"Yes, he's back. . . . He's upstairs asleep. I expect he'll sleep all day. I've had the doctor. It's just exhaustion and the after-effects of heavy drinking. He's got a chill, too. He'll need nursing. . . ."

"Jessica, it hasn't made any difference—has it?—to what you said last night."

She threw out her hands in a little gesture, half deprecating, half despairing.

"Oh, Martin——"

"Listen, Jessica," he said urgently. "You agreed with me last night. You agreed that you'd done all that could be humanly expected of anyone, that you'd sacrificed yourself to him long enough."

"I know, Martin. And then——"

"And then he came home," suggested Martin bitterly, "and you felt that, after all, he needed you more than I do. That's what happened, isn't it? Well, I can go off the rails, too, if that will give me a better chance with you. It's quite easily done. I could come to you in the state he does—or worse—if that will convince you that I need you."

"Don't be bitter, Martin."

"Last night you'd decided to come with me."

"I know."

"And his just coming back like this has made you change your mind."

"I think I should have changed my mind anyway," she said slowly. "I think that even last night the sane part of me knew that—oh, Martin, it would be too heavenly to be true. To be with you for the rest of my life. . . . It's one of the things that are too wonderful ever really to happen."

"But why shouldn't we take our happiness when we get the chance?" he persisted. "It's the only chance we shall ever get. I shall never love anyone else as long as I live. . . ."

"Nor I," she said breathlessly.

"Jessica," he pleaded, "don't throw away the happiness of both of us for no reason at all Darling . . ."

He put his hands on her shoulders, and she turned away from him sharply, as if she could not endure his touch or the pleading in his eyes.

"*Don't*, Martin. It isn't only that Brian's come back. There's something else. . . ."

"What else can there be?"

"I've got the sack from Cliff End School."

He stared at her in surprise.

"But I thought——"

"That they couldn't get on without me? I rather thought that, too. But evidently they can. I had a letter from Mr. Orton by this morning's post. Mrs. Orton's always hated me, of course. Well, she'll be rid of me at last."

"What reason does he give?"

"Oh, the usual one. Reorganising the staff. Going to have a 'Mam'selle' in my place. I don't suppose for a moment that he will, but it's as good an excuse as any for kicking me out."

"That makes no difference, of course," he said. "You were going, anyway. It only leaves you free to come with me at once."

"No, it doesn't, Martin. I'd thought of Brian staying here if I—went away, and keeping on with his vegetable-growing. I'd persuaded myself that he'd be all right here, even if I went. But—they don't want Brian either."

"Does he say so?"

"Yes, he says that, now the numbers of the school have increased so much, he's afraid he'll have to make other arrangements for the vegetables. The numbers haven't increased, but that's neither here nor there. . . . Don't you see what it all means, Martin? I can't leave Brian now. I might have done if this hadn't happened. But we shall have to go away from Merlin Bay and start fresh somewhere else. I must get another job. I—*can't* leave him now. You do see, don't you, Martin?"

"Yes," he said slowly, "I see. . . ." Some women could have done, of course, but not Jessica. "What will you do?" he said.

She squared her thin shoulders, and he saw again that something unconquerable that he had glimpsed in her when first they met.

"Oh, don't worry about me," she said. "I'll get a job all right. Of some sort or other."

He sat down on a chair and put his head on his hands. A sense of defeat weighed down on him like some tangible load. It was useless to plead with her. She had made up her mind. Fate had been too strong for them.

"It's damnable," he said through his teeth.

She knelt and put her arms round him, holding him tightly to her.

"I know . . . I know."

They clung to each other in silence, then gently she freed herself.

"Martin."

"Yes."

"You're going to-morrow, aren't you?"

"The others are. I shan't leave you a moment before I must."

She sat back on her heels looking up at him.

"Listen, Martin. I want you to go to-morrow—with the others—as you'd arranged to."

"No," he said angrily. "I won't promise that. I couldn't bear it."

"You must," she insisted. "Martin, for my sake, you must. I can't go on unless you promise. I shall love you all my life. I shall never forget anything about you—not a look or a word." Her fingers wandered lightly over his face. "I shall remember the way your hair grows here and the way your cheeks go here ... and your mouth ... and your chin. ... I shall live on it for the rest of my life, and it will be all I shall have to live on. But, oh, my dear, I love you so much, I long for you so much, that—if I can't have you properly—and I can't—we must break it off now. I've got to work hard and I couldn't if you were there, if I thought I might see you or hear from you the next morning. It would take all the strength out of me. It would be torture for both of us. Martin, will you promise?"

He was silent. The blood had left his face, making the furrows in his cheeks look like two black gashes.

"Martin, do promise," she pleaded. "If you really love me, promise. Go back next month when your leave's up, as you'd meant to at first. Put—how many miles is it?—" she smiled tremulously, "between us or I shan't be able to bear it. You'll be with me—right inside me—till I die, but, my dear, don't make it harder for me than it must be."

Still he said nothing. "Go back next month." Back to the old loneliness, a thousand times more damnable now than it was before.

"You're asking a lot of me," he said at last.

"I know, I know. I'm asking a lot of myself, too. ... Will you, Martin? For my sake. It's the only thing I've ever asked of you."

"Very well," he said.

He caught her in his arms and kissed her hungrily. She strained herself to him as if she would never let him go.

Violet was in the hotel bedroom packing a box that she was sending off by Luggage in Advance. Florence was fluttering about, trying to help, taking the wrong things out of the drawers, and putting them back into the wrong places. But Violet was being unusually kind. The terrifying moodiness that had hung over her the last week or so seemed quite to have vanished, and Florence basked happily in the sunshine of her kindness.

"I've so much enjoyed the month, and I'm so grateful to you for asking me."

Florence's heart expanded rapturously to her affectionate tone.

It was lovely to be *sure* that she was Violet's friend. Once or twice in the last few weeks she hadn't been *quite* sure. . . . To-day had been lovely altogether. This morning Rosemary had come to the hotel and presented her with a little box of shells.

"It's a good-bye present, Aunt Florence," she had said solemnly, "because you're going away to-morrow."

And all day the warm happy feeling of being loved and wanted had pervaded Florence's heart. The children *did* love her. She *was* surrounded by affection and devotion. . . . That bleak feeling of uselessness and loneliness she sometimes had was just her imagination. And, now, on top of it, Violet. . . . It was almost too much. Florence thought vaguely that happiness ought to be meted out more sparingly. It took one's breath away, made one feel dizzy, when it came all at once like this.

"It's been a lovely holiday," she said, forgetting all those strange under-currents of emotion that had made the holiday anything but lovely.

Violet went to the window and looked out at the sea that lay like a strip of painted silk in the sunshine.

"Is your mother being in for tea?" she said.

"No, she's gone to the Forresters'. She said she'd be staying there for tea. Martin said he'd be out, too."

Violet smiled at her.

"It's naughty of me, but I'm glad. Just you and I alone together for our last tea here."

There was a silence in which Florence felt that she was soaring off into the air like a balloon.

"I told you about the box of shells Rosemary gave me, didn't I?" she said when she'd returned to earth.

"Yes," said Violet, summoning her patience to refrain from saying that this was the sixth time she'd mentioned it in the last hour.

"When Pen told Val about Agnes," said Florence, "she said, 'Jesus will help her to walk straight, won't he?' Wasn't it sweet?"

"Wasn't it!" said Violet, who had already heard that, too, several times, and added, "Our last day is certainly a day of local excitement, what with Agnes Bevan—poor child!—and Mrs. Kemsing arriving."

"And Mr. Heath coming back," said Florence.

"Yes," agreed Violet with a little smile. "Mr. Heath coming back."

"Perhaps he really *had* only been to London on business," said Florence, trying conscientiously to Believe the Best of people. "I think the other was probably just an unkind rumour."

"Perhaps," said Violet. "By the way, did I tell you that a friend of mine wrote to me asking me to recommend a school for her boys?"

"No."

"Didn't I? I got the letter the other day. I'm going to recommend Cliff End School. I do so like what I've seen of it."

"That's *sweet* of you, Violet," said Florence. "Roger's got on so well there. I think it was wonderful, his winning the Obstacle Race; don't you?"

"I like all the staff so much," went on Violet slowly, "especially that charming Mrs. Heath."

If anyone ever said that she'd had anything to do with Mrs. Heath's dismissal, Florence would now be able to disprove it.

"So do I," said Florence expansively. "I like them all. It's all been so lovely, hasn't it?"

"Every day of it," agreed Violet.

A faint cloud came over Florence's face.

"The only thing—I do think Martin might have been a little more sociable," she said. "I suppose it's living in the East. One must make allowances."

Violet drew Florence down onto the bed by her and took her hand.

"Florence, dear," she said, "I want to tell you something because you're my friend. My only *real* friend, I think. The sort of friend one can always rely on, whatever happens. One hasn't many friends like that."

Florence's pale goat-like eyes dazzled with tears of joy, and on her face hung that silly smile that had so often made Violet long to slap it. . . . But now she only put both her hands round Florence's and pressed it affectionately.

"You know what I told you about Martin, dear, before I came down here?"

Florence, still too deeply moved for speech, nodded vehemently.

"Well, dear," said Violet slowly, "I don't want anyone to know this except you. It's the sort of thing that a woman doesn't tell even to her best friend, but I feel that you probably guess the truth already, and—well, you mean so much to me, dear, that I can't bear to have any secrets from you."

Florence uttered a little bleating sound expressive of gratitude and undying devotion.

"Martin proposed to me on the third day, I think it was, of our visit."

"Oh, Violet!" stammered Florence, recovering the power of speech with a rush. "What did you say?"

"I told him that I wanted the rest of our visit here to make up my mind. I told him that I couldn't make up my mind in a minute about an important thing like that. I said, 'I'll give you my answer at the end of the month. And, Martin,' I said, 'I want you to leave me alone to think it out by myself. It may be hard for you but will you promise to leave me alone?' He promised, and he's kept his word. I will say that for him."

Looking back over the month, Florence had to agree that he had kept his word.

"I gave him his answer last night."

"Oh, *Violet!*" gasped Florence. "What was it?"

"I'm sorry, Florence. I've been watching him and—he isn't the man I'd looked forward to meeting, the man who fell in love with me five years ago. He's coarsened. He's lost the fineness, the—spirituality he had then."

Florence listened open-mouthed, deeply impressed and affected. That Martin was coarse was doubtless true. All men were. She'd always felt it. She didn't even remember the fineness and spirituality in Martin that had made Violet love him five years ago.

"So I've said No," went on Violet, with a note of reluctant finality in her voice. "I told him so last night. I said, 'I'm sorry, Martin, but we could never have been happy together. I couldn't make you happy and you couldn't make me happy.' He was terribly upset, but in the end he accepted my decision. ... Of course, the month's been a strain for both of us. You've probably noticed that we've both been a little nervy."

Yes, Florence had noticed that. ... She was ashamed of the disloyal suspicion she'd had that Martin was avoiding Violet because he didn't like her as much as he thought he was going to. She realised now how ridiculous that was. Of course Martin wanted to marry Violet. Any man would. ... But Florence couldn't be really sorry that Violet had refused him. She had a feeling that, after all, she would be nearer Violet as a friend than she would have been as a sister-in-law.

"You see, dear," went on Violet, "I can't compromise. I can't lower my standards. I just *am* like that. If Martin doesn't quite come up to my ideal—and he doesn't—it would be cruel to both of us for me to marry him. I'm not one of those women who want a husband just for the sake of having a husband. I have enough strength of character, I'm glad to say, to stand alone.

'I am the master of my fate,
I am the captain of my soul,' "

she quoted with a brave gay smile, then suddenly wondered if she'd got it the right way round and murmured as if in continuation, "captain of my fate ... master of my soul."

"I do think you're wonderful, Violet," quavered Florence emotionally.

Violet looked at the flushed credulous face and drew a quick sigh of relief. Florence believed the story of the proposal. She almost believed it herself. In a short time, she knew, she would quite believe it. She rose briskly.

"And now, dear," she said, "let's go down to tea."

"It's gone so quickly," said Mrs. Paget dreamily. "I can hardly believe that I've been here a whole month ... and yet I feel I've been here all my life."

"But you must come again," said Ruth.

The old lady shook her head.

"No, I shan't see either of you again. It's been perfect—meeting you like this. You understand, don't you, Michael?"

He was watching her with a smile that swept her back over the gulf of years.

"Yes . . . I understand."

"Let's say good-bye now. Good-bye, my dear."

Ruth bent down and kissed the withered cheek.

"Do you know, when I think of you when you aren't here I always think of someone young."

"That's because I'm so old, my dear," said Mrs. Paget.

"I'll get the bike out," said Michael.

When he had gone Mrs. Paget looked round the little room.

"I shall always remember it just like this," she said, "with the sun pouring through the window and the sound of the sea. . . ."

"Won't you write to us?" said Ruth.

Mrs. Paget shook her head.

"No, that would spoil it."

"The steed's ready," called Michael.

Ruth came down to the gate to tuck her into the side-car.

"I don't know what's the matter with me," she said. "I want to cry. . . . But, of *course*, you'll come down again."

"Good-bye, my dear," said Mrs. Paget.

She put her hand on Michael's arm as they neared the little shop that had been the fisherman's cottage.

"Stop here, Michael. Let's say good-bye here."

"Mayn't I take you on to the hotel?"

"No, let's say good-bye here."

He helped her out of the side-car and they stood together just outside the shop.

"It's where I saw you first, isn't it?" she said, "and thought you were Michael. . . . Once we stood here together—Michael and I—and watched the sunset over the sea and he said,

'He that holds his sweetheart true, unto his day of
    dying,
Lives, of all that ever breathed, most worthy the
    envying."

Where does it come from? I never know where poetry comes from."

"I think it's from one of Thomas Campion's."

"I'd forgotten it till the other evening, and I suddenly seemed to hear him saying it again." She gave a little breathless laugh. "It's upset me, coming here, Michael. I don't know whether I'm an old woman or a young one."

"I can tell you that," he laughed. "Gallivanting over the countryside on motor cycles!"

"Let's say good-bye now."

He bent down and kissed her and she clung to him for a moment.

"You've been very sweet, Michael. God bless you. It's meant a lot to me."

"And to me. . . . Good-bye, my dear."

She watched him out of sight, then turned slowly to go to the hotel.

Martin was passing without seeing her, walking blindly, looking neither to right nor left. His sallow face was grim and ravaged, set in deep lines of unhappiness and strain.

Brian had awakened from a feverish sleep, calling out in terror for Jessica, and she had begged Martin to leave her.

"I shall have to be with him now. Dearest, it's no use your staying. I'd rather you went."

"Martin . . ."

He turned his sombre gaze on her.

"Oh, Mother. . . . I didn't see you."

She put her arm through his and they walked together towards the hotel without speaking. Long-forgotten memories were springing to life in her heart. She saw Michael kneeling by her bed the day Martin was born, Michael holding Martin in his arms, guiding his first footsteps, teaching him to ride, to play cricket. . . . Michael had been so proud of him. Once or twice she had felt almost jealous. Suddenly the happy, eager little boy was more real than the tired man by her side.

Through the window of the hotel they could see Violet and Florence sitting over a tea-table in the drawing-room, and on a common impulse they walked round the building and down to the beach. It was empty except for a youth who looked like Tim Bevan at the further end of the bay.

"Let's sit down," she said, and went to where a fallen rock formed a seat at the foot of the cliff. He sat down on the sand at her feet. In the silence the estrangement of his long absence faded away, and they drew near to each other. Tenderness for him welled up from some hidden source, filling all her being. She seemed to hold the child he had been in her arms again, cradling his head on her breast.

"Are you very unhappy, Martin?" she said.

"I'm more unhappy than I've ever been in my life," he said.

"But not sorry you came."

It was a statement, not a question.

"I shall be glad always that I came."

"I never thought she'd go away with you," she said quietly.

He looked at her in dull surprise.

"I didn't think you knew. . . ."

"Oh yes . . . I knew."

He said nothing, but comfort unbelievable seemed to flow to him from the small figure sitting so upright and motionless beside him. . . .

Stella was hurrying along the path that led to Four Winds. She couldn't wait any longer. Mrs. Kemsing had been there for nearly an hour. They *must* have come to some decision by now. After all, it was her business, too. She wished that she had broken down the barrier of his chivalry and *made* him discuss the situation with her. She knew that he loved her. It wasn't only his kiss. It was the way he looked at her, the way he spoke to her. It was everything. . . .

His wife, of course, would be beastly to him. She saw again the beautiful cruel mouth of the photograph, and her heart burned with protective love. She imagined herself standing by him, proudly confronting the woman who had wrecked his life and saying, "This is my place now for ever."

Perhaps he hadn't realised that she was willing to face the publicity of divorce for him. He was so unselfish, so chivalrous. . . .

She hurried up the little path, then stopped, her heart beating unevenly. She didn't know what she was going to say. . . . She couldn't just burst in on them without having thought of something to say.

Suddenly there came the sound of a woman's voice through the open window—silvery-sweet with a ripple of laughter in it.

"And what mischief have you been up to down here by yourself?"

She turned swiftly and saw them through the open French window. The woman was standing by the easel that held her portrait, looking at it. She was the loveliest woman Stella had ever seen, tall and slender and beautifully dressed, with deep black hair and violet eyes. And her mouth wasn't cruel. It was soft and lovely. . . .

He followed the direction of her eyes.

"Oh, that!" he said carelessly. "Let me tell you, woman, the sum-total of my love passages with *that* is one solitary kiss."

"Perhaps." There was laughing reproach in her voice. "But she's in love with you and you know it and you've been encouraging it."

He considered this, then grinned suddenly—a mischievous grin, like a small boy caught out in a not very serious fault.

"Have I? I don't know. Perhaps I have."

The woman's eyes were still fixed on the portrait.

"She's very sweet."

"Oh, she's adorable as a child, but ghastly when she tries to be grown-up. I can't tell you what I've endured. After all, if you will leave me here alone . . ."

"Dearest, I had to go to see Mother."

"Well, now you've come don't let's waste time talking about snotty little schoolgirls. You haven't even kissed me yet."

"I thought I had."

"Not properly. . . . Oh, my darling, it's been hell without you."

He put his arms round her, and Stella could just see his face as he bent his lips to hers. ... She hardly recognised it—hungry, yearning, stripped of its smiling urbanity.

She turned and went swiftly to the gate. Her body was on fire with shame and humiliation. She felt as if she had offered herself to him and been refused. She ran blindly down the lane towards home. She wanted to get as far away from it as she could. Sea, cliffs, sands swam blurred and formless before her eyes.

To Pen the day had been a nightmare. It wasn't only Agnes Bevan's death. That wouldn't have affected her very nearly. It didn't touch the small enclosed world that was her only real life. The nightmare had begun by her finding an envelope in one of Susan's drawers with a map of the Kingdom on it. She had stood staring at it, remembering Susan's quick denial when she asked, "Do you still play the Kingdom game?"

The date on the envelope showed that the map had been drawn during their half-term holiday (it was the envelope of a letter she had written to Gordon just before half-term). They must have been playing the Kingdom game together during the half-term holiday. It wasn't the untruth she minded as much as the necessity for the untruth. They wanted to shut her out. She'd thought that she had the key to their minds, and she hadn't. She had joined in the game once as a matter of course, but now they didn't want her any longer. She felt a hurt that was quite disproportionate to the occasion. It was as if they had disowned everything she had been to them, everything she had done for them. ... And on the top of it had come Mrs. Egerton's visit—Mrs. Egerton, large and moist and apologetic.

"I've only just heard of it," she said, "or I'd have come about it before. Very unkind of her it was, and I told her so, but, there, you know what children are. They don't mean anything. ... And it was so kind of little Rosemary to come round the very first evening she got back and bring those shells and all, and for them to send her away and say they didn't want her—well, it was downright unkind. ... I do hope you didn't think I knew of it. Not till this very afternoon, I didn't."

Pen had stared at her in amazement, remembering how Rosemary had returned almost as soon as she had set out, remembering, too, her "Yes" when she had asked if Beryl had not come back yet.

The child must have been desperately unhappy—but why hadn't she told her? The feeling of bewilderment, of desolation, grew heavier. How could they shut her out like this, when all she wanted was to help and protect them?

She got rid of Mrs. Egerton as best she could ("No, of course, I knew it was nothing to do with you. Rosemary was a bit upset, but she's quite got over it now. Children do such odd things, don't they? It doesn't do to take any of it too seriously ..."), then went into the front garden where Charles was weeding the small flower-bed.

"Charles ..."

He stood up.

"Yes."

She didn't really want to go to him for comfort, but she was so deeply hurt that she had to go to someone.

"You know that time when Rosemary went to Beryl's on the day——"

A constrained expression had come over his face, and she broke off to stare at him.

"Did you—know?"

"Well, yes," he said. "The little blighter sent her away, didn't she?"

"Did Rosemary—*tell* you?"

"Yes," he admitted uncomfortably. "She—she didn't want to worry you, Pen."

But Pen only stared at him with a set anguished face. And then Stella came, and Pen forgot all her own troubles in the blank misery of the childish blue eyes, the tragic curves of the young mouth.

"Stella, *darling*," she said. "What's the matter?"

"Nothing," said Stella stonily. "Nothing"

"Stella!"

The tenderness in Pen's voice broke down her defences, and, though she fought for control, her lips suddenly began to tremble. Pen's perceptions were intensified by her own unhappiness and she guessed what had happened. Ever since Charles's warning she had been secretly uneasy about Stella's visits to Arnold Kemsing, though resentment at what she had looked upon as his "interference" had prevented her from admitting it to herself. And she knew that to-day his wife had arrived. Stella had fallen in love with him, and his wife's return had shown her how hopeless her love was. Perhaps she had not even realised that he was married.

"Darling," she said, drawing the tense slender form into her arms, "I understand."

Sobbing, Stella flung her off.

"Oh, *stop* understanding. I hate you understanding. . . . I can't bear it." She ran to Charles, clinging to him as if for protection, and went on between her sobs, "Take me away, Daddy. . . . I hate being here. . . . I've told Mummy, but she won't listen. I want to have a job . . . to work at something. . . . Can't I go to London and learn a job of some sort? . . . I can't stay here. . . . I won't. . . . I'm so unhappy. . . . I'm so unhappy."

"That's all right, old lady," said Charles, holding her tightly to him. "Pull yourself together, there's a good girl. . . . It's all right. . . . We're all leaving here anyway and going to live nearer London. . . ." He met Pen's eyes over Stella's shoulder. "Aren't we, Pen?"

Pen had gone very white. She made a helpless little gesture of surrender.

"Yes," she said.

"Then you can take up any job you like in reason," Charles went on.

"Thank you," sniffed Stella. "I've been such a fool. I——"

She broke away from Charles's embrace and went out of the garden and down the path to the sands. She wanted to be alone—right away from everyone. She glanced around cautiously. There were Granny and Uncle Martin sitting together at the foot of the cliff. They mustn't see her like this—eyes red, cheeks tear-stained. She went round the bay to the other end. There was a place among the rocks where she and Tim had sat once—before this dreadful month. She didn't see that Tim was there till it was too late to draw back, but anyway she didn't really want to draw back. She'd come here to be alone, but somehow Tim didn't count. She felt alone, with him, and his being there held at bay the horrible feeling of unwantedness that was like a physical pain.

He looked at her gloomily. He was so wrapped up in his own troubles that he didn't even see that she had been crying.

"Hallo," he said.

"I didn't know you'd be here," she said, and sat down by him on the smooth hard sand, gazing out to sea.

"I suppose I oughtn't to be," he said, "but I can't stand it indoors any longer."

With an effort she tore her thoughts from her own troubles.

"Is it as bad as that?" she said. "But surely it's better than if she'd lived for years and years."

"Oh, it's not that," he said. "I shouldn't really mind—that, though I daresay it sounds awful to say so. It's—" he sat cross-legged, his elbows on his knees, his chin resting on his hands, "she hardly knows I exist. She's just waiting for *him* to come."

"Your father?"

"Yes. . . . I've stuck by her through it all, and he's let her down, and now—no one exists for her but him. She's just—waiting for him. She looks on me as if I were a child. She doesn't want to be bothered with me. It's as if she were—dead and waiting for him to come and bring her back to life. She's thinking of him, remembering the time when they were happy together before they knew about Agnes. I don't mean that she doesn't care about Agnes. She cares terribly. But she's right inside a sort of prison and no one can get through to her but him. She won't let me even try . . . and I've stuck to her all the time and he's let her down."

Stella wasn't listening. She had had a sudden vision of Arnold Kemsing and his wife and the little studio. . . .

"Oh, *Tim!*" she said. "I'm so unhappy. . . ."

He held her close, uttering childish words of comfort while she sobbed against his shoulder. Then she drew away from him and wiped her eyes on a rather grubby handkerchief that she drew from her knickers' leg.

"I'm sorry," she said in a choking voice. "I'm an awful fool." She turned to him with a watery smile. "I was looking at that Blake book you gave me last night, Tim, and there's such a lovely grasshopper . . ."

His grim young face relaxed.

"I know," he said. "It's where Satan smote him with boils, isn't it?"

Rosemary, Roger, and Valerie were playing shop at the bottom of the garden. Pen, finding Rosemary picking up cigarette ends from the road, had put an end to the tobacco shop, but there was a good supply of tea (sorrel), cauliflowers (hedge parsley), and greens (clover of any sort), and Bear presided at an improvised counter on the other side of which sagged the motley crew of Rosemary's "people," who were the customers.

After the first day Rosemary had been surprised to find that she was rather relieved than otherwise by Beryl's defection. She had a new exciting sense of freedom, as if she were released from some bondage. She needn't go up to Beryl's every evening. She needn't read to Beryl, play with Beryl, help Beryl with her home-work, strive to please and placate Beryl. She had a lovely feeling of belonging to herself again. And—strangest of all—the glamour had faded from Beryl. She wasn't a sort of fairy princess any longer. She was a fat and rather disagreeable little girl. Rosemary didn't want ever to be friends with her again. She had been terrified the day when Beryl and Carry had quarrelled and Beryl, following her speculatively with the large blue eyes and seizing at last her opportunity, had whispered, "Will you come and play with me after tea, Rosemary?" Rosemary had shaken her head, shyly but quite firmly, and to her relief Beryl and Carry had made up their quarrel the next morning.

She had kept for herself half the shells that she had collected for Beryl and given half to Aunt Florence as a good-bye present.

Roger thought it babyish to play shop and had at first refused to join in the game, though he felt secretly flattered by Rosemary's insistence that Bear should fill the important role of shopkeeper.

He had brought out his Meccano set and pretended to busy himself with it, ostentatiously aloof, but at last, when he couldn't hold out any longer, he said carelessly, "I'll come and play with you if you really want me to, Rosemary."

"Oh, *do*, Roger," said Rosemary eagerly. "That'll be lovely. You'll talk for Bear, won't you? Here's some money for change. Grass is a penny, and clover leaves sixpence, and dandelion leaves shillings. ... Then Val can talk for Hetty and Kanga and Roo and Wilfred, and I'll talk for Owl and Minnie Monkey and the others. Minnie wants heaps of vegetables because she's got some of the monkeys from the Zoo staying with her—the ones that laugh—and they eat a lot."

A sudden memory of Agnes came to her, clouding the sunny untidy little garden—Agnes drowned by the sea that all that day had lain so calm and smiling. ... She had cried bitterly when she heard about it this morning, but already it was a long way off, and Agnes had never seemed quite real.

"Come on, Val. Roo can have the first turn because he's the littlest."

Absorbed in the game, they hardly heard Mummy and Daddy and Stella talking in the front garden.

Stella sounds excited, thought Rosemary subconsciously, while the conscious part of her turned soil into coffee and moss into brussels sprouts. Is she crying or laughing? She must be laughing. Anyway, it doesn't matter. She's grown-up and one can't even pretend to understand grown-ups. ... Hawthorn leaves would do for watercress and little round stones for potatoes. ...

It was after Valerie's bedtime when Mummy came out. She looked grave, as if someone had been naughty, but not cross.

"Bedtime, Val," she said.

"Oh!" groaned Valerie. "It's such a lovely game!"

"Come along, darling."

"Let's stop now, anyway," said Rosemary. "I want to paint."

"I'm a *big* girl," said Valerie pathetically.

She always resented the extra hour that Roger and Rosemary had after she'd gone to bed.

She took Pen's hand and went in, dragging her plump sandalled legs reluctantly. Charles was at the foot of the stairs.

"You did mean what you said just now, Pen, didn't you?" he said. "About going to live nearer London."

She looked at him. She'd tried to hate him, to feel that it was all his fault, but somehow she couldn't.

She gave him a faint tremulous smile.

"Yes," she said. "I did mean it."

www.ingramcontent.com/pod-product-compliance
Ingram Content Group UK Ltd.
Pitfield, Milton Keynes, MK11 3LW, UK
UKHW030703020325
455687UK00006B/57